GOING THROUGH THE CHANGE

GOING THROUGH THE CHANGE

CHANGE

MENOPAUSAL SUPERHEROES - BOOK 1

SAMANTHA BRYANT

For any woman who has ever felt betrayed by her own body.

THINGS GET HAIRY FOR LINDA

L inda Alvarez had just been to the beauty salon yesterday, but all those weird hairs were back, like they'd never been tweezed and waxed away. She had eyebrows like Frida Kahlo *Por Dios*, and practically a five o'clock shadow. *Thank God David had already left for work.* She'd have time to take care of it before he got home.

David had been her rock through all this menopause garbage. He'd fetched blankets and brought her ice as she changed temperature four and five times in an evening. He hadn't complained about the extra money she was spending at the beauty shop or commented on the way her body seemed to be shifting around her, reshaping into something else entirely. *Something much thicker around the middle than she had ever been before*, Linda thought ruefully. She was lucky to have him, she knew.

Come to think of it, it wasn't just the hair today. She looked really different. There was something different about her jawline, and her favorite pink T-shirt hung oddly on her, like it was too tight in the shoulders all of a sudden and didn't quite reach her waist. Had it shrunk in the wash? She hadn't changed anything about the way she'd been washing it.

She grabbed the new bar of soap she'd picked up at the farmer's market last weekend. She'd bought it from the daughter of her old neighbor. Ms. Liu had moved into the old house after her mother died. Linda had been meaning to bring her a welcome package of some sort, but Cindy kept strange hours, and Linda had not yet caught her at home.

Despite living down the street from the older Mrs. Liu all these years, and spending a fair amount of time visiting the old lady, Linda had only rarely seen the daughter. She had been using Cindy's teas and lotions for years, though. Cindy's mother had kept a booth for her in the local market and would hawk her daughter's products and fill the buyer's ear with praise of her brilliant child.

Cindy worked the booth herself whenever she was in town. Linda wasn't sure if she liked the younger Ms. Liu. She had a gruffness to her and didn't seem to understand how to talk to customers. But she did like the things the woman made. Whether it was psychosomatic or not, those products worked. Her cramps went away, her blemishes cleared up, her mood lightened. Ms. Liu was a genius.

The new soap was called "Nu Yu." It had a picture of a woman drawn in lines out of calligraphy on the wrapper. The woman's legs were impossibly long, and her stride was the length of the wrapper. Ms. Liu had said it would let the inner person shine through. Linda assumed that was just a New Age spin to sell to the hippies who came to the market, a play on the idea of inner beauty, something like that.

Whatever. Even if it had a silly name, the soap was just as wonderful as all of Ms. Liu's other products. It smelled marvelous and made Linda's skin tingle. She wondered what was in it that made her feel so alive when she used it. She unwrapped the new bar and reached into the now-steaming shower to set it in the soap dish atop the little remnant of the previous bar.

Linda peeled off her clothes with some difficulty. They seemed to cling to her tightly. She dropped the poor maligned pink shirt on the floor and stepped into the shower. She'd start by getting good and clean and exfoliated, and then she'd figure out what to do about her crazy hormone hairs.

Her grandmother had suffered from the same problem, she knew.

When she got too old to take care of it herself, Linda used to come by the assisted living place and wax her upper lip on Saturdays, so she would look her best for church on Sundays. Linda tried to remember how old her Abuelita had been when she started having the mustache problem, but she couldn't remember. Probably Abuelita had suffered with it for a long time, and Linda only found out about it when she needed help to take care of it. Maybe she had only been forty-eight, too. Luckily, there were products for that.

Linda rolled her neck and let the water wash over her, grateful for the warmth and the white noise effect of the water beating against the tiled walls. It was easy to let her worries fade when she was in the shower. She stretched out her arms above her head and ran the new bar of soap over her arms and into the armpits—hairy, again, of course. Really hairy! *Caracoles!* She was sure she had shaved just yesterday.

She grabbed onto the top ledge of the tile wall for balance, surprised to find out she could reach it easily, and grabbed the pink Daisy razor out of the little hanging basket just outside the tub area. If she was going to keep growing hair this quickly, maybe she'd need to check into some electrolysis or something. The *peluquería* was good with waxes and such, but she was going to need a more permanent solution. When she stood again, after shaving her legs, she knocked her head into the shower spigot. Weird. Maybe David had left it set lower than usual?

A few quick strokes and her pits felt smooth again. Linda rinsed out the razor, grimacing at the amount of dark hair swirling around the drain. Even her feet looked strange to her today, more spread out. She thought that only happened in pregnancy. Or maybe it was time to see the eye doctor. She might have to upgrade from her simple readers to bifocals or something.

Turning her back against the warm stream of water, Linda ran the bar across her upper chest and shoulders. It felt so smooth and hard. So did her torso. Maybe her time on the treadmill was paying off. When she ran her hand up around her breasts, she gasped a little. She'd never been a busty woman, but her breasts seemed to have all but disappeared. Surely, this wasn't more *cambio de vida*. She'd never heard of anyone losing her breasts because of menopause. Maybe she should call the doctor and see if she could be seen this afternoon.

More tense now, Linda continued her washing. At least the soap felt good and moisturizing. It made nice creamy suds in her hands. There wasn't any jiggle across her belly when she ran her soapy hand across it. Her belly hadn't felt tight like that in a good fifteen years, not since the last baby, the one that had come by emergency C-section.

Then Linda dipped her hands lower to clean between her legs. Her eyes flew open. Something was definitely not right. It felt—it was just like—Linda looked down and screamed. There, resting against her thigh was, unmistakably, a penis.

PATRICIA AND THE 58 YEAR ITCH

Patricia O'Neill pulled out her cell phone to check the time. She turned it over on the table before it could suck her into the barrage of e-mail and looming meeting reminders. She ran her hand up the back of her short, red hair, wondering vaguely if the new shade was too vibrant for her skin. She had always loved her red hair and wouldn't let a little thing like going gray keep her from it. But she also seemed to keep getting paler the older she got, like pigmentation was only for young people. Her stylist seemed to think she could pull it off. Patricia hoped she was right.

Cindy was late again. Cindy Liu could never seem to understand that not everyone had endless free time. Ever since she had retired, she had been wholly unreliable. Still, it was going to be nice to see her. Patricia wasn't having an especially good day, and lunch with an old friend might be just the thing to turn the day around.

Patricia tucked her phone back into her Louis Vuitton bag and gestured to the waiter for additional coffee.

As he poured, the young man complimented her on her hair. "It's good to see an older woman with some style!" he said.

Patricia looked the boy over. Facial piercings, sarcastic T-shirt, and a sleeve tattoo. She wasn't sure it was a good thing that he liked her hair, but she decided to be gracious and thanked him, even though he'd just called her old.

"I think I'll go ahead and order. My friend is obviously late."

Setting the pot on the table, the waiter obediently pulled out a small notepad and stood, pencil poised. That was when Cindy finally arrived.

"Oh good, you got some coffee!" She slid into the other side of the booth, took Patricia's coffee cup from the middle of the table, and began loading it up with sugar. "Can you bring some more cream, please?" She poured the remaining three plastic tubs from the bowl into the mug.

"And a fresh mug for me," said Patricia.

Patricia crossed her arms and glared at her friend who was still busy doctoring the sugar level in her coffee. She noted that Cindy had started dying her hair as well. The streaks of gray she'd been letting grow were gone. "How can you even drink it with all that crap in it?"

Cindy laughed. "Well, I don't actually like coffee. It's just a vehicle for cream and sugar as far as I'm concerned."

Patricia shook her head. "They have tea, you know."

Cindy made a face. "They do serve something they call tea." She shuddered, gripping Patricia's hand in mock terror. "It comes in bags!"

Patricia had to laugh at the dramatic show. "It's good to see you, Cindy. Even if you are late."

"I'd say my timing was pretty good. You already had a table, coffee, and a menu. Besides, you're the boss, aren't you? Who's going to complain if you are late returning from lunch? One of the privileges of old age, I guess."

"Old schmold. Speak for yourself, old-timer."

Just then, the waiter stepped up, serving Patricia her fresh cup of coffee and setting a new bowl of creamers between them. The women quickly made their selections, and he scuttled off.

"Do you remember the good old days, when we used to go to Jerry's late at night and share hot fudge cake?" Cindy asked, reaching for another creamer.

"Good old days?" Patricia snorted. "You mean when we dug

through all the couch cushions in the lounges to find the two dollars we needed to buy one? You can keep those kind of good old days. I'll take these days, thank you." She paused, looking thoughtful. "Unless, of course, I can have my old metabolism back, too. I swear I have to buy new suits every time I miss a workout."

Patricia and Cindy had been friends for decades. They met when they drew each other in the freshman lottery for dormitories. They were an unlikely match. Patricia was a field hockey player from Illinois, known as The Amazon, for her height, strength, and attitude toward men. Cindy was a five foot tall Chinese-American girl from Springfield, working on her second bachelor's degree. They may have looked odd standing side by side, but Patricia and Cindy understood one another.

Patricia hadn't known many people in her life who understood her. She was thrilled that, after all these years, her best friend would be living in the same city she did. Until recently, they'd seen one another only a few times a year, whenever Cindy came to visit her mother or Patricia could travel to wherever Cindy was. When Cindy inherited her mother's house, she announced that she would build her own laboratory in the basement and move to Springfield. Now that the renovations were finished and the lab was ready, they'd be able to see each other regularly.

"Tell me about your new lab," Patricia said before picking up her sandwich and taking a big bite.

Cindy grinned around the bite of her salad, ignoring the bit of chicken that fell back onto the plate. She rhapsodized for ten minutes about the various sorts of machines she had purchased. She was especially pleased about an isolation chamber she had purchased from a company in Germany. It gave her complete environmental control, she said, down to the percentages of different gasses in the air.

Patricia didn't really understand what such a device might be used for, but she understood loving the tools of your trade, and was pleased for her friend, who was finally getting to build a dream lab. She wished Cindy could have had it when she was younger and would have more time to use it. It didn't seem fair to finally grasp your dreams as you were becoming too old to hold them for any length of time.

As Cindy continued describing her lab equipment in loving detail, Patricia had the thought her friend sounded like she was in love. She never spoke of other people with the same love and admiration that she spoke of her equipment. Not since Michael. Had it really been thirty years since Michael died? Odd that Cindy had never loved anyone else.

Not that she was one to talk. Patricia had never married, either. Then again, she'd never even been tempted. She thought men were pleasant enough company, in limited situations. She didn't mind having one take her places from time to time, or even share her bed for a night or a weekend, but she certainly wasn't interested in letting one into her life. The trade offs were not worth it.

The women ate in silence for a few bites, each pondering her own concerns. Patricia squirmed in her seat a little, rubbing her shoulder blades against the cushions of the booth. It didn't really help with the itching but made her feel like she was doing something. Her skin had been a problem for a few months now.

She'd been to see her doctor, who said it was a form of eczema and gave her a useless cream to apply. Like she hadn't been down the "sensitive skin" primrose path before. It came with the hair, apparently. That, and her temper problem. When she asked about a hormonal component, he had brushed her off, saying her skin condition had nothing to do with menopause. Her estrogen levels were still acceptable, and he didn't feel they needed to start her on hormone therapy. Was she still taking her calcium supplements?

She was looking for another doctor now.

Patricia didn't take it well when people tried to brush her off. Unfortunately, it was happening more now that she was nearly sixty. Everyone seemed to think she should retire. She'd overheard a conversation at work the other day about whether the old battle-axe was ever going to retire or if she'd just die at her desk. Her boss had recently suggested she take some more vacation time. He'd said she should enjoy life at her age. At her age, indeed. Like he was any younger, the pig.

"What's wrong, Patricia? You're as wiggly as a six-year-old girl."

"It's my back. I've got this skin thing going on." She waved her hand dismissively.

"You should come visit me at my lab. I'm working on a cream that might help you."

Patricia accepted the offer immediately. She was dying to see the new setup, anyway. "I can come tonight. How's seven-thirty?"

LINDA FLOORS HER HUSBAND

Linda was bundled in blankets, hiding on the couch in a cave made of fleece and wool and cotton when her husband came home. She had cried the afternoon away.

"*Qué pasa, mi amor?*" David asked, sitting beside her and resting one hand on her arm, probably trying to guess where her shoulder was. His voice was soft and gentle, his tone kind. He was so patient.

But there were limits, she knew. How could she even begin to tell him what was wrong?

Linda pulled away when he moved to tug the blankets away from her face. "No!" she said, grimacing at the way her voice sounded. It was like she had swallowed a ball of cotton.

"Are you sick?"

"No, no, it's the *cambio de vida*, the menopause."

David tugged on the blanket hood Linda had constructed and peered inside to find her face, but she kept it shadowed. His large brown eyes were full of worry, but he didn't ask any more, just sat patting her arm and waiting. Linda appreciated his silence. She rocked herself back and forth, letting silent tears fall down her cheeks and into her coverings.

After a few minutes passed with only the sound of Linda's occasional hitching sobs, David stood and went into the bathroom. Linda nearly called out to him not to go in. She had not cleaned up the mess she had made. The shower curtain was torn from its hooks and hanging off kilter. All the sink bottles were still on the floor from when she had shoved them aside to get better access to the mirror. The mirror she had then broken in a sudden fit of rage, punching it just over the image of her own face. She'd been shocked at her own violence and even more shocked when her knuckles began to bleed. The first aid supplies were probably still spread across the sink and counter as well.

She was going to lose him. Her David. Her *vida*. This wasn't just aging, a little sag, or another skin problem. It had been hard enough to talk to him about ordinary woman stuff. He was so old-fashioned. He thought of periods and childbirth and hormones as mysterious things just this side of magic. Things men were not meant to comprehend.

Linda had tugged him gently into this century in the thirty years of their marriage. When the children were school age, she took a part-time job at the school "to be there for our *niñas*." When their daughters were old enough to date, she made him a part of the conversations about what good girls do and do not do. She had recently heard him echoing her comments about husbands and wives as partners to one of his coworkers. He had come so far! But this...

Her heart was breaking at the thought of David leaving when he found out she had become... whatever it was she had become. Was there a word for that? *Una mariquita?* A girl-man? She couldn't help it. She sobbed aloud.

David came out of the bathroom and knelt in front of her, wordlessly holding out a washcloth still hot from the sink. He knew she found a hot cloth soothing when she was upset. She reached out a hand and took it from him, pulling it into the cave she had constructed from blankets.

She was nearly naked beneath. She couldn't find any clothing that would fit her; her body had grown so huge. She was clad in a beach cover up that now only came to her hips and a pair of boxer shorts one of the girls had given David as a joke one Father's Day. They were red with huge white hearts all over them.

When she continued to weep, David sat back down beside her and simply pulled her to him. She wrapped her arms around him, turning her face away from his so he couldn't see her whiskers. He rubbed her back with the palm of his hand in a slow circle, cooing soothing sounds and loving words into her ear.

Twirling around, Linda suddenly grabbed David, pulled him to her, and kissed him. She knew it might be the last time she would ever get to. David murmured surprise, but soon was kissing her back. For just a moment, she felt normal, a wife loving her husband in their home and getting loved back.

Then she felt it—not a tingling, not exactly. More of a tension, but warm. Not a hot flash, more like a rush of warmth. And it was down there.

She pulled back from the kiss and threw herself to the other end of the couch, where she curled her body into a ball.

David reached for her, obviously confused. "Linda? *Corazón?*"

Linda fumbled in the blankets to find the source of the warmth. What was going on? It was like a spring inside her had tightened. She gasped when she dared to put her hand into her pants—she knew exactly what this was. It was the thing that grew on her. The *pinga.* The manhood. And it was stiff.

Linda howled.

David jumped up and rushed to her side. "Linda? Please, *cariño*, tell me what's wrong? Do I need to call an ambulance?"

"They can't help me. No one can help me." She sobbed without restraint.

David took an angrier tone. "Linda. Tell me what is wrong."

Linda sat up on the couch and let the covering fall back. David's eyes widened.

"Can you still love me, David? Can you still love me if," Linda stood, revealing the extent of her change, "if I am a man?"

David hit the floor, passed out cold.

PATRICIA HAS AN ITCH SHE CAN'T SCRATCH

Patricia let out a low whistle as she walked into the laboratory in Cindy Liu's basement. There was nothing about the rest of the house to suggest the state-of-the-art beauty of what she found there. In fact, the rest of the house was run-down, dark, and looked like it belonged to a blind eighty-year-old woman, which, Patricia guessed, it had, until recently. There were doilies on the end tables, for goodness sake. Cindy must have just moved in and left everything exactly as it had been when her mother lived there.

But down here? That was a different story. Everything was chrome or white and sparklingly clean. There were stations for everything imaginable. Chemistry equipment, animals in cages, herbs and minerals, the touted isolation chamber from Germany, a desktop computer station with four different monitors, and a rack full of machines. Even if the devices were things she only half-recognized and understood, Patricia could see the quality of the equipment. She knew quality by its smell. One wall featured a row of glossy cabinets beneath a giant corkboard on which charts and graphs of various sorts were hung and spotted with post-it notes with Cindy's spiky handwriting on them. It was a fully working lab, and Cindy was obviously utilizing it to the fullest.

"Wow! You weren't kidding, were you?" Patricia said.

Taking the opening and running with it, Cindy told Patricia all about the experiments she was running, and the range of treatments she was developing. Patricia was amazed by the breadth of her friend's work. She seemed to be running about fifteen experiments all at the same time, mostly connected to The Change, as she called it. Patricia already knew her friend was a world-renowned expert on women and aging, but she tended to forget Dr. Cindy Liu could well be described as a genius as well. Giving the tour had made her breathless, and Patricia had laughed, enjoying her friend's energy and enthusiasm. She looked great. Obviously, this move was good for her.

Cindy's eyes glowed with pride, and she gestured broadly at the room. "Do you realize the work I can accomplish here? What I have already accomplished here? I have a lifetime of experiments waiting for me."

Patricia tilted her head and looked at her friend with concern. "A lifetime?"

"I know what you're thinking, Patricia O'Neill. I'm too old to be talking about a lifetime in the future." Cindy waggled a finger at her, which had the unfortunate effect of making her seem like a grumpy old lady, which was counterproductive to the argument she was trying to make.

Patricia grimaced. She hadn't wanted to say it aloud, but that was exactly what she had been thinking. Neither of them were what you might call a spring chicken anymore. Cindy was almost a decade older than Patricia. She might have another ten or fifteen years before this kind of work was beyond her physical and mental capabilities, if she stayed healthy and was fortunate. It was hardly a lifetime.

"You'll see, Patricia. My best work still lies ahead. But, tonight, let's see what we can do about your skin. Take off your jacket and blouse. Let's see what we have here."

Patricia complied, cooperatively taking a seat on a massage chair, so her itchy upper back was exposed for Cindy's examination. Cindy pulled up a small rolling cart with a variety of tools on it, including a large magnifier. She ran her small hand gently over the bumpy patch between Patricia's shoulder blades. "What did your doctor say about this?"

"Eczema. He gave me the same cream that didn't work for me last time."

"You should have come to me sooner. Conventional doctors are either useless or an impediment to health." Cindy spit the word "conventional" like it was a nasty bit of gristle in a steak.

Patricia bit her lip. They'd had this conversation many times, especially in the years right after Michael died, and Patricia had no desire to plough the same fields yet again. The worth of conventional medicine was one of those "agree to disagree" subjects that was best left alone if they didn't want to end up shouting at each other.

It was true Michael had been misdiagnosed, and that the misdiagnosis might have contributed to his death. But Patricia didn't believe that meant the entire medical establishment had to be written off. Doctors had kept her father alive for many years, after all. She'd had conventional medicine to thank for the rebuilding of her shoulder as well. But Cindy saw things in black and white terms, at least on this topic.

"My former doctor is an asshole; I'll give you that," Patricia conceded. "I fired him. He waved me off when I suggested the root cause might be menopause."

"Good for you! What does he know about it, anyway? He's just a man. For him, it's something he read in a book. We live it. We are women. It's all hormonal at some level." She paused, filling a dropper with a pale green liquid and holding it over Patricia's bare back. "This is going to sting."

Cindy dripped some kind of liquid onto the affected area. Patricia flinched. It did more than just sting.

"Sorry," Cindy said.

Patricia forced her shoulders to relax. The apology showed how far Cindy had come. Once upon a time, she would have told Patricia to stop being such a baby, or not said anything at all, giving her entire focus to the sample she was collecting and ignoring the human it was attached to. Comparatively, this might be described as a proper bedside manner.

Rolling the worktable aside, Cindy told Patricia she could dress. While Patricia buttoned up her blouse, Cindy busied herself sanitizing instruments and closing and labeling sample containers. Then she went to one of the side cabinets and pulled out a small jar of a greenish paste. She unscrewed the lid to the jar and sniffed the contents.

"I'm afraid this stuff doesn't smell very nice. I'm still working on making it more palatable in that sense. But it has proven very effective on my test subjects. I think it will help you."

Patricia took the jar and examined the contents. It definitely didn't look as nice as the clear ointment her doctor had provided. This stuff was green with flecks of brown in it and smelled of something dank and root-ish. Patricia found she kind of liked the smell. It reminded her of the barn at her grandfather's farm somehow. She touched the cream, rubbing a small amount between her fingers. It was a little gritty. "Do you have anything that will help me apply it? It's kind of hard to reach the spot."

"Apply it? Oh, no, Patricia. You've got to eat this, two tablespoons, twice a day."

Patricia felt the color drain from her face at the thought of consuming the nasty stuff.

Cindy snorted and punched her on the upper arm. "You are so gullible, Patricia! Of course, you apply it to the skin. Let me get you a paddle I've developed for application." She walked away, laughing to herself.

JESSICA LIGHTENS UP

J essica Roark was feeling sorry for herself again. She had spent the afternoon watching weepy movies, a favorite solace, but Nathan would be home soon with their boys, and it was time to pick herself up and get a move on. She sat up and gathered up the used tissues in her hands.

She couldn't explain why she watched things like this, knowing they would make her cry. She found it soothing somehow. Maybe it was that she could cry over someone else's problems instead of her own. In this movie, the young man reminded her of herself, before her surgery, when she wasn't sure what her prospects might be. He was hurting and angry and lonely. But he found love, and through love, hope.

When Jessica got her cancer diagnosis, she was already five years married. Her husband had stuck by her, of course. What else could he have done? But it was hard on him, which was hard on her.

Nathan Fellicelli had steadfastly insisted to anyone who would listen that his wife would beat this "cancer thing." It was a way of being supportive, she supposed, but Jessica felt an incredible pressure to show him and his connections she was that kind of strong. She needed to be a good poster girl for the corporate fundraiser, the bravely smiling woman who refused to be a victim.

That didn't leave much room for tears or talking about your fears. Unable to talk about how she really felt without disappointing her husband, Jessica found she didn't have much to say to him. The silence was growing daily. It didn't matter that she had beaten it, in the end. It had changed how they saw each other.

Unlike the girl in the movie, Nathan had difficulty seeing past the illness, to see Jessica herself, more than the external effects of her struggle on him and their children. Maybe it wasn't fair to compare her husband to the fictional love interest of a cancer patient in the film, but Jessica found she was doing so anyway, and her husband was coming up short. She was tired of being fair. She wanted to throw a good temper tantrum and let it all out.

Because he had known her before, known what she had been like, and loved the old her, he mourned the pre-cancer Jessica. Maybe that was the difference. That Jessica had been a lot of fun. She had hosted parties, volunteered in the right charities, represented her husband proudly at formal events.

She had been beautiful, too, glamorous, even. Jessica tugged at her worn yoga pants ruefully. It was hard to care about things like fashionable clothes anymore. It was even harder to listen to the inane chatter at dinner parties and events. It all felt so empty.

The girl in the movie didn't lose the man she had once known; she met him when cancer already had him in its sights. Jessica supposed Nathan had lost the woman he used to love, even though she was sitting on the couch today. She wasn't the same person.

It was true. Part of her was missing, something more metaphorical than her ovaries. Nathan was trying to believe she would find it, and be her old self again. Jessica didn't miss her old self the way he did, but she wasn't that fond of this new self so far, either. She wanted to be fun again, but she didn't seem to enjoy the same things she once had, and she hadn't yet figured out what might bring her joy now.

Sighing, Jessica hauled herself off the dark leather sofa, automatically straightening the blanket she had pulled over herself as she watched TV and putting the remote back into the drawer in the coffee table. She looked back at the couch. It looked showroom ready. No sign it had been used. When she stood, she noticed an odd sort of tickling sensation in her stomach, but she tried to ignore it. She was probably just being paranoid again.

She'd been back to the doctor what seemed like hundreds of times since her oophorectomy, three days before her thirty-second birthday. She kept feeling strange things and panicking. She'd never been so aware of every little thing her body did before. Now, every gurgle, moment of dizziness, or racing heartbeat sent her running to her oncologist. The doctor was nice, telling her it was better to be safe than sorry with her history, and they were always happy to run any tests she wanted for reassurance.

Nathan, on the other hand, was becoming less nice. Jessica guessed there was a time limit for grieving for your lost ovaries, and she was past it now. He was right. All this moping about wasn't changing a thing. She had survived, after all. The boys needed her back. He needed her back.

It was time to step back into her old roles, pick up her life where she had set it down. They were lucky. They had already had children before her diagnosis. They didn't really need a third child. Their lives were full. It was time to get back to normal. He was ready to get back to their lives now that she had beaten this thing. Wasn't she?

In the kitchen, Jessica picked up the tin of herbal tea her mother's friend had made for her and began brewing a cup in her little Adagio teapot. "It will help with the depression," Ms. Liu had written on the card in her bold, spiky, oddly slanted script. "Make you lighter." Jessica didn't know if it was helping or not, but it was very soothing and smelled wonderful. She couldn't really remember what was in it, other than some special kind of ginseng. She'd drunk kind of a lot of it, though. She held the cup under her nose for a moment to savor the smell and then stood staring out the back deck while she drank it.

Some new birds had come to the little station she'd built for them last summer. She'd imagined standing at the window with her children watching the birds, but the boys were not very interested—they'd rather be outside chasing the birds away just to watch them fly. Maybe if she'd been able to have that third child, the daughter, she would've been more contemplative, more like Jessica.

Mostly, Jessica watched alone, and was the only one to notice the little birds coming to enjoy the treats and the bath. A small yellow finch was there now, picking at the seeds she had put out that morning. He turned to her for a moment, cocked his head, jumped into the air, and was gone. Jessica gasped at the effortlessness of it. So beautiful. She felt a kind of giddiness in her gut, like she had been swinging at the park and had gone weightless for a second, a feeling like she might just vault into the sky.

Just then, she thought she heard a car door slam. *Shit!* The house was still a mess. Jessica stacked the teacup next to the other used ones from the past couple of days and hurried to the living room. Just as she crossed the threshold into the living room, her bare foot caught under a rug and she went flying. She braced herself, tucking into a safety roll automatically. It took her a moment to realize she hadn't hit anything.

After a few seconds, she opened her eyes to find she was hovering, midair, about two feet above the glass coffee table. Jessica stayed absolutely still, afraid to move. If she fell into the table, she was going to be horribly hurt. Could she move? She took a deep breath and kind of aimed herself at the couch. Her body drifted a little that direction and then just sort of hovered again.

Okay. This has to be some kind of dream. Right? She must've fallen asleep on the couch. So, if it was a dream, she should be able to figure out a way to move. *Maybe it's like swimming.* Jessica stretched an arm out tentatively in a sort of Australian crawl. When she pulled back, her body shot forward a foot or two, bumping her into a picture frame above the couch and knocking it askew. *Okay. Maybe crawl stroke is too strong.* She decided to try a gentle breaststroke, and her body bobbed gently forward. *That's better.* Another stroke. *This is actu-*

ally kind of fun. Maybe it was a good dream. The light bubbly sensation in her stomach was really strong now. She felt good. Effervescent. She decided to enjoy the dream.

She bobbed around the living room and toward the stairwell. She didn't notice she was continuing to rise until she bumped her head on the lighting fixture. She pushed off from the ceiling with her arms and went back down a bit, back to hovering halfway between the ceiling and the floor. She worked her way into the open two-story foyer and peeked out the window above the door. *Yep, Nathan is home.* He and the boys were closing up the mini-van and heading for the door now. She noticed she could read the decorative plate on the front, "Mama's Taxi." Jessica frowned. She'd taken a vivid dreaming seminar her junior year. You weren't supposed to be able to read when you are dreaming.

Jessica swam her way over to the banister a little awkwardly and grabbed on, trying to pull herself down. She could get her upper body down, but her abdomen and legs stubbornly floated upward. It was like the empty space in her belly had filled with helium, and gravity had lost its hold on her. She was going to scare the kids. Heck, she was scaring herself. *How can I get and stay down?* She blew the locks of blonde hair out of her eyes, noting the color had darkened as her hair grew back in.

She heard Nathan's key in the lock and tried again to pull herself down. She tucked her ab muscles and folded herself at the waist, like she'd done in gymnastics class, pleased to find that it didn't hurt to do so. She pushed herself down and was relieved when her feet made contact with the ceramic tile. The relief quickly gave way to panic, though, when she simply bounced up, like the floor had been a springboard. She lost her hold on the banister and sailed toward the ceiling.

Nathan came through the door, calling her name. Jessica was quiet, holding on to the chandelier with one hand, floating there, looking down at them. From her ceiling view, her children looked wide and squat, like they'd been designed by Duplo. The bald patch on the back of Nathan's head was clearly visible and much wider than when she had last noticed it. Somehow, this made her want to giggle. She stifled the laugh, not wanting the boys to notice her. She let Nathan get the boys settled in front of the TV and then hissed his name when he came back to toss his keys into the bowl by the door. "Nathan! Don't scream—I'm up here!"

HELEN IS HOT AND BOTHERED

Helen Braeburn sank into the overstuffed recliner chair with a sigh of relief. It was wonderful to get off her feet. She'd shown that prissy little rich girl seven different houses today, just so she could go with the first one; the one Helen had told her was perfect for her needs. Why couldn't young people just listen? They could've saved several hours of time and Helen's aching feet.

She bent forward over her paunchy stomach with a grunt and unlaced the bright pink sneakers she had recently started wearing everywhere, much to her daughter's embarrassment. Helen had to laugh at the idea that her twenty-three year old daughter, with white girl dreads and a tattoo snaking from the shoulder to the wrist around her right arm, found her, with her pink sneakers and otherwise perfectly ordinary appearance, embarrassing.

She let the sneakers fall to the side of the chair and tossed the socks down the hall, vaguely in the direction of the laundry alcove. Then she pulled the handle, leaned back, and clicked the button to start the kneading massage feature. It felt good to get her feet up. In spite of the sneakers, her feet still ached, and she thought they looked a little swollen. Her days of wearing pretty little flats were definitely over. She felt like they looked silly on her, anyway. Like putting a sweater on an ugly dog. Besides, knee troubles had come on with the new tire around her middle. Kitten heels weren't going to help that, either.

Now that George was gone, the bastard, she was kind of glad he had insisted on buying this monstrosity of a chair. At the time, she had thought it ridiculous. "Who are you, Ward Cleaver?" she'd said. She had tried getting rid of it along with all his other belongings after he'd decided not to come back from his midlife-crisis cross-country motorcycle ride. The chair was so damned heavy that no one seemed to want to do the work it would take to move it from the third story condo, at least not for free. And Helen was done spending money on George.

So, the chair remained. It had become her favorite place in the condo. She moved a short bookshelf, a small table, and good reading lamp around it, running a multi-plug extension cord under the rug so she could charge her iPad, Kindle, phone, and laptop all without getting up. The table held a stack of books to read, the remote controls for the television and stereo systems, a little bowl of butterscotch candies, and her unsorted mail. There was a blanket over the back of the chair in case she got chilly.

Chilly was definitely not the problem today, though. Helen pulled her hair up, like it would help. Her hair felt stiff, and she wondered if she had just smeared makeup into it. Her stylist would just love that. Strawberry blonde highlights combined with age-defying pasty-white foundation. Lovely.

Helen tugged at the front of her blouse and pulled it in and out like she could fan herself cool. But she knew better. This wasn't an external heat, this was her burning up from within, and all she could do was wait it out. She hated waiting.

Oh wait, there were those new supplements Mary had picked up for me at her little food co-op thingy.

She picked up the box, wondering when that girl was going to get a real job. The supplements were conveniently chair-side with the unsorted mail. The box was bright orange with an ornate yellow font. "Surge Protector." Helen snorted. Well, at least this Dr. Liu who made this stuff had a sense of humor. She read through the label quickly. Lots of hippie-sounding stuff like black cohosh and kava and primrose oil and more sciencey-sounding things like isoflavones. She didn't really know what any of it was, so she read the bio of Dr. Liu on the side panel instead.

"Dr. Cindy Liu has been on the cutting edge of natural remedies for menopausal symptoms for twenty years. Her newest product will bring instant relief to many women suffering from hot flashes." Helen studied the small black and white picture of Dr. Liu. She looked normal enough, small-boned, delicate face half hidden behind large glasses. She seemed to be wearing a lab coat over a nondescript crew-necked shirt. In the tiny picture, there was no way to tell if she was thirty or sixty years old, though Helen assumed she must be nearer sixty if she could really claim twenty years of experience. Dr. Liu's hair was dark and trimmed in the smooth around the face hairdo favored by so many Asian women. She looked directly at the camera, smiling.

Helen considered the orange box again. *Sure, why not? It probably wouldn't make it worse.* And everything at that co-op place was so healthy. That was probably why it tasted so awful.

Helen looked around and realized she had neglected to bring out a glass of water this time. Damn. She really didn't want to clamber back out of the chair to take these things. Could she dry swallow them? *Jesus. No.* They were huge. *Horse pills.* Those chalky kind, too. Bright orange with yellow spots. Weird looking things, for sure. *Ah, here we go.*

Helen found a half-full bottle of water squeezed between stacks of books. It probably wasn't too old. She gulped down the pill.

"Bleah! Horrible!" Helen downed the rest of the water, trying to get the taste out of her mouth. When that didn't work, she grabbed one of her butterscotch candies to suck on. It was a weird combination at first, but then the taste of the pill began to fade.

"Ooh." Helen had the oddest sensation. It was like a cooling ray had run down her body, starting with a sort of tingly sensation in her scalp and then spilling down her neck and shoulders and out her feet.

It was like the heat was being pulled out of her body. She imagined just wadding up the heat ball and chucking it over her head and behind her into the kitchen.

Wow! These things are pretty good, Helen thought. She'd have to let Mary know how quickly and well they worked. Maybe now she could enjoy some TV. She found the other clicker, turned on the system, and began clicking through the channels. She stopped when she found a good one about baseball players getting their chests waxed. Lots of bare muscle to admire.

She was startled out of her enjoyment of grown men turned to jelly by a little wax when the smoke detector started beeping. *Damn!* She'd have to get up to deal with it or her neighbors would call the super on her. Probably the batteries needed to be changed again. It always went off to announce that it needed batteries.

As she hauled herself out of her comfortable seat, she thought she smelled smoke. Impossible, since she hadn't cooked anything in days. But when she turned around, she saw that there were actual flames in the kitchen. *Shit!* Her laptop was in there. She ran into the kitchen and snagged it off the counter. *It's okay!* She hugged it to her chest. It was warm but not yet hot. It would probably be okay. Thank God! She was terrible about remembering to back it up, and her whole life was in there.

But when she turned around, she saw the flames had now spread across the doorway. Helen looked around the room for the fire extinguisher and saw its empty holder on the wall. She hadn't replaced it after that little grease fire a month or so ago. This wasn't good. The air had visible smoke. Not just that wispy stuff, but black puffs. Helen was sure it was the curtains. That filmy, sparkly stuff had to be full of things that turned toxic when they burned. She crouched low in the room. That's what you were supposed to do, she was pretty sure. Something about the air being better down low?

Helen thought she must be in some kind of shock because she seemed to feel just fine. In spite of the smoke, she wasn't having any trouble breathing. Her eyes weren't even watering. *Weird.* She'd still better get out of there. She braced herself and scuttled for the lowest point of fire. She figured she'd have some burns, but it would be better than dying.

When she made it to the living room, she grabbed her striped tote bag and dropped the laptop in it. With one quick arm sweep, she knocked the contents of her side table into the bag. She grabbed her shoes and had just reached for the doorknob when a fireman burst through the door, his face blackened around his protective mask. He grabbed her by the arm, tugged her through the doorway, and then tossed a blanket over her shoulders. Before she knew what was going on, she was outside, standing with all her neighbors in a sort of circle near an ambulance.

"Ma'am. Are you okay, ma'am?" a young man in a white coat was yelling into her face.

Helen nodded, confused.

The young man pulled over a little bag full of medical instruments and leaned toward Helen. "Let's check you out. Are you having trouble breathing?"

Helen shook her head. "I'm fine."

The young man sat her down on a sort of metal stool and took the blanket off her shoulders. He pulled out various gadgets and examined her. As he worked, Helen watched her neighbors. They were a mess! The old fart across the hall was attached to some kind of respirator. The nice young lady with the best view in the complex was sobbing into the shoulder of a tall man in a long black jacket, the latest in a long string of handsome guests Helen had admired in passing. People she didn't even know lived there were all gathered around, whispering, crying, and moaning.

"Unbelievable!" The paramedic pulled his stethoscope down and looked Helen in the face. "Ma'am, I don't know how you did it, but you are absolutely healthy. Jack said your shirt was actually on fire when he dropped this blanket on your shoulders, but I can't find a mark on you. It's some kind of miracle."

JESSICA GETS DOWN TO EARTH

Jessica peered down at her husband, trying not to think about how far below her he really was. She felt sick with fear. He was looking around all over. Everywhere but where she was, hanging on to the chandelier above his balding head.

"Jessica?" he called. His voice seemed to bounce off the empty walls.

Her hand slipped, and she had to grab the light again to avoid floating all the way up to the skylight. There was nothing the least bit fun about this dream anymore. It was becoming all too real.

"Up here," Jessica hissed through clenched teeth.

Nathan peered around the back of the staircase. "Higher!" she said. If he didn't see her soon, the boys were going to hear. She shook the chandelier, making the dangling crystals shake. They were seriously dusty, and the released cloud of dust made her sneeze.

That's when he looked up. His eyes went wide. "What the—"

"Shh! Help me down! I don't want the kids to see this."

That was when three-year-old Max peeked his head around the corner. "Frankie," he yelled to his brother, "Mama can fly!" His grin was so broad it seemed his face might split in half.

Jessica tried to smile back, but the best she could manage was a weak twitch.

Coming at his brother's call, Frankie barreled around the corner, nearly sliding into the china closet when he tried to stop. "Whoa! Mama, how'd you get up there?"

"Right now, I'm just trying to get down, honey," Jessica said, keeping her voice and face as calm as she could. She burped. She was so scared she was sure she was going to throw up. Her husband had moved to the doorway between the two boys. He put one hand on each of their shoulders. The three of them stood there with identical mouths hanging open.

"Any ideas?" Jessica asked, trying not to sound as frightened as she was.

"Can't you come back down the same way you got up there?" asked Frankie. He was so rational for a five year old. Mama's future scientist, Jessica always said.

"I don't think so, honey. I don't really know how I got up here." Jessica gulped back a salty ball of tears that seemed to fill her throat. She tried to signal to Nathan with her eyes to get the boys out of there, but he was just standing there like a slack-jawed idiot. She willed him to snap out of it and get the kids out of the room, so they could work this out together. They used to be so good at solving problems together.

"I just tripped and sort of didn't fall," she told Frankie, who was still studying her with a curious gaze.

Jessica thought about her flight across the living room, how she'd thought it was a dream. That light tickling was still there in her belly. Like she had swallowed something effervescent and it still bubbled in her gut. It wasn't painful. Just sort of strange. She burped again.

As she tried to analyze the feeling, her legs suddenly dropped liked gravity had remembered they were there. She was no longer holding on to the chandelier in order not to float away. Now, she was hanging from it, and she was starting to fall. "Nathan!" she squealed. One hand was already starting to slip. Her hands always got damp when she was scared. It had been a real problem when she'd been doing competitive gymnastics.

Nathan moved. He was standing below her now, waltzing in a sort of circle, trying to make sure he stayed under her. "Boys," he yelled, "get back in the doorway. Stay out of the way!" His eyes were still on the boys when Jessica lost her grip and plummeted from the ceiling. The collision knocked him to the floor.

She lay there, breathing hard for a moment. When she opened her eyes, she saw the chandelier's wild swinging. "Nathan! Get up! The chandelier is going to fall!"

He didn't respond. Christ. He must've knocked his head when she landed on him. She scrambled to her hands and knees, grabbed him under the armpits, and hauled with all her might, trying to keep one eye on the boys and another eye on the chandelier. She was sure she saw dust and plaster breaking away around the joint that connected the fixture to the ceiling. "Frankie, take your brother to the couch, now!"

Frankie knew the tone that meant Mama was not to be disobeyed. He grabbed his little brother by the arm and yanked him around the corner to the living room. Jessica kept tugging on her husband, moving him a few inches with each tug. She'd just gotten his head and shoulders through the doorway when the chandelier fell and cracked the tiles in the foyer. The crystals spun off the fixture and scattered across the room, but none shattered.

"Plastic," Jessica muttered. "I knew it!" Then she called back over her shoulder, "Frankie, bring Mama her phone, Little Man."

LINDA FLEXES HER MUSCLES

Linda held the teacup gently in her hands. It was the last one from her favorite set—the ones with little pink roses and gold edging on the delicate handles. She'd broken all the rest getting used to her larger, stronger hands as she hid in her house like some kind of hunchback these last few days. She and David had told their children she was very ill. Lupita, the oldest, still called every day, but, especially with the way Linda's voice was changing, it wasn't hard to convince her not to come over. Linda sounded terrible.

She couldn't actually get her finger inside the tiny handle of the teacup, so she held the entire thing in the palm of her hand, like the little bowls the soup comes in at Japanese restaurants. Not pretty, but it worked. She should probably just invest in some bigger mugs, but she hated to give up the reminder of who she used to be.

Linda stood suddenly, the motion seeming to make the entire dining room shake. She felt ponderous and huge in this new body, but now, five days after the initial transformation, she was finding there were things she liked about it. Crossing to the kitchen, she opened the top cabinet and easily reached the extra box of hibiscus tea she'd stowed there. When she put it up there a month or so ago, she'd had to haul out the folding step stool from the garage to reach the shelf.

31

Even better, when she had dropped a sock behind the washing machine while trying to get the thrift shop smell out of the new clothes David had picked up for her, it had been a simple thing to tug it out away from the wall and reach behind with her new long arms to pull it out. There had been a pleasure in exerting her muscles that way; a pleasure she had never taken in lifting the ten and twenty-pound weights she used at the gym to fight upper arm wobble. She wondered how strong she was now. A washing machine was a heavy thing, and she had tugged it forward with one hand, like it was nothing.

～

L inda went back to the dining room and looked at the piano. It had been in the same corner for fifteen years, ever since she and David bought it for their youngest daughter who said she wanted to learn to play. Viviana had never learned to play. She'd lost interest within weeks, and the piano had sat there collecting dust and knick-knacks ever since. David always put her off about getting rid of it. "It's too heavy to move," he'd complained.

Was it? Linda wondered. *Was it really too heavy?* Quickly, she moved all the little objects from the top and laid them gently on the dining room table, working as rapidly as she could without breaking all the little pieces of ceramic her children and grandchildren had made. She made short work of the surface and then stood looking at the piano another minute or so, hands on her hips.

It was what they called a studio piano. Plain brown wood without much decorative detail, but quite solid. Her brothers still grumbled about all the aches and pains it gave them to move it into the dining room from the little moving truck she'd hired to haul it across town. Jorge swore it was the start of all of his back problems. But men were such babies. They acted like every little ache and pain was the end of the world. Linda knew it couldn't be that bad.

She blew on her hands and bent at the knees like she'd seen the men do whenever there was heavy lifting to be done. She put her hands under the keyboard and lifted. There was the smallest feeling of resistance and a cracking sound. She let go. That wasn't going to work. She'd just end up yanking the keyboard off.

What if she lifted from the top? She put a hand between the piano and the wall and pushed it out into the room. The little metal wheels screeched, but the piano moved. Linda wondered vaguely if the wheels were rusted immobile.

She stretched her arms out and grabbed the two ends of the piano at the top. The piano lifted off the ground easily, but then the top flopped open and she dropped it, cringing at the sounds of all the insides crashing. That couldn't be good for the soundboard.

The problem was there just wasn't really a good way to get a grip on the thing. Linda stalked around the piano, thinking. She moved to one end and sort of hugged the piano, one arm along the dusty back that had been against the wall and one arm along the front where the music would have sat. She squeezed her arms toward each other, thinking of a pair of tongs or maybe a pair of pliers. She stretched one leg out behind her and pulled the piano toward her chest. To her great surprise, the instrument shifted in her grip, and suddenly, Linda was standing in her dining room with a piano in her hands. "Hah," she cried aloud. "Hah!"

She walked toward the front door, with a sort of shuffling step, leading with the hip, leaning the piano toward her chest so as not to damage the walls. Once she cleared the doorway into the living room with its higher ceilings, she sort of shrugged the piano up higher so she could take more of the weight on her shoulder. *This is easy!* she thought.

❧

L inda set the piano down when she got to the foyer, leaned against it, and contemplated the door for a moment. She hadn't ventured out much yet. In fact, she'd been a hermit since it happened, afraid to be seen by the neighbors if she did so much as weed her garden. Where was she going to go with the piano?

She opened the door a crack and peeked out. No one. A little wider. She poked her entire head out and didn't see anyone. It was ten o'clock in the morning. No one was home. Everyone was at work or school or running errands. There was no one to see her. Even Cindy Liu, the soap-making lady who lived a couple of houses up and kept the strangest hours in the neighborhood, didn't seem to be moving around.

Linda reached up and pulled the little ratchet on the screen door that held it open, enjoying the added inches of height yet again. She could put the piano in the truck and sell it at Ms. Taylor's junk shop three streets over. David's truck was in the driveway. He had taken the Honda when he went to stay with his sister, Isa. He'd said he needed some time to think. Linda said she understood. It wasn't exactly true, but she knew it wouldn't have helped to beg him to stay or try to make ultimatums.

She frowned, thinking of David at Isa's house. She didn't like the idea of him under his sister's influence. She hated to think what kind of assumptions Isa was making about what was wrong in their relationship and how she might pressure David. David swore he wasn't telling Isa anything, that he just kept telling her he didn't want to talk about it, but Linda knew that wouldn't stop Isa from making up her own theories about what was wrong in her baby brother's house.

At least David was still coming over every night. He wouldn't look Linda in the eye most of the time, but he made sure she had groceries and clothes she could wear. Each night, he sat across the table from her, drinking the mug of chocolate she made for him. Linda was sure he was aching in the same way she was, lonely and confused and angry.

Last night, he'd said he missed her, asked if she thought her condition was going to last forever. Her heart had leapt with hope, but she had to admit she had no idea how long this was going to last. She didn't even know what had made it happen in the first place. He'd nodded thoughtfully and sipped his chocolate without saying anything else.

Linda rubbed her jaw and found it rough as if she hadn't yet shaved today, even though she'd already shaved twice. She snorted. Wouldn't Isa be surprised to find out what was really coming between her and her husband after all these years? Not another woman—not even another man, not exactly.

PATRICIA'S INTERN GETS UNDER HER SKIN

Patricia rushed out of her boss's office, so furious she could hardly see. Why did he do these things to her? It was bad enough he insisted on calling her Patty, no matter how many times she corrected him. *Patricia, please.* But an intern? It was a good thing she had a thick skin.

Patricia rubbed at her forehead as if she could reach the headache forming somewhere deep behind her right eye. She had worked for this man for how long now, twenty years? A good ten years before that for his predecessor. He knew damn well she preferred to work alone and absolutely detested any kind of group project or partnership. Yet, this was the third time he had assigned her an intern to mentor. Always women, too. Or really, girls. Skinny little milksops with no real backbone. He actually used the word nurturing, like she was a freaking wet nurse. Didn't he remember that she had sent the last one home in tears? And this one was his own niece. She was going to have to coddle the ninny.

It made her skin crawl just thinking about it. Literally. Damn that scaly skin. She'd have to stop and see Cindy about more of that nasty cream for those patches on her shoulders and arms tonight. The cream, she had promised, would alleviate the itching and let her skin finish its metamorphosis, whatever that was supposed to mean. Sounded flaky to Patricia. What was she, Madame Butterfly?

The cream had made things less itchy, but, at the same time, the patches of skin seemed to grow thicker and had spread onto her shoulders. It was affecting the fit of her blouses.

On the phone, Cindy had advised patience, talking about menopause as a process, and one that shouldn't be shunted aside with drug regimens, but Patricia wasn't a patient woman. She wanted results, yesterday if not sooner. She wished the whole Change would just happen already. She didn't need this transitional time of wonky periods and skin flare ups. Cut to the chase already. She wondered if Cindy had anything that could just jump her ahead in the process. Nothing wrong with a good shortcut.

When Patricia got back to her office, the intern was sitting in the little chair outside the door. She stood when Patricia approached. The girl had already reached out a hand, a big insipid grin on her milky white face before Patricia was anywhere near the reach of a clammy and weak handshake. Patricia held up a manicured hand in return, "Not yet. I'll call you when I'm ready." She shouldered past the little twit, threw her folio on her desk, and thundered over to the coffeepot by the window.

She was so enraged she slopped coffee on her sleeve. "Damn it," she yelled.

The door creaked open behind her, and the twerp peeked her head in. "Ms. O'Neill?"

Patricia turned and glared.

The girl came in, uninvited. "Here, let me see that." She reached for Patricia's sleeve. "Ah, on this lovely ecru jacket! Is this Armani? That's going to stain." The girl set her little beaded purse down on Patricia's desk. "Take it off."

Patricia stared at her. The girl stood with her hand out, waiting. "Give it to me. I'll get it taken care of." The girl reached out a little limp hand but smiled at Patricia with such startling confidence that Patricia obeyed, shrugging off the jacket and letting her take it.

The girl nodded. "I'll be right back." She bounced out of the office, leaving a scent of something floral behind her. Patricia snorted to herself. She probably couldn't make it worse.

Patricia sat down at her desk to wait. She was typing away at a report on her laptop about thirty minutes later when she heard the door click open again. She looked up, and there was the intern, holding Patricia's jacket in a dry-cleaner's plastic bag in one hand and a cup of coffee in the other hand. "The barista downstairs says this is your drink." She placed the coffee just beyond the stack of papers at Patricia's right hand. "And the dry cleaner across the street has emergency service for ten dollars. You can pay me back later."

Patricia smiled in spite of herself. "Thanks."

"Now, Ms. O'Neill, what on earth is wrong with your shoulders?"

Patricia's smile disappeared. She stood and put on the jacket. She threw the plastic covering towards the garbage can and missed. The intern picked it up and tossed it in. Still kneeling, she looked up, all wide-eyed concern. "Seriously, Ms. O'Neill, that looks like it hurts!"

Patricia buttoned her jacket and smoothed it and then stared at the girl silently. She had best let this go. Running her dry cleaning was one thing. Picking up the coffee was nice. But they were not friends. "What did you say your name was?"

The girl fluttered a bit. "Oh, I'm Suzie. I assumed Uncle Mike had already told you about me."

"Suzie, huh?" Patricia sneered. "Not Susan? Sue?"

"Nope, I'm Suzie," she said brightly.

"That's enough for today. Be here at eight o'clock tomorrow." Patricia sat back down and focused her attention on her computer screen. She could feel the girl looking at her but decided to ignore her. Eventually, she really did lose herself in her work. When she looked up, the girl was gone. Patricia was surprised to find that she was disappointed.

LINDA WALKS LIKE A MAN

L inda pulled up in front of the used furniture shop on the avenue and sat behind the wheel for a minute. Would Ms. Taylor recognize her? Linda had shopped here many times. Dawn Taylor, the shop owner, lived in the neighborhood, too, and while she and Linda weren't friends, they were friendly.

They talked about their children when they ran into each other at the weekend market in front of the library. Dawn was always worried about her son finding a nice girl to settle down with, and Linda was happy he had never caught the eye of her daughters. Beau Taylor wasn't interested in nice girls. Linda wondered how such a nice lady had ended up with such a wolf of a son.

Linda flipped down the truck's visor and opened the mirror. Her own soft brown eyes looked back at her, but that was the only part of her face she could recognize. Even her jawline was different now. Her nose might have been the same, but it was hard to tell when the rest of the face was so changed. Her cheekbones seemed to have moved higher in her face, her chin elongated, the whole face widened.

Linda had pulled her long hair back into a tight, low ponytail like she'd seen some of the younger men wearing. Some shorter strands fell forward on her cheeks. That was attractive on a woman but looked strange on her new face. She'd have to grow them out. There was no way she was going to cut her hair short. She tucked the hairs into the ball cap as she pulled it on. It was one of David's ball caps, a plain blue one with a little green paint on the visor part. She sighed at the sight of her face. No, Ms. Taylor wasn't going to recognize her. That was a man in the mirror.

She stepped out of the truck and tugged at her clothes, adjusting the legs of the jeans, and then bent down to check her face in the side view mirror one more time. She smoothed her eyebrows and checked her teeth. It was kind of nice to give up makeup, though she did miss lip-gloss.

She'd been wearing sweatpants at the house, but felt she should wear jeans if she was going to venture out. They felt strange. Or really, she felt strange. She had a struggle figuring out how to zip up the pants without snagging that thing in the zipper. Somehow, it always seemed to be in the way, dangling out the front flap in the boxer shorts or reacting to a change in the air and stiffening for a moment.

She'd already figured out that sitting worked differently, and that men weren't exaggerating about how much it hurt to take a hit to the *cojones*. David had tried to advise her on proper hygiene and care, but they had both been so embarrassed by the conversation that they had ended up talking about baseball instead.

Simply walking in jeans made Linda oddly aware of all her new parts. And they itched. She wondered if that was normal. If normal was a word a person could use for any part of this. She was starting to get all the jokes about the Lower Brain and other head. Sometimes, it really was like that thing had a mind of its own. It always wanted attention. Just like a man.

Linda smoothed the soft, gray T-shirt over her hips, wondering if she should've worn one of the button-down shirts David had brought her. She hoped she didn't look too disreputable. She took a deep breath and opened the door to the used furniture shop. A little bell above the door rang. Linda waited by the door, not wanting to chance moving around too much in the crowded shop. She was always underestimating her size and bumping into things, and Ms. Taylor wouldn't appreciate it if she broke the little ceramics and dishes lining the tables near the door.

Ms. Taylor came out from the back of the store, pulling a work apron over her head and leaving it by the cash register. "Can I help you?" Ms. Taylor smoothed her hands over her hair and tugged her blouse down, displaying her impressive cleavage more prominently. Her voice was honeyed, and she gave Linda a very obvious once-over. Linda was shocked. Maybe Beau wasn't so unlike his mother, after all.

Linda took a step backward, bumping her head on the bell dangling at the top of the doorframe. "Um, yeah," Linda said and then coughed, like she could make her voice sound like her own if she only cleared her throat. "I've got a piano in the truck. Can you take a look?"

"Does it play?"

"Yes. It probably needs tuning, but it works."

"Okay, honey. Let's see what you've got." Ms. Taylor laid a hand on Linda's elbow and gestured toward the door. Linda wondered if this kind of thing happened to her husband when he was out without her. She wasn't sure if she was supposed to hold onto Ms. Taylor's hand or something, so she just turned and led the way to the truck.

~

Standing on the sidewalk, Ms. Taylor stood on tiptoe to look at the piano in the truck. "It doesn't look too bad, on the outside at least." She smiled back over her shoulder. Linda put her hands in her pockets and looked at her feet, trying to remember to stand centered on her two feet and not leaning into one hip. She was pretty sure Ms. Taylor was flirting with her, and she didn't know what to do with that. She'd never been on the receiving end of this kind of attention before.

Ms. Taylor moved to the back of the truck and lowered the tailgate. "Give me a hand up?"

Linda moved to her side and offered a hand. Ms. Taylor took it daintily and steadied herself as she stepped into the truck bed. She lifted the keyboard cover and plunked out a little bit of Für Elise. "Piano lessons when I was eight," she said, winking at Linda. She climbed to the back of the truck and held out a hand for an assist.

When Linda offered her hand, Ms. Taylor bent forward and took her arm, resting a hand on one of Linda's shoulders and the other on Linda's bicep. "Little help?" she said, her face suddenly awfully close. Linda could smell Ms. Taylor's perfume, something floral that she wore a little too much of.

Linda lowered her hands to Ms. Taylor's waist and lifted her easily off the truck, pulling her into the air and putting her down as quickly as she could and nearly tripping over the curb as she backed away. Her arms flailed for a moment, and she bit her tongue to keep from squeaking in surprise. *Men don't squeak*, she reminded herself. She tucked her hands into her back pockets, feeling all elbows and awkwardness, and hoping the pose looked appropriately masculine. "You are a strong one, aren't you?" Ms. Taylor said, admiration in her voice. "Yeah, I'll take the piano. I'll give you two hundred dollars?"

Linda nodded.

Even though there was plenty of room to get around Linda without touching, Ms. Taylor managed to bump her breasts against Linda's elbow, causing Linda to pull her elbows in on herself. She fought the urge to rub the spot where she'd been touched. That thing in her pants stirred a little. *Dios mío.*

"Pull your truck into the alley behind the shop, and I'll have my son come help you get it out and into my back room," Ms. Taylor called over her shoulder, pushing one hip out in a pose Linda recognized as one designed to highlight the view from behind. Linda knew she didn't need the help, but thought she'd better accept it all the same. Normal people couldn't pick up pianos alone.

SUZIE IS A GIRL AFTER PATRICIA'S HEART

W hen Patricia arrived at seven forty-five the next morning, Suzie was already sitting outside the office waiting for her. "Didn't we say eight o'clock?" Patricia asked, mock confusion in her voice.

"Yes, but I believe early is even better than prompt," Suzie answered.

Patricia barked a short laugh. "You might just do okay then. Let's get started."

Patricia had spent some time thinking it out the night before and had chosen a few tasks she didn't enjoy very much herself but still needed doing—some filing, some running different things around to different parts of the building, and reading the reports from the various project groups that reported to her to see where her attention was needed today. She spent only ten minutes explaining and then settled in at her desk and ignored the intern. She figured even if Suzie screwed it all up, none of it would take her long to fix.

She was surprised to look up from her work only an hour later and find Suzie standing by her desk. "Do you need something?" she asked, unconsciously scratching at the scaly patch on her upper arm. It itched, but she could hardly even feel her own nails digging at it.

She hadn't made it to see Cindy the night before. She'd have to go today after work. She stopped scratching when she saw Suzie staring.

"No. I'm done," Suzie said. "Your filing system could use some revamping, though. You might consider digitizing some of these old files that only exist as paper so they can be search-able. The tech department can set me up a scanning station for that this afternoon if you'd like me to take care of it for you."

Patricia liked the idea of a long-term project that would keep the little twit out of her hair. She liked even better that Suzie had already checked on how it would be done. She liked a self-starter. Maybe this girl had some promise after all. Patricia thought about her old friend Cindy and how no one would suspect the steel lining her backbone, either. Books, covers. All that jazz. Though the cover of this particular book was very blonde, very wide-eyed, and very young. That would take some work on her part to get past. "Okay. That could be useful. What about the errands and the reports?"

"I used the in-office courier service to return the items to their owners. As for reports, it seems like the teams are mostly on track, but, reading between the lines, I think Marcie Henderson is bullshitting you. She doesn't have her deliverables, and she's just hoping you won't ask for them today. Looking back at old reports, she's very good at never actually saying she has things ready but leaving it open for you to assume she does."

Patricia stood up and walked over to the window-side coffeepot again. She sipped her coffee silently, considering. She'd had a bad feeling about Ms. Henderson for a few months now, but everyone else seemed so sure she was the one to ride this particular wave into the future that Patricia second-guessed her instincts. She paced a little, trying to release a little of the tension through movement. She felt oddly wound up over this. And being wound up seemed to make her skin worse. When she ran her hand across the back of her neck, there were nodules, almost like bones. They went back down when she took some deep breaths and rubbed them.

She sat back down in her desk chair and spun back toward Suzie, tapping one mauve lacquered nail on the side of the mug. She wriggled in her chair to scratch her upper back against the rough material. Damn, it itched again today. Suzie was giving her the oddest look, like she really wanted to ask something. Patricia waited for a beat, but no thought was forthcoming. "It's interesting you would pick Ms. Henderson as the case needing my attention. Pull the documents for her group. Let's look at them."

~

Hours later, Patricia and Suzie had their heads bent together over the same screen looking at the graphs they'd made showing the history of missed deadlines, dropped balls, and outright lies coming from the "cloud group" headed by Marcie Henderson. The workers were obviously in over their heads, unable to do the work they were being asked to do and doing their best to keep that under wraps.

An analysis of the employees in the department showed that some were quite productive, but the tasks they were given didn't make sense. It was like the big picture was entirely missing, like the boss was just throwing out tasks without knowing how all these pieces would fit together. Suzie had been so proud, laying out the charts she made.

"I do love a good chart," she said. "They just make things so clear!"

Patricia had to agree. It was nice to work with someone who appreciated a good visual organizer the same way Patricia did.

"It's her," Patricia shouted, slamming a fist on the stack of papers. "These guys could do this if they just had a leader who knew what was going on." She tapped her finger on a file for one of the new guys, one only three years out of grad school. "I think this is our man. Get him in here for a conversation this afternoon. Don't let Ms. Henderson know about it."

Suzie jumped up to make the call and then looked at the clock. "Oh, Ms. O'Neill, I don't know that we'll reach him. It's six-thirty already."

"Try anyway. Set something up for first thing tomorrow morning.

That's probably better, anyway." Patricia gestured at one of their charts. "Ms. Henderson tends to arrive late. We can talk before she arrives."

Patricia swung her blue Donna Karan jacket across her shoulders and removed her new Diane von Furstenberg purse from the desk drawer. "I've got to go. My spin class starts at seven. I get cranky if I don't get my exercise." She winked as she closed the door. "You wouldn't like me when I'm cranky."

LINDA'S FAMILY MATTERS

L inda was in the kitchen, reminding herself to breathe. In the living room, just on the other side of the swinging door, she could hear Carlitos, her favorite grandchild asking again for *abuelita*. The sound of his voice tore at her heart. What if he couldn't accept her? Would she lose her special boy? He was only three. There was so much he didn't know yet, so much she still wanted to show him.

She knew she was stalling. The food was ready. Everyone was here. Even Isa, her husband's nosy sister. Isa hadn't been invited, but of course, she knew the entire family was gathering today, so she had stopped by to return a long-ago borrowed dish, and David had, of course, invited her to stay. She, too, was dying to know what was going on that had her brother and his wife behaving so secretively.

Linda smoothed her hair down, retying the ponytail at the base of her neck. She checked her reflection in the dark face of the microwave and then licked her finger to smooth her eyebrows back down. She looked good, she supposed, but she didn't look like anyone's mother or grandma anymore. She was just barely getting used to this face herself, and she'd had more than a week to look at it in the mirror.

She sighed. She knew David was right. It was time to tell them. She missed her grandchildren. She couldn't hide from her daughters forever. She closed her eyes to pray for support. She hadn't been this nervous since her first blind date with David back when she was sixteen years old.

It was time. She wiped her sweaty hands on her apron one more time, took a deep breath, and pushed open the door into the living room. The room went silent in an instant. The sound of Linda's soft leather shoes seemed impossibly loud on the hardwood floor, and she forced herself to keep walking, her eyes trained on the ground to avoid meeting all the eyes trained on her. She stopped, standing in front of the silent television, and raised her face to her family seated in the living room.

All three of their daughters looked at each other and at her and back to each other again. None of them spoke. Viviana pursed her mouth and crossed her arms. Lupita reached behind her for her husband's hand, drawing it to her shoulder. Estela covered her mouth with one hand, her lacquered nails curled into her cheek.

Carlitos turned to see what his mother was staring at. The twins stopped in mid-struggle over the electronic game they had been unsuccessfully sharing to gape open-mouthed at the stranger in their midst. The other children were too young to understand what was happening, but they knew their parents were upset and clung to them. The baby cried and Paul handed him back to his wife. He looked to Viviana to explain, confusion and questions all over his face, his pale skin reddening as it did when he was nervous. Her other two sons-in-law looked at David and at Linda and back again.

Linda felt sick to her stomach. Would no one speak? Her gaze darted all over the room, seeking the face of each of her family in turn, but only David met her eyes squarely. She very nearly turned on her heel and ran back into the kitchen to hide.

Then Isa stood up, clutching her little black church purse in her hands like she might have to use it as a weapon. "Is this him?" Isa's voice shook. "Is this the man that is coming between my little brother and his wife?"

David laughed. Everyone in the room turned to look at him.

"Don't be ridiculous, Isa." He walked to Linda's side and took her arm, just as he always did. She smiled down at him gratefully and patted his hand on her arm. "Don't you know your own sister-in-law?"

Isa sat down hard on the arm of the chair. She didn't seem to notice her knees were spread in a decidedly unladylike manner. "*Mi cuñada?*"

David moved to her side, taking her elbow to guide her into the cushioned part of the chair. "It's true, Isa. This is Linda, my wife."

Isa's mouth gaped open like some kind of fish. Linda continued to smile nervously, plucking at the lace around the pocket of her apron.

Her daughters had turned toward each other, forming a circle of knees as they all tried to talk at the same time. "Is Papi crazy? What can he mean? Where's Mamá? Who is this man? Should we call the police?" Viviana's voice was the most strident, rising above the cacophony. "Who is this man, Papi? Why is he wearing Mami's apron? What's going on here?"

Linda's mind spun, trying to come up with something she could say or do that would show them all she was herself.

Linda reached out for Viviana's hand, and her daughter snatched it back. "I don't know who you are and what you think you are doing here, but I will find out. Come on, Paul!" She turned on her heel and left.

Linda followed to the porch, calling after her, but Viviana didn't even turn around. Paul stood outside the car for a moment after the baby was buckled in, looking back at the house and Linda standing on the porch. His face was a mass of turmoil. He and Linda had always been close, and Linda could see he wanted to hear what she and David had to stay. But he did what he had to for his *familia* and took his wife home. Linda was heartbroken and proud of Paul at the same time. It was important to choose your wife's side, even if she might be wrong.

When Linda came back to the living room, wiping tears on the sleeve of her brown T-shirt, everyone was standing in a circle, talking at the same time. David was trying to explain that it had just happened. Hovering at the edge, unsure how to help, Linda eventually just sank into her chair, the blue floral one, and let her head fall into her hands. After a minute or two, she felt a small, warm hand on her knee and looked up.

"*Abuelita?*" said Carlitos, looking confused.

Linda knelt, putting her face near his and nodded silently. "*Soy yo, Carlitos.*" The room grew quiet again, all eyes focused on Carlitos and Linda.

Carlitos tilted his head as he always did when he was thinking deep thoughts. He was an old soul, Linda had always said. The boy laid one hand on each of Linda's cheeks, looking very seriously into her eyes. "*Abuelita*, did you make my favorite cookies?"

"Of course, I did. *Biscochitos y marranitos, también.*"

He nodded. "And are you going to be a boy now?"

"Yes, Carlitos, I think I am."

"But you are still my *abuelita?*"

"*Soy tuyo, querido.* I am yours. *Siempre.*" Linda's voice cracked. She couldn't stop the tears.

David crouched beside her. "Wait till you hear how this happened, little monkey." He scooped up his grandson and gestured at the group. "Come on. Mami made tamales. Let's eat!"

There had never been such a quiet and restrained dinner at the Alvarez house. At times, all Linda could hear was the sound of silverware on plates. David did his best to explain simply and gently what had happened, but each time he tried, he had to keep starting and stopping the story when a new outburst of disbelief derailed the telling. Linda didn't blame the children for their doubt and confusion. It was beyond strange.

No, Linda had not had surgery. It had just happened. It seemed to have been caused by her soap. At first, they thought it was temporary, so they hadn't said anything. Yes, they were pretty sure Linda was going to be a man from here on out. Yes, they were staying together. David had gripped Linda's hand when he said that, and her heart had soared.

Carlitos and the other grandchildren had the least trouble. By the time they had finished off dinner, they were focused on what kind of cookies Abuelita had made this time. Magdalena, the quieter of the twins, had whispered to her sister that she didn't know why their grandma would want to be a yucky boy. Her sister reminded her that grownups did things that didn't make sense all the time.

As people finished eating, they spread out across the house. Linda and David played politics, talking to each person in turn, making sure each of their loved ones got a chance to ask what they needed to ask. Linda called on all her patience as she proved to each individual that she was indeed Linda Alvarez on the inside, no matter what her outside looked like. She answered hundreds of questions that only Mami would know and recounted childhood stories for each daughter and how-we-met stories for *los yernos*. Her sons-in-law, wisely, in Linda's opinion, looked to their wives and followed their leads. Isa had been silent long enough that Linda worried she might have had a stroke. Her worries were relieved when Isa took a second helping of dessert. Whatever she was thinking hadn't affected her appetite.

It had taken all afternoon, and Linda was hoarse from talking so much, but one by one, her children, all but Viviana, had come to terms with it, each in her own way. Lupita, ever the big sister, was already texting Viviana, trying to get her to come back and at least listen, but Viviana wasn't answering. Linda tried to have faith they would win her over, given time.

She was glad they had decided not to talk about her strength just yet. As it was, all this talking took all day. Come suppertime, their luncheon guests were still there. Linda had refused to cook a second meal for so many people, so they had ordered pizza.

It was nearly nine that night before Linda and David were able to convince their family it was time to go back to their own homes. Three of the grandchildren had to be carried out, having already fallen asleep. Having seen the last daughter out the door with a quick hug and kiss, Linda collapsed on the couch, exhausted. She put a pillow over her head and blessed the silence. As she rested, David was collecting all the pizza boxes and flattening them. He hummed as he walked through their home, and Linda smiled in spite of her exhaustion. It had been worth it.

HELEN IS BORED AND DANGEROUS

Helen shifted a pile of magazines so she could sit on her daughter Mary's futon. It was a terrible futon. The cover was a pink floral. Helen was pretty sure the background was supposed to be white, but it was yellow. It smelled awful, like patchouli and old lasagna. Helen looked doubtfully at a reddish stain on the edge nearest her left thigh. She hoped it was a food stain, but it really looked like blood. She shifted closer to the magazines. *Mother Jones. Whole Earth Catalog. Ms.* Not a fun read in the pile. Helen sighed and picked up the *Ms.* magazine. She missed her chair.

Mary had insisted her mother stay with her while the insurance stuff was straightened out. The initial investigation said the fire had started in her kitchen, but they couldn't find a direct cause—no appliance shorting out, no stove left on, no cigarette left burning. None of the usual causes. The investigator distrusted "freak accident" as an explanation, but right now, it was all they had, so they were taking more time.

Looking at the futon again, Helen really wished she had opted for the hotel like she had first planned. She sniffed the air. She thought she smelled cat even though her daughter didn't have one. Giving up on *Ms.,* Helen picked up *Bitch* magazine. She flipped through page after page. Angry articles about politicians. Single mothers. Transsexuals. Rape. Ads for cloth pads and (shudder) menstrual cups. Thank God she was past all this. She hadn't had to buy a pad in over a year now. For the last few months, after Mary had started working at the co-op, she had to hide her paper products in a locked cabinet in the bedroom to avoid lectures about landfills and seventh generation and blah blah blah blah blah. Helen was as green as the next person, but there were some things that were too much to ask.

Looking around the basement apartment—her daughter insisted on calling it a flat like they were living in London or something—Helen prayed the insurance would clear soon and she could get into a new place. She was going to shop for a bottom floor condo this time. No more stairs or creaky elevators for her. If she really wanted to get Mary's goat, she could buy into that new complex they'd built right in the middle of downtown, the one Mary and her friends had spent the summer picketing and trying to stop construction of.

Helen was bored. She paced the small apartment again, picking up the knick-knacks and tchotchkes and putting them back down. Her daughter was no housekeeper. The stuff was so dusty it was easy to see right where the piece had been. She looked at the small bulletin board over the desk in the corner. There were photos of people she didn't know, mostly smiling kids with facial piercings and large backpacks, probably spending their parents' money on travel adventures. Helen had almost turned away when she spotted it: a picture of George, her ex-husband.

She pulled it off the board. He had his arm around a small brown woman with a broad white smile. He was wearing a leather headband around his forehead. He looked tanned and strong and happy. Helen's blood boiled. The bastard. She turned the picture over. "The pic you asked for. Hope you can come visit again soon! Love, Elaine." The picture curled in her hand, the edges seeming to melt. Helen dropped the picture in surprise and then picked up the melted mess and put it in the garbage can. She reached in and shuffled the other garbage around to hide it. That was weird.

Helen sighed. Mary was a good kid. Of course, she would keep a relationship with her father. She also would protect her mother's feelings by not making that known.

Helen knew she was fortunate to have such a good daughter. A daughter who wanted her there in her apartment, who offered her a futon to sleep on, no matter how ratty. But she had to get out of this apartment. She had really enjoyed living alone, and it was killing her to schedule her life around her daughter's.

It had only been three days, but three days could be very long. Mary got up early and did yoga in the living room, so Helen had to get up early, too. Mary ate vegetarian, so Helen had to eat vegetarian for any meals they shared, if you could call them meals or call it eating.

She'd have to call the insurance agent again. What was taking them so long to process her claim? She definitely should've taken the offer of the hotel. But Mary really wanted to help, and she'd thought the few days together might be good for their relationship. They hadn't been as close since George had left. Mary said she got tired of hearing her mother sound embittered. Helen got tired of having to put a happy face when she didn't feel it. So, here she was, suffering through a stay with her daughter in the name of family.

Not that Mary hadn't made any concessions. She had cleared a corner of the tiny counter so Helen could plug in a small coffeepot, even though she thought coffee was evil. Apparently, it was grown on the backs of slaves or something like that. Oh, and it would give her eye spasms and migraines, hurt her blood pressure, and mess up her digestive system. Helen listened politely and sipped quietly from a mug that said, "We're still angry!" in big, black letters atop a green female gender symbol, and tried to get used to the flavor of the new coffee Mary had brought home—the one with the big "FREE TRADE" sticker to seal it.

Helen knew Mary was a good girl and all this came from a desire to make a difference. How could you fault a young person for caring? It was just hard, being in her line of sight all the time, having all her little habits criticized. Unfortunately, Mary's self-assurance made her more than a little condescending toward her mother. Helen held her temper pretty well, she thought. But it was irritating.

At least, Mary had been pleased in one respect. She was happy to see Helen was using the Surge Protector pills and no longer taking the "unnatural" hormone supplements her doctor had given her. Helen didn't argue about the hormones. While she thought calling them unnatural was a stretch, given that estrogen was something your body produced on its own, anyway, she didn't miss the pills and the strange way they made her feel. And Helen had honestly been able to say the co-op supplements helped with her symptoms.

Last night, when they had been sitting in lawn chairs out in the green space with some of Mary's friends, Helen had another good one. She'd tried to be cool and not make a big deal out of it, but she was sure she was changing colors. Finally, she'd excused herself and came back with a pill and glass of cold water. Just like last time, there was this feeling like ice running down her head and trickling down her body. Helen imagined puffing the heat out the open toes of her Ecco sandals.

Suddenly, there was a little fire by the feet of one of the boys, the one with the pretty blue eyes. Too skinny for her taste, but Mary seemed to like the skinny ones. He jumped up, whooping in surprise. Mary dumped the rest of her drink onto the fire, and it went out easily. Just to be sure, Helen stomped on the ground a few times. That was weird.

Standing in her daughter's living room, Helen looked back at the wastebasket that held the melted curls of the photograph. Something was definitely strange around here. She was starting to think it was her.

JESSICA TRIES TO STAY GROUNDED

J essica watched as the paramedics raised the table with Nathan strapped to it and pushed him through the still-open door. Max had one damp and mildly sticky hand wrapped around her knee. Frankie had hooked one hand into the back of Jessica's pants and had his only recently abandoned thumb firmly in his mouth. Jessica rested one hand on each downy, blond head, grateful for the comfort in their warm bodies against hers. She felt as if they were the only things anchoring her to the ground. Thankfully, that seemed to be only a metaphorical anchor. She didn't seem to be in danger of floating away again.

As soon as the paramedics left, Jessica freed herself from the grasp of her sons and knelt in front of them. "Everything is going to be okay, boys. The doctors are going to help your Daddy." Big tears fell down Max's chubby cheeks, and Jessica rubbed them away with her thumbs. "Really, baby. It's going to be okay. I promise." She leaned her head against his, forehead to forehead, their private signal for serious reassurance. She reached for Frankie's hand, and Frankie nodded emphatically without removing the thumb from his mouth.

"Frankie, can you put your shoes and jacket on and help your little brother with his?"

Frankie nodded again.

When the boys left the foyer, Jessica took a deep breath and slid her foot across the tile floor in practiced graceful steps, like she once would have made across a gym mat on the way to her floor routine event. She was afraid to lift her feet, afraid that if she stepped down too hard, she'd spring back up into the air again. The bubbling sensation in her stomach had completely disappeared. She hoped that was a good thing, a sign she would stay on the ground.

A few more sliding, ice skating steps and she was at the side table, where her purse and keys were. It was a very solid table with an antique marble top. Holding onto it made her feel secure. She looked at the swirls of marble and pondered her dilemma. She had to get to the hospital with the boys. She really didn't know what had made her float, or what had made her stop. She didn't know if it would happen again or if it had been some bizarre fluke, a dream somehow made manifest or a paranormal event.

What she did know was that there wasn't time to figure it out now. Nathan was at the hospital. Her family needed her. Hearing the boys coming toward the front hall again, she gripped the table and bounced a little on her toes. Nothing. Gravity was once again on her side.

She sighed. She'd have to take her chances. She pulled out her cell phone and dialed her mother.

～

They hadn't been in the family waiting area long when the boys spotted Grandma coming through the doorway and ran to pummel her with exuberant hugs.

Max yelled, "You should have seen it, Grandma. Mommy was flying, and then she fell on Daddy!"

Eva Roark lifted an eyebrow at her daughter, and Jessica looked around the room nervously and did her best "Kids-what-can-you-do?" shrug.

Eva frowned and reached into her pocket. "Here, Frankie. I just got a new cell phone. Why don't you and your brother figure out how it works for me so you can teach me later?"

The boys ran back to the bench seat, already squabbling over who got to hold it and wondering loudly if this one would be able to show movies. Eva watched them, smiling, but concern quickly clouded her face when she looked back at Jessica.

"How is he? What's happened?"

Jessica took a deep breath, trying to decide what to say. "We're waiting to hear. They're still examining him, I guess. All they've done is take our insurance information so far." Jessica realized with a guilty start that she hadn't really been worrying about Nathan that much. Tears suddenly sprung to her eyes. What kind of wife was she? It hadn't really occurred to her that he wouldn't be all right. He had to be, didn't he? They'd already been through so much with her cancer. It wouldn't be fair if he wasn't all right. Things were supposed to go back to normal now.

"I'm so glad you're here. The hospital is no place for the boys." Jessica patted her mother's arm as if to reassure her, but really, the touch was to comfort herself. "I've already had three age-inappropriate questions about transgender issues thanks to daytime television."

Eva grabbed her daughter's hand and gave it a squeeze. Jessica looked down at their joined hands and considered what to say next. She wanted to tell her mother about it all. If anyone would believe her, it would be her mother. Anyone else would call the guys in white coats. But here in the waiting room didn't seem like the place or the time.

"How did the accident happen?" Jessica jumped at the sound of another voice. She looked up into the curious, penetrating gaze of an Asian woman who had taken the chair beside her. It took her a long moment to realize it was Cindy Liu, her mother's long-time friend, the one who made the tea she enjoyed. The two women had met when Jessica was just a baby and had been friends all of Jessica's life.

"Ms. Liu, how nice of you to come," Jessica began. It seemed impolite to comment on the strangeness of tagging along to a family hospital visit, but Jessica was taken aback by the woman's presence in a private moment. Even if she had been visiting when Jessica called, the courteous thing to do would have been to excuse herself and call to check in later. Of course, Ms. Liu had not always been one to follow societal expectations or to read social cues well. Jessica had sometimes wondered if her mother's friend might have a form of autism or some other disorder that kept her from understanding how her behavior affected others.

"What did your son mean? You were flying?" Ms. Liu seemed oddly intense. Jessica squirmed beneath her gaze, looking to her mother for help. Her mother just shrugged, as if to say, "You know how she is."

"Um, well, it's a strange story..." Jessica hoped to avoid having to make up the public story right there on the spot.

~

A nurse came into the waiting area and called, "Mrs. Fellicelli?" Jessica raised her hand, so relieved by the nurse's timing that she almost shouted. "It's Roark. But I'm married to Nathan."

The nurse nodded and held the door open for Jessica to pass. Jessica squeezed her mother's hand and went through the door.

The nurse led her around several corners and up a small staircase and left her outside the door of a hospital room. At least the quick pace hadn't given her time to worry about whether she might float off toward the ceiling again. Jessica hoped she wasn't expected to find her way back to the waiting room alone. She had no idea where she was now.

She stepped into the room the nurse had indicated and found a doctor leaning over her husband. She knocked on the doorframe. The man stood, clicking off the small light he had been using and dropping it into his jacket pocket. He extended his hand in greeting. "Mrs. Fellicelli?"

Jessica opened her mouth to correct him and then abruptly decided to let the mistake go. What difference did it make if he got her name right? He could tell her Nathan was going to be fine. She nodded.

"I'm Dr. Hofstedder."

Jessica took the proffered hand and shook it quickly, anxious for the man to get past the pleasantries and just tell her how Nathan was. "How's my husband?"

The doctor stepped to the side, and Jessica saw Nathan lying in the bed. He looked oddly small and had a variety of monitors attached to him, but from his regular breathing, he seemed to be sleeping, not unconscious. His color was good. She leaned over and brushed his hair back from his forehead in what she hoped looked like a loving gesture instead of just her not knowing what to do with her nervous hands. She gripped the side rail of his bed, hooking her fingers beneath.

The doctor placed a hand on her elbow and said quietly, "He's resting. Let's talk in the hall."

Jessica gave her husband's hand a squeeze and turned to follow the doctor and then stopped. Her foot hadn't made contact with the ground. *Shit.* She grabbed at the doctor's arm, tugging him back, keeping a strong grip on Nathan's bedrail with her other hand. "Is my husband going to be okay, doctor?" Her voice sounded a little panicky, but Jessica hoped the doctor would just think she was worried about Nathan. If she pushed down hard with her arm, she could force her feet to rest on the floor.

The doctor gently tugged his arm free from her grip, and Jessica turned her body so she could hold on to the railing with both hands. It was a relief to be able to use both hands; the one arm had begun to tremble from the force she was exerting to hold herself in place.

The doctor seemed puzzled by her fervor but offered reassurance. "Yes, he'll be fine. He's got a concussion, but I think you'll be able to take him back home tonight as long as you can stay with him to make sure his condition doesn't change." The doctor cocked his head at her curiously. He was probably just surprised that she hadn't obediently followed him into the hall, but Jessica still felt paranoid that he could tell what was going on with her. Her chest felt tight and her stomach queasy. She was one step away from telling him what was happening and begging for help when she farted.

Jessica had no idea what the connection was, but as soon as she farted, her feet settled back into her shoes and onto the floor. She smiled, feeling the knot around her heart loosen. "You had me at 'fine,'" she said and turned back toward Nathan, trying to compose her face into a look of wifely concern, but really just wishing the doctor would go.

"Mrs. Fellicelli?" The doctor hesitated, and when he spoke again it was with a nervous laughter in his voice. "It's the oddest thing. He said you fell on him when you were flying around the chandelier."

Jessica tried to keep her face neutral. Her smile felt overly wide as she tried to laugh without giving way to hysteria. "Well, you did say he had a concussion, right?"

PATRICIA IS PUT TO THE TEST

Patricia walked in to Cindy Liu's lab without knocking. Some people might consider that rude, but Patricia thought knocking was just unnecessary. After all, Cindy knew she was coming. She was there exactly when she said she would be, seven o'clock. There was no need to play parlor manners games. They'd been friends a long time, after all. She calculated quickly. She'd started college in 1973. Had it really been forty years?

Patricia thought about the first time they met. The Resident Advisor had gathered all the new fresh-women into the lounge for a meet and greet. Though both Patricia and Cindy had been by the room and dropped off their belongings, they hadn't yet met, somehow missing each other throughout the afternoon as each wandered in and out and around campus. They had only just introduced themselves and realized they were each other's roommates when the RA asked them all to sit down and started her spiel. The RA had directed them through a silly activity designed to help them get to know each other, an icebreaker with a cutesy theme. Something about flowers, Patricia thought she remembered. "These are the friendships you will cherish all your lives," she had rhapsodized, fluttering her hands at the gathered young women and seeming almost as if she might cry.

Patricia had felt embarrassed for her. She thought a person should have more self-control than that, especially in a position of leadership. When other women got teary, Patricia had to fight to keep herself there in the room. Her every instinct told her to flee the melodrama and false sisterhood. Turning to the side to hide her consternation, she found herself looking into the face of her new roommate Cindy Liu, a very similar look of disgust and dismay on her face.

Patricia was much too polite, at age eighteen, to say aloud what she was feeling, but Cindy, a few years older, had no such qualms. As the meeting went on, she began to draw caricatures of other students and slyly show them to Patricia, who had bitten the inside of her cheek to keep from laughing aloud.

That RA had annoyed them both with all her hokey sentimentality, but in the end, she had been sort of right. Patricia couldn't remember the other women in the room at all. But she had cherished her friendship with Cindy all her life.

~

Moving aside a sheaf of papers on Cindy's worktable to make a place to put her purse, Patricia complained, "Cindy, these patches on my back are getting thicker, and now they are on my arms and chest, too. What the hell is in this cream you've been giving me?"

Cindy held up one finger, and Patricia knew that meant she needed to finish something. She huffed, impatient. After all, she was on time. Cindy should have been ready for her when she got here. She swung around and started peering into the animal cages. There was always something interesting going on with Cindy's lab animals.

"What's up with this one?" Patricia pointed at a small, white rabbit. The label on the front of the cage said, "Roxie" but you could see that "Rocky" had been crossed out beneath. "She didn't like her name?"

Cindy clicked at her computer a few more seconds and then looked up. "Sex change," she said, picking up a black cloth and dropping it over the lizard cage she'd been working with. Just as the cloth fell, the lizard seemed to catch fire. It must have been a trick of the light.

Patricia blinked. "You mean it used to be a boy rabbit, and now it's a girl?"

Cindy nodded but didn't offer any more information. "Let's see what we have. Take off your jacket."

Patricia sighed. She was used to Cindy clamming up like that. She never liked to talk about what she working on until after she completed her experiments.

Removing the jacket was more difficult than it should have been. The patches were thick enough that they were making the sleeves snug against her biceps, definitely thicker than when she had first come in. In fact, they couldn't properly be called "patches" anymore. They were more like plates one might have seen on an armadillo or, more accurately, a triceratops. Patricia couldn't see the ones on her back, but she knew the eczema, or whatever it was, must have been spreading because of the itching. She resisted the impulse to turn and rub her back against the support beam behind her and tried to be patient as her friend examined her.

Cindy rested the pen she was holding against her cheek and tilted her head thoughtfully. She had that look of studied indifference that could only mean she was considering something deeply. She also had, Patricia noted with surprise, a face-lift. She wouldn't have expected her friend to indulge in that kind of vanity, but there was no denying her face had fewer lines than it had just a few days earlier. She looked all of fifty years old, maybe a little less. Patricia knew she was in her later sixties.

"Come, stand here in the light." She walked around Patricia in a circle three times, clicking her pen open and closed, leaning in close and changing her angle as she walked. She picked up a petri dish and a scalpel and scraped off a piece of the plate on Patricia's upper arm.

"What the hell, Cindy! You've got to warn me before you do something like that. What kind of doctor are you, anyway?" Patricia clapped her hand protectively over the platelet on her upper arm, but there was no bleeding, no external sign that the area had even been cut.

"Did it hurt?"

"Well, no." Patricia examined her friend's face, looking for a clue as to whether or not she should be frightened by the lack of pain response. It couldn't be a good sign, but how bad a sign was it?

"How about this?" Cindy grabbed the other upper arm and squeezed, none too gently. Patricia saw Cindy's knuckles whiten as she tightened her grip. "Can you feel that?"

"Not really."

"Sit down." Cindy pulled out a low-backed stool and pushed the taller woman down on it. "Close your eyes, and tell me when you can feel my touch."

Patricia obliged. Long seconds passed. Patricia felt nothing. She sighed, growing impatient. "Are you going to start?" Suddenly, there was a loud pinging sound reverberating around the lab. Patricia opened her eyes. Cindy was glaring at her and rubbing her fist. The knuckles were reddened. There was an array of little hammers laid out on the table in front of her.

"You'd better put some ice on that," Patricia suggested, gesturing toward the quickly swelling knuckles. "What did you do? Hit yourself with one of those hammers?"

Cindy wrinkled her brow. "Did you really not feel that? None of that?"

Patricia shook her head. "Not a darn thing. What did you try?" She was getting more and more worried but trying to stay calm and let her friend do her work.

Cindy gestured at the hammers and flexed the fingers on her sore hand. "I got mad. Stupid of me, using my own hand. You're as well armored as a tank, Patricia O'Neill."

Patricia snorted. "I doubt that. But I'm worried there's something wrong with my nerves if I can't feel you hitting me with a hammer." She tried to make it sound like a joke, but there was a chill going down her spine. This might have been much more serious than she had first thought.

"Let me try something else." Cindy crossed the lab to the desk under the window and pulled something out of the top left-hand drawer. "Stand over there," she ordered, gesturing at a wall lined in soft white cushioning. Patricia obeyed. "Now turn around, so your back is to me."

Patricia stood still, waiting. She heard a sound she felt she ought to be able to identify, sort of a "shoom." At almost the same time, she felt an impact on her left shoulder. She spun around, excited, "I felt that!"

There was Cindy Liu, lowering a handgun with a silencer, and stepping out from behind a policeman's riot shield.

"You shot me?" Patricia growled with anger. "What the hell were you thinking?"

Cindy smiled, an ear-to-ear grin that made her look like an evil twelve-year-old. "I'm going to need to get a blood sample and a few more scrapings. This is amazing!"

HELEN LETS OFF STEAM

"**M**om! Guess what?" Helen turned from the window where she'd been standing and thinking, sipping the coffee she had snuck out to buy from Starbucks. Quickly, she dropped the labeled cup inside an oversized ceramic mug that had been on the counter and hoped her daughter wouldn't notice the disposable cup from the evil company. She turned and put on her best curious face.

Mary was practically fluttering; she was so animated. Helen hoped she wasn't in love. The last one was almost twenty years older than her and had been an exercise in biting her tongue for Helen.

"Dr. Liu is coming to Our Market! If you come back to work with me this afternoon, you can meet her."

Helen breathed out. Good. Not about a man this time.

Helen must've looked blank because her daughter went on. "You know, the lady who makes the supplement. The one that helped so much with your hot flashes?"

"Oh! And she'll be there today? I do have a few questions for her. Let me go get my purse." Why not? She didn't really have anything else to do.

~

An hour or so later, she was seated in an outdoor picnic area that had been temporarily re-arranged into a sort of forum. There was a makeshift podium under the large cedar, and the benches and tables formed a loose sort of semicircle around it. Helen sat almost exactly in the middle—alone. She hoped someone else would show up. She was early. She'd had to come early to share a ride with Mary because Mary didn't see the sense in two people driving separately to the same place. "Wasteful." So, she had arrived with an hour or so to kill.

She'd circled the tiny market twice, buying overpriced lip balm she didn't need, the little gluten-free bag of cookies she was nibbling on now, and an ice tea that was oddly pink but not that bad with enough of that weird brown raw sugar they had. That left forty-five minutes. She'd already read all the magazines. They were the same ones all over Mary's apartment. She should've brought her laptop. They had wifi, more reliable than Mary's, and she could've caught up on her e-mail and checked to see if she had any showings upcoming.

The office had automatically given her a week off as soon as she'd reported the fire. After all, there were more agents than buyers in this market. Helen knew they were hoping she'd just retire and leave it to the Barbie dolls and former athletes. Their solicitude was insulting. Those glossy young professionals didn't understand how she out-sold them year after year.

Helen knew part of her success was her age. People trusted what she said. She seemed like someone's mom, rather than like someone who was trying to sell you a new car you didn't need. She wasn't slick. She played to those strengths. She wore sneakers. People liked that.

After a while, a woman came and sat beside her, chomping on some kind of rolled up Asian thing. Helen estimated the woman as forty-five years old. Chinese-American. Some kind of Asian-American, anyway. She wondered if she might be related to Dr.

Liu. Maybe her daughter? She wore her hair in that same bob Helen remembered from the picture on the box of Surge Protector supplements, but this woman didn't wear glasses. She was pretty in an unpracticed sort of way. She didn't appear to be a woman who spent a lot of time on her appearance, but she also wasn't a slob. There was something poised about her that made Helen feel a little frumpy.

"Smells good," Helen said conversationally, gesturing at the roll the woman was eating. "Did you buy that here?"

The lady nodded, holding a hand in front of her mouth and said, "It's a samosa. They make decent ones here."

Helen nodded politely. Mary had brought some of those home for dinner two nights ago. Helen had choked half of one down, claimed she wasn't hungry, and snuck out later for a fast food burger. She knew she should eat healthier, but all the whole grain, gluten-free, vegetarian stuff made her want to run for the border. "Are you here for the talk?"

The lady nodded, continuing to chew.

"I don't know much about this Dr. Liu, but I've been taking one of her supplements: Surge Protector."

The lady was suddenly much more interested. She turned in her seat, regarding Helen with avid eyes. "Does it work for you?"

"It really does. It's almost like a cooling ray. It feels strange but really does take care of the hot flashes."

"How does it feel?" The woman seemed really interested now. Maybe she was thinking of taking it herself. She seemed too young, but maybe she was just well preserved.

"Well, the first time I took it, it started with a tingling in the top of my head and then sort of melted down my body in fingers of coolness. Weird, like I said, but very quick and very effective."

"So, where did the heat go?"

Helen started. That was a weird question. A question that had been bothering her, nagging at the back of her mind. Especially since the little fires seemed to still be following her. She'd had to put another one out in the bathroom just that morning. "Interesting you would ask that. It is definitely like the heat leaves my body entirely." She thought about the way she directed the heat, gave it a direction to flow. She wondered again about her condo fire, and how it started, and how she'd come out unscathed.

The woman looked at her. There was something unsettling in her gaze. Something measuring and analytical. Helen smiled, disarmingly, she hoped. "I've started taking it daily, just sort of proactively. I've had fewer hot flashes, and when I get them they're not as severe. It's like the pills gave me control over the heat. I can just visualize the heat leaving me and it does."

"Visualizing, huh?"

Helen nodded.

"Any side effects?" The lady wasn't making eye contact now. Her entire body language had changed. She was tense. She appeared to be watching the small white dog digging at the roots of the rhododendron, but Helen felt she was listening very intently to her, that Helen's answer mattered a great deal.

"Um," she began. They were interrupted when a man stepped to the podium and began to thank them all for coming. Helen looked around and realized a small crowd of fifteen or so people had gathered while she'd been focused on her conversation.

"So, without further ado, let me introduce Dr. Cindy Liu."

The woman next to Helen stood, smiled apologetically, and walked toward the podium.

Helen wasn't sure what she had expected Dr. Liu to be like, but this wasn't it. She definitely appeared younger than she had in the picture on the box of Surge Protector pills. Helen wasn't sure what to make of that, but, other than surprising youth, there was nothing particularly striking about Dr. Cindy Liu in person. She was small and thin but gave an impression of strength. Helen guessed the doctor must be about her own age, give five years or so. There was no visible gray in her hair, though, so either Dr. Liu was a devotee of a beauty salon somewhere or had lucky genes when it came to hair.

Helen also wasn't sure how she felt about the mild subterfuge Dr. Liu had just used to get her uncensored opinion. On the one hand, it was smart to take the opportunity to get unfiltered feedback on her products. On the other hand, it felt sneaky. While she hadn't lied, she also hadn't offered the truth. It would be interesting to hear what this woman had to say.

Dr. Liu smiled as she walked to the front. She looked at the small crowd of people and stepped around the podium. "Come," she said, gesturing with her hand. "Let's just make a circle of chairs up close. I'm too old to stand up here to talk to you when we could just sit and have a chat."

Helen hesitated only a moment and then joined the other Our Market customers tugging the chairs nearer each other until it looked like they might play musical chairs. Dr. Liu had apparently sent the young man who introduced her after some refreshments, because he re-appeared with a tray of small paper cups filled with a fruity smelling iced tea and served everyone before taking a seat himself.

Dr. Liu sat and waited until everyone was resettled and then cleared her throat. Her voice was louder than it had been when she was talking to Helen individually, but not overpowering, just the right tone for a group this size. "Let me start by saying that conventional medicine is not as advanced as we might like to think. It does not have all the answers. It is definitely not harmless. There are nearly one hundred thousand deaths a year from medical mistakes."

Someone gasped and Dr. Liu looked approvingly in the gasper's direction. "How many of you know someone who has suffered at the hands of so-called 'modern medicine?'" After a brief pause, Helen noted that nearly everyone had raised a hand—herself included. "Would anyone care to tell their story?" Eight of the sixteen people shot their hands into the air. Helen smiled to herself. Dr. Liu knew her audience. Our Market customers loved to share what they thought they knew.

During the telling of the tale, Dr. Liu gave every appearance of watching the speaker, a white haired man whose voice shook with emotion as he described the misdiagnosis and untimely death of his wife. Although she seemed to be listening attentively, somehow Helen felt as if the doctor was really watching her. She shifted a little in her seat. Wasn't it a little late in the day to be so warm? She shifted some more and groaned a little to herself. What terrible timing for a hot flash. There was no discreet way to excuse herself or slip out when they were all seated in a tight, little circle like this.

She closed her eyes and breathed slowly. Breathing was the one part of yoga she had taken to when her daughter had bought her those classes last year. Relaxation and focus through breath control. She felt the now almost familiar icicle-like sensation moving down her head and arms and out her fingertips. She imagined the heat disappearing into the paper cup of tea she was still holding and felt the cup grow warm in her hand. The tea began to bubble and some rolled down the sides over her fingers. She could feel that the liquid was boiling hot, but somehow it didn't actually hurt her hand.

Helen opened her eyes. She could see steam rising from the disintegrating paper cup, and through the steam, Dr. Liu's sharp gaze, focused on her.

CINDY ADDS FUEL TO HELEN'S FIRE

Helen stood around what seemed like forever after the talk, waiting for the other audience members to take their personal moment with Dr. Liu. She felt strange, waiting like some kind of over-age fan-girl, but she knew the doctor had seen what she did with her heat. Once she knew the doctor had seen her, she had hardly heard a word of the talk. She wasn't sure if she should be nervous or excited. It was like going on a blind date. She had no idea what was going to happen. It was thrilling.

What did all these freaks and geezers have to say that was so important, anyway? It's not like there was a book to get signed or anything. But Dr. Liu just nodded patiently through each tale of woe, like she had all the time in the world. The only sign of impatience Helen could see was that the doctor kept changing her position to keep Helen within sight at all times.

She didn't want Helen to walk off anymore than Helen wanted to leave without learning what Dr. Liu knew. Helen needed to be the last one to talk to her. So, she stood waiting.

She hated waiting. It made her miss cigarettes. Cigarettes gave you something to do while you waited. But the rage of self-righteous youth would fall on her like acid rain if she dared light up here beneath the tree at the Market. No one smoked without irony anymore.

Patience is a virtue, she reminded herself and then laughed at her own sanctimonious tone. Virtue is boring was more like it. She had just decided it wasn't worth waiting when she felt a hand on her elbow, and there she was, the lady of the hour.

"I think we need to talk," Dr. Liu said, gesturing with her head toward the podium.

Helen followed her. "You think?" Her laugh died in her throat when Dr. Liu just nodded curtly. Great, she didn't have a sense of humor. This should be fun.

"I'd love to run some tests with you. Would you come with me to my lab?"

Helen's eyebrows shot up. She had a vision of Dr. Liu, lightning crackling behind her head yelling, "It's alive!" She decided not to share. "I drove here with my daughter, so I don't have my car."

The doctor nodded. "I can give you a ride. It's not far."

Helen considered for a moment. It was strange to think of going to a stranger's home, but strange was getting to be ordinary. Who better than Dr. Liu to help her figure out what was going on? It was a risk. But, sometimes, risks paid off.

Helen nodded. "Sure. Just let me tell my daughter where I'm going. You'd think she was my mother or something."

Dr. Liu's impassive face killed the conspiratorial laugh, and Helen disguised it as a cough. Guess the good doctor didn't have kids.

A few minutes later, she was back in the parking lot, looking for the gray van Dr. Liu had described. Unfortunately, there were four similar vans in the parking lot. Helen was scrutinizing the bumper stickers, trying to guess if Dr. Liu was more likely to be "Another Mama for Obama" or the "Coexist" written in religious symbols. Luckily, it was neither. Dr. Liu pulled up in a beat-up van with no bumper stickers and rolled the window halfway down, where it became stuck. "Hop in," she called, like they were teenagers on their way to the mall.

Helen opened the door and hesitated before climbing in. The passenger seat was covered in a towel. Judging by the condition of the rest of the seats, Helen decided it would be best to sit on the provided towel. She pushed some small boxes and bags off to the side with her ankle as she got in, making room to set her purse down in the footwell. At the last minute, she decided she'd better hold the purse. One of the bags had been sticky in a soft and particularly disgusting way. Resting gingerly against the seat back, she reached back for the seatbelt, only to find a scrap of torn and jagged cloth. It looked like something had bitten through the strap.

As discreetly as she could, Helen slid her fingers into the assist handle, or as her daughter called it, the "oh shit handle," above the door. She was glad she did, because Cindy Liu drove like a crazy woman. She careened out of the parking lot like they were being chased and sped off through the quiet streets.

Helen lost track of the direction pretty quickly. Dr. Liu took a strange route, cutting through parking lots and circling around. Helen was pretty sure they'd gone through the same intersection twice. She was now gripping the oh-shit handle fiercely enough that her fingers were beginning to hurt. She was just working up her nerve to comment on the ride, when Dr. Liu pulled into a hidden driveway and threw on the emergency brake. "Here we are!"

~

Helen half-expected a castle on a lonely hilltop, but Dr. Liu's house was a simple, white cottage. The plants around the house were grown up and untended, but the house seemed to be in good repair. The porch featured a couple of rattan chairs with floral cushions and a porch swing. The only oddity seemed to be the soaped-over windows of the basement.

The house reminded Helen of the kind of house her mother once had, that everyone's mother had. The real estate agent in her assessed the house automatically as lacking in curb appeal. It would need to be re-sided and landscaped to get a young couple to even look at it. Her guess was Dr. Liu had inherited it from her parents and hadn't changed a thing since.

"Come in! Come in!" Dr. Liu was gesturing from the porch, where she stood holding the door open.

The house was dim. Once Helen's eyes had adjusted, she glanced around the room. It seemed perfectly ordinary at first. There were some slightly worn, old-fashioned furnishings of the sort Helen's mother had favored—big, overstuffed, and covered in ugly floral upholstery. None of the lamps seemed to match the furniture or each other. The rug looked brand new, and the geometric pattern was at odds with the chintz and doily look the rest of the room featured. Helen now knew for certain that Dr. Liu had inherited the home and never bothered to make it her own.

Gradually, Helen became aware of a fluttering, clucking sort of noise somewhere to the left of her. She turned her head, thinking Dr. Liu might have a pet bird or something. She found, instead, a mouse, floating in midair. The mouse seemed to be in some distress, wriggling frantically. Helen stared, fascinated. It looked like a perfectly ordinary mouse. What kind of trick could this be?

When Dr. Liu returned from whatever corner she had disappeared to in those few seconds, she reached for the mouse. Taking it in her hands, she walked it over to a bird stand where she strapped the rodent's leg to a small leather strap. Helen could see several other remnants of various straps, dangling from the stand, all chewed through.

"Sorry. It's one of my experiments. He has achieved flight, but he can't control his movement. Maybe I should have tried a more intelligent lab animal."

Helen consciously closed her mouth, hearing her mother in her head, "Close your mouth dear, a lady doesn't show her surprise." This day just kept getting more and more interesting.

"My lab is in the basement. Shall we?" Dr. Liu stretched an arm toward a door, standing open off the living room, and then turned to lead the way.

Given the condition of Dr. Liu's car and home, Helen was surprised to see the lab looking, well, like a lab. It was a brightly-lit room, clean and institutional looking, full of white cabinets and metal racks of various sorts. As she let her gaze wander the room, she saw what she thought of as normal science stuff. Petri dishes full of gooey-looking samples were lined up on a long table against the wall. A rack holding test tubes was on a shelf above. A tall shelf held a variety of implements Helen recognized as Bunsen burners, a microscope, and beakers, and other things she wasn't sure of the use for.

There was a large mortar and pestle and a rack of little glass jars full of what looked like items from a spice rack intermixed with something you might find in a witch's brew. She knew what some things were, like ginger root and cloves, but other things she couldn't identify at all. There was an interesting smell lingering in the air. Something musty, or maybe just really old.

Under the soaped-up window on the far wall was a computer desk. The entire wall was lined with charts of various sorts. It looked like a professional workspace, but Helen suspected there was more here than met the eye.

When her gaze found Dr. Liu again, she was wearing a lab coat and blue latex gloves. She unwrapped a syringe and laid out vials on an empty table. "Could I get a blood sample?"

Helen said, "Not just yet. Let's talk a little first. I know you saw what happened with my tea. So, why am I here? What do you want from me?"

Dr. Liu laid down the syringe and turned to Helen. "I would think it obvious. You've been taking my supplement, and it works very differently in you than in most women. I want to know what it's doing to you and why."

Helen paced a few steps, hesitating. "Are there some other tests we can run first? Something a little less invasive and personal than giving you my DNA in a vial?"

Dr. Liu pursed her lips. She seemed to be considering something deeply. "I am very anxious to look at you under a microscope, but I suppose we could start by letting you show me what you can do. Want to start a fire for me?"

"It doesn't work like that."

"Like what?"

"I can't just make fire whenever I want. It's more like I can release the heat when it's already there."

"I see. Have you tried?"

"Tried what?"

"Making fire when you're not having a hot flash?"

Helen had to admit she had not. She had experimented with dispersing the heat in different ways. The first time, she was now pretty sure, had been at her condo. She had just tossed the heat out without concern about where it landed. That hadn't ended so well. But other times, she had been able to focus the heat in certain directions. The heat had never hurt her. She'd suffered no burns or effects from smoke. The same could not be said for her clothes. She'd thrown away several blouses and pairs of pants in the past few days because of small holes or melted fibers.

When she boiled her tea at the talk that afternoon, she had even controlled the speed, so the tea had come to a boil and slowly turned to steam and disappeared. The cup had even sort of survived. If it had been a cup meant to contain heat, Helen suspected she could have done it without damaging the cup.

Could she do it just anytime? That was an interesting question, indeed. "Let's try it," she said aloud.

Dr. Liu led Helen to a corner of the lab where there was a sort of glass stall, not that different from a shower. "This is reasonably fireproof. It's where I tested the—" Dr. Liu seemed like she wasn't sure she wanted to reveal whatever she had started to say. Helen was finding Dr. Liu more interesting all the time.

Helen set her purse on a small table and looked into the stall. "What do you want me to do?"

"Tell me how it feels, what you do when you push the heat out of you."

Helen thought. She remembered the icicle feeling dripping down her body from the top of the head, down her arms, and out her fingertips. She remembered focusing the energy out her toes that time in her daughter's yard. "When I'm already hot, it's like I can just imagine the heat leaving me, and it does. The other times, it made actual fire. Today, at the co-op, that was the first time I made it come out as heat without flame."

Dr. Liu was typing notes in a netbook she had pulled from somewhere. "What did you do differently today?"

Helen laughed. "It's gross, but it's like when you have to fart, but you're in a public place, so you try to let it out only a little at a time, without any noise. I think I was controlling how fast it came out. Slower, it's just heat. Faster, it's fire."

Dr. Liu typed faster. "And you say you're taking a daily dose of my supplements? How many tablets a day is that?"

Helen nodded. "Yes. At first, I was taking Surge Protector multiple times a day—whenever I got a hot flash. And I was having a lot of them. When they started happening less often, I slowed to taking just one a day, which seemed to keep them at bay." Helen paused, thinking. "One time, I had one at night. I was upstairs, the pills were downstairs, so I didn't take another pill. I went into the bathroom and tried cool cloths on my neck. It wasn't working. I wished I could just push the heat out, someplace safe, like the sink. Then I felt it." Helen could almost feel it again, thinking about it.

"I raised my hand and felt the heat coming out my palm. Then there was this little ball of fire in the sink. It sort of rolled around in the bowl until I turned on the faucet and put it out. It singed the washcloth I had left hanging over the basin, but otherwise, didn't hurt anything. I went back to bed. The next day, I wasn't even sure it had really happened."

"So, you've sent out your heat a variety of ways: projected away from your body, a fireball, general fire all around, and slowly, as heat?"

Helen nodded again.

"I think it's time to see if you can call it at will." Dr. Liu pointed toward the booth.

Helen hesitated only a moment. She had to admit she wanted to know. Could she do this? She stepped in, and Dr. Liu closed the door behind her.

Helen looked around. The walls appeared to be ordinary glass. "Won't I just melt the glass?" she asked.

"It's grade four fire-resistant glass. It should be able to withstand your fire for up to thirty minutes."

"And if it fails?"

"There is a sprinkler system in the ceiling and a gaseous fire suppression system as a backup."

"Good. I'd hate to burn the house down. The insurance people might doubt the condo fire was an accident." Silence. If they were going to spend time together, Helen was going to have to teach that woman to respond to a joke. In the meantime, she was excited about trying this.

She sat down cross-legged in the middle of the stall and rested her head in her hands. Could she raise the heat if it wasn't already there? Helen closed her eyes and breathed in and out slowly, finding her center like she'd been taught in yoga class. She imagined a ball of fire in her cupped hands, spinning gently. The yellow and orange flames rolled around themselves like an Ouroboros, a dragon consuming and feeding itself endlessly. It was beautiful. She opened her eyes. There, in her hands, was the ball she had imagined.

Dr. Liu was practically pressing her nose against the glass. Helen raised her hands high, the ball spinning slowly. She stood, wobbling a little since she couldn't use her hands to push herself up. She willed the ball to spin faster, and the ball began to whip around in her palm. Helen noticed her palm felt no heat, just a light tickling sensation as if someone were running a feather duster across her hand. Then she threw the fireball down at the ground in front of her feet. A small wall of fire spread in a line in front of her toes. Helen raised her arms, and the wall grew to knee high, and then waist high, and then filled the space in front of her. It felt wonderful. Helen realized she was laughing.

"Can you bring the flames back down?" Dr. Liu's voice came through a speaker somewhere in the stall.

"Down? Why would I want to do that?"

"The flames are hotter than the grade of the glass! Can you bring them down yourself or should I engage the system?"

Helen imagined the fire becoming smaller but nothing happened. She imagined the wall rolling itself back into a ball. Nothing. She pulled at the flames with her mind, trying to pull them back into her body. Nothing. Her head hurt from the effort. She started stomping out the flames with her feet, but the fire was burning faster than she could move.

For the first time, she felt afraid. Was she going to burn up in there? She started to feel dizzy. The box was fully sealed. Was she even getting any oxygen? The flames began to look strangely like liquid. As she fell to the ground, she was dimly aware of a sound, like there was a leak in her inner tube. *It is very warm here at the beach today,* she thought, just before she fell into darkness.

JESSICA IS DEFIED BY GRAVITY

J essica's weekend started out okay. Nathan was feeling more normal, eating and complaining, which was a good sign. So, Jessica's guilt over injuring him when she fell from the chandelier was somewhat assuaged. Of course, they hadn't really talked about how he ended up in the hospital yet, or what was happening to her. There was this look on Nathan's face every time his accident was mentioned, as if he felt a little queasy.

Jessica thought it best to leave that topic for another day. It wasn't as if talking about it would help. Jessica didn't know any more than he did about why she'd had these incidents. They had just happened. It's not like he could help her find an expert to consult, either. Jessica was sure there wasn't a Google entry for floating women, at least not one that would be helpful.

As for Nathan, he seemed to have convinced himself it had not really happened, that it was just his concussion talking. The fact that the boys had seen it, too, and had taken to incorporating flight around the house into their imaginative play, didn't make him accept the truth. He just smiled tensely when Frankie and Max ran by the bedroom with capes and shouted about flying just like Mommy. She didn't blame Nathan for feeling freaked out—she was pretty freaked out herself—but she was annoyed he so blatantly ignored her role in the whole thing.

He hadn't once asked if she was okay. It was becoming increasingly clear Jessica had used up Nathan's supply of understanding and support with the cancer year. He wasn't ready for any more drama.

Jessica wasn't interested in babying him along. She had enough on her plate, worrying about what might trigger another incident. While she might wish for a partner to work this out with, Nathan wasn't going to be that for her. She would deal with this herself.

When she'd made it to Saturday with her feet still firmly on the earth, Jessica began to relax a little. She had stayed grounded. She began to hope she could pick up the boys and her life and pretend this had never happened. Maybe her flight was a one-time incident, a freak event. The lightness she had experienced at the hospital had not reoccurred, and it had now been several days.

But a simple trip to the grocery store dashed those hopes like jellyfish in the surf. Jessica had been examining packages of ground beef in the meat section when she'd felt the lightening sensation in her belly, the same tickle she'd felt before taking flight in her living room. She closed her eyes and prayed silently, "Please, God, no."

But God wasn't listening. When she took a step toward the grocery cart, her foot bounced against the floor, and she felt herself rising. Grabbing at the nearly empty cart didn't help. It simply started to rise with her. Luckily, she was still near enough the meat counter to grab it. With all her strength, she pulled herself down and wedged her body inside, pushing her hands up against the top of the case to hold her bottom down in the shelf with the meat. She looked like a stone monkey stuck in the middle of the pillar to hold up the structure. But this wasn't funny.

Stuck, she buffeted against the cold metal. She huddled there for long minutes, willing weight back into her body, straining the muscles of her arms against the force trying to suck her into the rafters with the lost balloons and confused songbirds. She was trying not to panic and failing miserably. Anytime she peeked out, she could see other customers quickly changing their minds about needing any meat just now and backing their carts away.

Eventually, a manager had approached her. "Ma'am? Are you okay, ma'am? Should I call an ambulance?" He eyeballed the way she was wiggling around on the packages of ground beef. "You need to get out of the meat counter, ma'am. It's just not sanitary."

Somehow, she convinced him not to call an ambulance or the police. She told him she'd gotten lightheaded from going too long without eating and lost her balance, and now, she felt weak. He was still wary but seemed sympathetic. He said he'd go get something to help. He came back with a package of cheese crackers and a soda, which she drank gratefully with one hand, hoping he'd mistake her death grip on the meat case as nerves. He'd been so nice, crouching down and talking with her while she took care of her "blood sugar problem." Oddly, the soda did seem to help. She suppressed a gentle burp and suddenly felt much more normal. Still, she was loath to let go of the nice, sturdy meat case and try standing in open air.

Eventually, she could stall no longer. The light, bubbly feeling had abated. She'd have to take her chances, or he'd call that ambulance after all or maybe the police. She knew she'd never be able to shop there again.

She accepted the manager's arm and allowed him to help her stand. This time, she stayed on the ground. She moved carefully, keeping a tight grip on the grocery cart. The manager shadowed her for an aisle or two until he was called away to another problem. Jessica smiled at him with all the reassurance she could muster and shuffled her way to the checkout, afraid to lift her feet from the ground. But she'd made it.

The walk back to her van felt endless. She'd stood for long seconds at the exit doors, just staring at the long open expanse between the relative safety of the store and her minivan. She was terrified of what would happen if she lost her grip on gravity outside. What would stop her from just floating upward until she disappeared into the upper atmosphere and suffocated? It was only the impatient harrumphing of another shopper that made her take the first step into the open air.

She sweated enough in the ten yards or so walk to soak her thin T-shirt through.

When she made it back to her house, she parked in the garage and asked Nathan to carry in the groceries. She was less worried about his concussion than about herself now. While he'd brought the groceries in, she'd gone into the attic and found the chest with her father's old scuba gear in it. She had pulled out his weight belt and ankle weights and strapped them on.

She'd hardly taken them off since. Nathan hadn't asked. Either he hadn't noticed, or he assumed it was some kind of fitness thing she was trying. She was glad not to have to explain. She'd work this out somehow on her own.

HELEN AND DR. LIU GET ON LIKE A HOUSE ON FIRE

Helen woke on a sofa some time later. She was under an itchy blanket crocheted from some kind of yarn with sparkles throughout. She sat up with a start and looked around. Where the hell was she? The room was completely unfamiliar. She looked everywhere at once, searching for anything she recognized. That was when she spotted the mouse strapped to a bird stand, hovering four inches above it at the end of its tether. The sight of it soothed her. She knew where she was. She was still at Dr. Liu's house, somehow back in the living room.

She tried to stand but almost immediately fell back against the cushions. Her head hurt. What had happened? She stood again, this time more slowly, using the couch arms and the coffee table for support. She swayed a little but kept her feet. The blanket fell from her shoulders. Helen looked down and saw that her pants were full of holes and one leg of them had been cut away. Her shirt wasn't in much better shape. It hung in tatters around her.

She remembered the wall of fire she had been unable to bring down. Dr. Liu's backup systems must have worked, because she was here and alive. Other than the headache, she felt fine. How had that tiny little woman managed to move her up the stairs and onto this sofa?

Examining herself for signs of damage or injury, Helen noticed one of her arms was bandaged at the inside of the elbow. Dr. Liu must have taken a blood sample while she was unconscious. They'd have to talk about boundaries, and also about what she had learned. In spite of the lingering headache, which probably came from oxygen deprivation or dehydration, Helen was excited. She had done it! She had produced fire just because she wanted to. That probably meant she could do it any time she wanted to!

Concentrating on her hand, Helen tried to raise a fireball. It came, though it sort of sputtered like wood does when it is a little too wet to light well. Helen frowned. She hoped it was temporary. It had been exhilarating, the power of controlling the flames like that. She wanted to do it again. For now, though, she had to admit she was dizzy. Helen sat back down to gather the blanket. It might have itched, but at least it was all in one piece.

She had just settled the blanket around her shoulders when Dr. Liu entered the room, a large bronze edged tray in her hands. "Oh, good! You're up."

Helen nodded. "What time is it? Was I out long?"

Dr. Liu gestured at the clock above her left shoulder with her ear. Helen saw it was nearly seven o'clock. So, she couldn't have been out too long. That was good. She also saw the tray was laden with a tea set: a small pot that looked like it was made of stone and two of those tiny cups with no handles. Helen hated those kinds of cups, but the tea smelled wonderful, and she was grateful for the gesture. She reached for a cup as soon as Dr. Liu set the tray down. She also picked up one of the Surge Protector pills her host had included in a small bowl on the tray. Against the blue lacquered bowl, the orange and yellow pills looked like strange Easter eggs. She swallowed one of the tablets, hoping that was why her power seemed diminished—maybe she had used up the effects of the pill she had taken that morning.

Dr. Liu sat in the chair across from her and took a cup of tea for herself. They both sipped, thinking their own thoughts for a few moments before Helen spoke. "Well, that was interesting."

"Indeed! Interesting and exciting." Dr. Liu opened her eyes wide and leaned forward, her entire face rapt and a little predatory. Helen could almost see the thousands of questions spinning in Dr. Liu's brain and her plans to find the answers.

It made Helen a little nervous. "Usually, I like a little less excitement in my life. Women my age are supposed to be slowing down, you know." She laughed, hoping Dr. Liu would appreciate that self-deprecating sort of wit.

"Slowing down? We are just getting started!" There was a fervor in Dr. Liu's eyes. She stood, pacing with her cup of tea, sloshing it as she gestured. "I get so tired of hearing that. Like a woman has a shelf life that ends when she is too old to make babies. Babies. Nasty little parasites. We can create so much that is more wonderful than babies. My best work is yet to come."

Helen stared at the other woman. She had a point. Sometimes, Helen felt like she had spent her whole life waiting to be "old enough" and then had crossed over into "too old" without finding out what it was she had been waiting for. It was only now, with the tingle of fire still on her fingertips and the smell of sulphur on her skin, that she felt she knew what she wanted. "Of course, but I think I'm a little older than you."

Dr. Liu arched an eyebrow. "I'm sixty-seven."

"Sixty-seven? You've got to be kidding." Helen peered into the doctor's face, disbelieving. There was hardly a line on her face. Helen rubbed at her own cheek, thinking about the lines that had collected around her eyes and mouth. "Plastic surgery?" she asked.

Dr. Liu shook her head and then smiled slowly. "Ancient Chinese secret."

Helen spit her tea out in a burst of laughter. The woman did have a sense of humor after all. Helen grinned and wiped her face on the charred and holey remnant of her sleeve. Dr. Liu didn't laugh aloud, but amusement was clear on her face. She poured another cup of tea for them both. It had been a long time since Helen had felt like someone "got" her. She raised her cup in a salute. "I think this could be the beginning of a beautiful friendship," she quipped.

JESSICA FINDS TEA AND SYMPATHY

J essica arrived at her mother's house at the agreed upon pick-up time. The drive over had been uneventful, though she felt a rising sense of panic standing on the stoop. Even with the weights on, she couldn't help but imagine herself spiraling off into the sky and disappearing into the clouds above, never to be seen again.

She rang the doorbell and listened but didn't hear the expected stampede of her boys running to the door. That was strange. Had they gone out? She rang the doorbell again. This time, she heard quick steps clicking in the hall. The door opened, and Jessica was surprised to see Cindy Liu on the other side of it. "Oh, hello, Ms. Liu. I'm here to pick up the boys."

Cindy opened the door wider, inviting Jessica in, her gaze sweeping over her like a laser. Jessica smoothed down her long tunic top and patted the neckline, wondering what about her had invited such scrutiny.

Ms. Liu said, "Your mother had to run to the store, and the boys went with her. They'll be back in a few minutes. Come, sit down. I'll make you a cup of tea, and we can have a little chat."

"That would be lovely, thank you." Jessica pushed down her impatience. She didn't feel like chatting with her mother's old friend. She hadn't decided what to tell her own mother yet, and definitely wasn't interested in a heart to heart with Ms. Liu. She just wanted to pick up her boys and get back under the safety of her own roof.

But the boys weren't there, and there was no need to be rude. Ms. Liu had always been kind to her, in her own way. Jessica had often felt uncomfortable around her, but she figured that was just culture clash. It was important not to assume ill intent just because someone did things differently than you would, she reminded herself, echoing her mother's careful training in social etiquette.

"I just brought your mother some more of my special ginseng blend. Have you been enjoying it?" Ms. Liu seemed especially solicitous, and Jessica felt guilty for not wanting to visit with her.

"It smells wonderful. I've been drinking it like crazy. I'll probably need to get a new tin from you soon." Ms. Liu looked pleased at the praise for her tea and disappeared around the corner.

Jessica marveled again at how young Ms. Liu appeared. She knew she had to be at least sixty-five, like her mother, but if anything, she seemed to look a little younger than she had when Jessica had last seen her just a few days earlier at the hospital. She certainly moved like a younger woman. *There really must be something to the herbal remedies she concocts*, she thought.

Jessica sat at the table, staring at her reflection in the polished top. She wasn't pleased with what she saw. The woman in the reflection looked tired, and a little sad. She smoothed some stray hairs back into her stubby ponytail. Jessica missed her long hair. It seemed like a petty concern to someone who had survived cancer, but she had always been proud of her hair. She was grateful it was growing back but impatient for it to be long again and disappointed the hair was darker than it once was. She supposed she could go to the beauty shop and buy any color she liked, but she had liked being a natural blonde.

Feeling pensive, Jessica stood up and paced around the dining room, examining the artwork. Jessica's mother was always changing what was on the walls. The new display was Chinese characters, done in broad calligraphy strokes, simple black on white in red frames. They were displayed in a line.

Ms. Liu reappeared with the stonework tea set a few minutes later. "That one says *Qi*," she said. "Breath." She set the tray on a table and began arranging the cups and saucers. "The others are *xue, jing, shen* and *jin-ye*. Blood, Essence, Spirit, and, um, Fluids. They are the basics of Chinese medicine."

"Beautiful. Does my mother know what they mean?"

Ms. Liu laughed. Her laugh was surprisingly brash in such a small person, almost a bray. The sound of it made Jessica smile. "Probably not," Ms. Liu said. "She probably just likes the calligraphy."

"It is beautiful. Makes you sad that English doesn't use more art in the formation of its letters. It's like, why choose such dull script when you could have dancing figures to represent your words."

Ms. Liu nodded. "There is an efficiency to the English alphabet I enjoy, but, yes, it does lack artistry."

Jessica sat at the table and poured herself and Ms. Liu some tea from the small pot. Her cup already had some clear liquid in the bottom, but it was probably just water. Jessica raised her cup to her chin and inhaled. "The best part of this tea is the aroma," she said. Then she took a sip. "Or maybe the taste." Almost as soon as she sipped the tea, Jessica felt more relaxed. Even more so than usual.

"There's also the way it makes you feel. Lighter. Free. It's different for you, isn't it?" Ms. Liu seemed to be watching Jessica closely. It made her a little self-conscious, but she shrugged it off. After all, this woman had known her since she was a child. She was just curious.

"How is your husband, by the way? Is he recovered from his accident?"

Jessica looked up sharply. There was something in the way Ms. Liu had said "accident" that rankled her. It was somehow accusatory. It had, after all, been an accident, if a bizarre one.

"He's fine. He had a concussion, but there's been no problem in his recovery."

"How did he get hurt again?" Ms. Liu wasn't looking at Jessica now, but somehow, her attention seemed all the more focused for the lack of eye contact. "Your boys said you fell on him from the ceiling."

Jessica looked down at her tea, surprised by how strongly she wanted to tell Dr. Liu everything. "I don't think you'd believe me. I mean, I hardly believe it myself."

Cindy Liu reached across the table and touched Jessica's hand. "You might be surprised what I can believe. Try me."

LINDA IS A MAN'S MAN

David parked the truck and picked up the clipboard he had wedged into the dashboard to check the address. Linda stretched in the seat next to him and then ran her sweaty hands down the thighs of her jeans, both to dry them off and to pull the jeans away from her *pelotas*. She looked out the window at the house. It was easily double the size of the house she and David had raised their family in. It was beautiful but also cold. Carefully trimmed shrubberies flanked the small porch. The same kind, Linda noted, that grew next to every porch on the block. No flowers at all. No children's riding toys littering the lawn. It was perfect. She didn't like it.

She was playing it cool, or trying to, but really Linda was fluttering with excitement inside. When David had come by to check on her last night, he had stayed longer, and they had begun to talk the way they used to—him telling her little stories about his coworkers, his day, and his life in his hours away from her. He had told her about the trouble his boss, Randy, was in for installing inferior chandeliers in the homes David had helped build two years ago. David had shaken his head. He had often said Randy was cutting corners to make a dollar, and it was going to come back to haunt him. Apparently, some lady's chandelier had fallen in a freak accident, and she'd discovered the "crystal" chandelier featured jewels made of polished plastic.

So, he was being sent out to install a new chandelier really made of crystal, free of charge. Randy wanted David to handle it because David did good work and was known for being good at soothing angry customers. Linda had seen it with their daughters. There was just something in his demeanor that made a woman feel listened to and understood. And really, if a woman feels listened to, half the battle is already won.

David was worried, though, because it was a two-man job for safety, and Jorge, Linda's brother and David's usual partner for such things, was in the hospital and would not be able to help. He wasn't sure whom to call on. He felt that most of the other men in the crew were lazy or unreliable or both.

"These young men..." David left his judgment unspoken, but somehow, still quite clear to Linda.

"I could help you, David," Linda had offered. "I am really quite strong now, you know." She had rested her hand on top of his and was pleased he didn't flinch or tug away. She had wished he would turn his palm up and squeeze her fingers lovingly, but allowing her touch was a good start.

Linda hadn't told David about the piano, but she had told him about moving the dryer. She had stood and taken their dishes to the kitchen, pausing in the doorway to remind him, "You can rely on me."

~

Linda hadn't expected David to accept her offer, but she didn't give him a chance to back out once he had. She had been sitting in the living room waiting when he arrived in the morning, dressed for work in a plaid work shirt, jeans, and work boots, and holding two travel mugs filled with steaming coffee with milk.

She didn't tell him, but there was *asado de bodas* in the refrigerator. The stew had always been one of his favorites. She was hoping they might end this job with a quiet lunch together at the table.

And now, here they were, riding together in the little blue truck. She was going to spend the day with her David, working. She had never been able to watch his work and was excited about this new view into the other parts of his life.

David replaced the clipboard on the dashboard and turned slightly in his seat to smile at Linda. She sipped her coffee without breaking his gaze. He was still such a handsome man. She could see the boy she had married in his face, but liked the man he had become even more. He had a round face that became even rounder when he smiled. His eyes were so dark it was difficult to tell where his pupils stopped and the irises began. She felt she could swim into the depths of those eyes for days and never touch bottom.

Like hers, his hair was now sprinkled with gray, but she liked it on him. She reached out a hand and tucked a wild hair behind his ear. "You need a haircut, *mi amor.*"

"It's good to see your smile," he said.

Linda brightened, smiling more broadly. David placed his empty coffee mug in the holder and slapped his hands down on his thighs, a gesture he often used to say it was time to get moving.

"Okay, Leonel," he said, grinning at her and laughing quietly at the man-name they had finally chosen for her last night. "Let's go."

Linda followed her husband to the back of the truck and stood aside as he dropped the tailgate with a noisy clatter. She moved closer when he began to tug at the ladder and, reaching into the truck bed, picked up the other end with one hand and eased it forward to help. When the ladder was nearly out of the truck, she grabbed the toolbox with her other hand. It took David a moment to get situated with the new chandelier in one hand, and then they walked in tandem to the front door and rang the bell.

"Ms. Jessica Roark?" David asked when a short blonde woman answered the door. When the woman nodded, he continued, "I'm David Alvarez, and this is my partner, Leonel. We are here to install your new chandelier."

"Thank you! Randy called and said you'd be here this morning. Please, come in."

~

L inda stood in the foyer, steadying the ladder in a corner while David assessed the job. He pulled out a variety of tools from the chest and laid them out neatly on a soft rag on the floor.

As he worked, Linda let her eyes wander. It was quite an impressive foyer, with a two-story ceiling and wide staircase with a bend in it. The walls were painted a warm yellowy color and displayed paintings of brightly colored flowers. In spite of the color, the space felt lifeless, though, like it was for display only and no one really lived there.

Linda's eyes met those of the woman of the house. Ms. Roark was tiny, even smaller than Linda had been as a woman. She was maybe four-foot-eleven, thin-hipped, and slender. She wore her hair pulled into a ponytail, despite the fact her hair wasn't really long enough for it. She wore no makeup at all. Linda felt she could've used some. Her face was very pale, and there were dark circles under her eyes. Still, even with all of that, she was very pretty. Young, too. She couldn't be older than thirty. Linda found herself wondering about how they could afford such a place when they were still so young.

"Will the work be very noisy? My husband is resting upstairs."

David told her there would be some noise, but it wouldn't last long unless he ran into problems. Ms. Roark nodded and then turned to walk up the stairs. "I'll go close some doors, try to shield him from the noise a bit." As she moved to climb the stairs, her pant leg slid up, and Linda noticed the woman was wearing some kind of brace on her ankle. It was an oddly bulky thing and looked very worn, like it had been around a long time. Her walk was strange, too. She gripped the banister very tightly and pulled herself up as if her legs were very heavy. There was something not quite right about this woman.

"Leonel?"

Linda started, realizing from his exasperated tone that David had probably called her more than once. She had just failed to respond to her man-name. She walked to his side and listened carefully as he explained how to help him set up the special ladder and then walked over and picked it up from where they had leaned it. David's eyes widened. He must not have really believed her when she talked about her strength. To her, the ladder was no heavier than a load of laundry. She shrugged and set up the ladder where he indicated.

Standing next to her husband, Linda realized how much taller she had grown. David was tall for his family, five-foot-five, though he claimed five-foot-six on his driver's license. She had always been a bit smaller than him at five-foot-three. Really, the footstools all over their house were for both of them. But now, she was looking down at David and noticing some new gray hair around the crown of his head. According to the measurements on the ladder, she was around six-foot-two now. No wonder she had been so sore in the days after her transformation. That was nearly a foot of growth over the course of a couple of days.

David began the long climb up the ladder. Linda hovered at the bottom, keeping a steadying hand on the ladder and her eyes on her husband. It was a very high ceiling, and Linda was glad she was not the one who had to climb the ladder. Once at the top, David made a quick examination of the remaining pieces of the old chandelier, climbed back down the ladder, and began gathering tools. "Linda, could you go and find Señora Roark and ask her the location of the electrical box so I can turn off power to the fixture while I work?"

Linda nodded her agreement and stepped to the bottom of the staircase, craning her neck to peek at where she'd last seen the lady of the house. She couldn't see much because of the bend in the staircase, so she climbed a few steps to the first landing. At the top of the stairs, she could see a few baskets lined up against the railing filled with brightly colored bed sheets and clothing. Must be laundry day. Linda didn't miss those days when the children seemed to dirty six or seven outfits each day. It was nice having them grown and taking care of themselves.

When Jessica Roark appeared in the hall, arms full of yet more laundry, Linda called out, "Mrs. Roark?" Jessica jumped a little, and Linda had the distinct impression that her feet didn't make it all the way back to the floor. "I'm sorry to startle you. My hus—partner— needs to know where to find your electrical box?"

Linda expected Mrs. Roark to come downstairs and walk with them to the box. Most women didn't like for workmen to wander around the house unsupervised. But Mrs. Roark grabbed the railing and leaned down, gesturing and explaining to Linda where to go to find it. Linda nodded and turned to go back down the stairs, wondering what had the woman holding onto the railing with such force. Her knuckles were white.

Back downstairs, Linda led her husband to the electrical box in a little closet outside the kitchen. While he examined the switches in the box, figuring out which one to flip, Linda took a step into the room and peered curiously around. It was certainly big. There was one of those island stations in the middle with a pretty marble countertop and a small sink, with plenty of room all around it for movement. There was a fancy oven Linda found herself coveting—double ovens, plus a gas range with the changeable plates that would let you configure it however you wanted. The walls were a dusty red, almost an adobe-color, but more vibrant. A skylight lit the whole room with a lovely natural glow. Beautiful.

Still, as she looked at it longer, Linda wondered if anyone actually cooked in there. The countertops were clear of the devices, spice racks, and jars of kitchen implements that lined her own kitchen counters. Again, she had the strangest feeling that no one really lived here. The only place that looked used was the area by the dishwasher where a tiny teapot sat surrounded by used teacups left unwashed. She picked up the box of tea and was startled to see her neighbor, Cindy Liu, looking at her from the side of the box. Linda had not known Ms. Liu made tea as well as soaps and lotions. "Mood Lightener," read the logo. It was written in the same calligraphy as her "Nu Yu" soap.

David came behind her and put a hand on her elbow. He looked up at her. "I know. A waste of a good kitchen, huh? Most of these rich ladies don't cook, but they still want all the best in their kitchens." He gestured at the stainless steel refrigerator and pot rack stocked with pots that looked brand new.

Linda nodded. "I could make quite a feast in a kitchen like this one."

David patted her back. "You have always fed us well, *corazón*." Linda felt like she could fly. It was the first time he had called her by an endearment since the change. Even if it was just habit, even if he was disgusted by her new body, it meant he knew she was still herself inside this hulk. She was still his Linda. She took his hand in hers and squeezed. He smiled up at her.

They were standing there a few moments later when they heard heavy footsteps approaching. David pulled his hand back, an apologetic look on his face. Linda understood, though. There was no way to know how this *gringa* would take the sight of two men holding hands in her kitchen.

Mrs. Roark came around the corner, holding a basket of kitchen towels. Linda couldn't help noticing the towels all looked practically new, no signs of wear or even ordinary use. No sauce stains.

"Oh, hello," the woman said. "Did you find the electrical box?"

"Yes, ma'am," David answered, smiling. "So, now I'm going to remove the remnants of the old fixture and see what we need to get your new one in place."

Linda turned to follow, paused, and, turning to Mrs. Roark, said, "You've got a lovely kitchen."

Mrs. Roark smiled brightly. "Thank you. It's more kitchen than I need, but I hope to learn to use it all someday."

"It certainly is a good space. You could prepare quite a feast in there."

The woman looked a little surprised. "Do you cook?"

"Oh, yes. I've always been the cook in our family. It's just one of the ways I take care of the people I love." A strange look crossed the woman's face. Linda couldn't read it, but she could see the woman was very worried about something. "Hey, can I help you with that?" She took the basket from the woman's hands. "Maybe you should sit down?" She steered the woman toward the breakfast bar by the window. The woman moved strangely, shuffling her feet rather than raising them. When Linda touched a hand to the woman's back to direct her, she felt some kind of brace or belt under her thin T-shirt.

"Leonel!" David was calling her from the front hall.

Linda shrugged at the woman apologetically. "I can come check on you in a little while. But, for now, duty calls!" She turned and walked quickly to the foyer.

"Sorry, David. I was talking to the lady about her kitchen." She added in Spanish, "There's something strange about her."

David nodded in agreement, shrugged, and started to climb the ladder. "I'll need you to keep my ladder steady and maybe to pass a few things up to me once I get up there."

Linda manned her station, keeping her eye on her husband as he climbed the ladder once more. She watched as he removed the part of the old lighting fixture that was still affixed to the ceiling and took it when he passed it down to her. Her eyes were fixed on him as he examined the wires, so she didn't see what startled him. She saw it when he began to fall, though.

"*Madre de Diós!*" He stepped too far back and pinwheeled his arms for a long second before he lost his balance completely.

Linda moved under him, making a basket of her arms, and caught him as easily as she might have caught a child. She looked down into his face as he lay in her arms and thanked God she was there. Her curse was a blessing. She had saved him.

JESSICA DANCES ON THE CEILING

After the two workmen left the kitchen, Jessica leaned against the tall stool near the side counter. Her knees and legs hurt so much from trying to move about the house with the scuba weights on that she couldn't even lift them to sit in the chair. Looking around the kitchen, she saw several furniture items she could grab onto if she had gravity problems, so she decided to take the weights off.

She removed the weights and laid them out carefully on the counter next to her. She pulled herself into the backed stool and crossed one leg across the other knee, flexing and rubbing the ankle. There was a dark line encircling it and a reddened, sore-looking patch of skin just at the inside bone. She wished she had a better idea of how to deal with her problem, something that didn't come with new problems of its own.

She considered, again, Dr. Liu's offer to help her. Her mother's friend was an herbalist or something. Jessica had never been sure what exactly she did for a living, but knew that her mother swore by various products Cindy Liu had created over the years.

It was Dr. Liu who had concocted the licorice scented tea that had soothed Jessica as she recovered and grieved following her surgery, the same tea they drank together when they spoke two days earlier.

The tea had tasted a little different. Not bad, just different. Jessica hoped Dr. Liu wasn't changing the blend. She loved it the way it was.

It had been a surreal conversation. Jessica couldn't explain why she decided to tell Dr. Liu about her condition when she hadn't yet even told her own mother. Maybe she was just that desperate to tell someone, to get some reassurance she hadn't just lost her mind. After all, it sounded crazy. A person couldn't really just float away like a balloon.

But tell she had, when Dr. Liu asked her to. In fact, she had talked quite a bit, more than was usual for her. Jessica had always been somewhat reserved about her personal life. She had certainly never been accused of over-sharing, especially not to people she didn't know well.

But she found herself telling Dr. Liu all about her life—not just her condition, but also the way her feelings about her husband had changed and how she felt trapped in her life. Things she had certainly never told anyone before. It was like she couldn't help it. She was simply compelled to talk. Jessica wondered what had come over her. She was disturbed now to realize how much she had revealed. She wished she could take the words back somehow, erase them from the woman's memory. She'd had a headache the entire next day, which she thought came from the stress of knowing Dr. Liu knew so much about her situation.

Dr. Liu had listened intently as Jessica described her gravity problem. She didn't even really seem surprised, reacting as calmly as if this were a perfectly normal problem any person might have. She had asked a lot of questions about how it felt and about how Jessica had been able to move through the air and get back down. She'd asked if Jessica had any idea what had caused it, and Jessica had to admit that she did not. She hadn't done anything differently that day that she could think of. She'd sipped tea and watched movies all morning. That was all.

Dr. Liu had contemplated this information quietly for a while after that, picking up the box of tea and reading the list of ingredients as if she didn't already know what was in it. Finally, she had put it down and gripped Jessica's hand in both of hers, looking into Jessica's eyes with an alarming intensity. "I'd like to run some tests, Jessica. Would you come to my lab tomorrow? With a few tests, I know we can figure out why this is happening to you."

She couldn't have said why, but Jessica didn't want to go to Dr. Liu's basement laboratory. It was true she had been curious about it when she'd heard Dr. Liu describing it to her mother. It was also true she had not been to see it yet, though her mother had visited and had gushed about the amazing setup and the incredible work her friend was doing there.

Now, she was invited, and some part of her hesitated. She had told Dr. Liu she couldn't come at that time and promised to call to set up another time, stalling. There was something she didn't like in the focused attention of Dr. Liu. Something about her felt dangerous.

Still, obviously, Jessica needed some kind of help. It's not like she could take this one to Urgent Care and get some antibiotics. When she imagined trying to discuss it with a medical professional, she had images of straitjackets and long syringes dripping thick medicines. She should probably take Dr. Liu up on the invitation. It wasn't like she had a lot of options. Maybe she really could help.

Sitting in her kitchen and thinking, Jessica continued to rub and rotate her feet. It felt so good to take the weights off her ankles that Jessica became that much more aware of the belt around her waist. Taking a deep breath, and hoping this wasn't a mistake, she loosened the belt. Heaven! She stretched her body, arching her back and closing her eyes. Maybe it was because she had closed her eyes, but Jessica didn't see or feel this one coming. The next thing she knew, her cheek was pressed against the ceiling.

Jessica didn't know what to do. The upward force was so intense it took all her upper body strength to force a couple of inches between her body and the ceiling, so she could try and move herself to a position where she could grab something and get herself back on the floor. Maybe it was a reaction to the weights. A build-up of some kind. Maybe the condition was getting worse.

This time, Jessica wasn't afraid so much as angry. What the hell was happening to her? Hadn't she had enough trouble in her life? Her gymnastics career ruined at age eleven by a stupid knee injury during a three-legged race at field day. Her failure to find a career. Her father's sudden death. Her ovaries gone to cancer at thirty-two. Her husband and his impatience. Early onset menopause. Depression. She reached the doorway between the kitchen and living room just as she reached the end of her litany of woes.

Grabbing onto a section of the moulding around the wide door-frame, Jessica whipped herself around the corner. She hadn't counted on the force of her own movement, however, and lost her grip, flying into the middle of the room. *Déjà vu*, she thought, grimacing. There she was again, hovering in the middle of the living room, too far from the floor to reach it and too far from the ceiling to push off from it. Stranded again.

So, she did the only thing she knew to do. She tried to swim through the air over to the wall. At least she had the sense to get rid of the glass coffee table. She'd told Nathan that a crack had developed in the glass and it would cost too much to repair. He'd just nodded and turned back to his laptop. He never used the table, anyway. So long as she kept the house showroom neat and furnished in the sleek, modern style he preferred, he didn't take much interest in such things.

Jessica's awkward attempts to pull her way through the air were having some effect. She built up a small amount of momentum and felt herself buffeting forward. She panicked when she realized her trajectory was taking her toward the doorway to the front hall, where the workmen were. There was nothing she could do to arrest her movement, nothing she could reach. She stopped only when she reached the open doorway and was able to grab the moulding. A chunk came off in her hand with a gentle cracking sound.

Jessica saw it, the moment when the nice man from the contractor's office looked up and saw her floating along the ceiling. She heard him call out something in Spanish and then watched helplessly as he stepped backward and started to pinwheel his arms. She willed herself forward, but her body wouldn't cooperate. She continued to bob along the ceiling like some kind of abandoned balloon. Useless. Even her voice failed her. The poor man!

When the man on the ladder fell, Jessica cringed, waiting for the sound of impact. It was so far to fall! But the sound never came. Jessica pushed off from the ceiling and spun herself toward the doorway so she could see what had happened. The other man, the big handsome quiet one—Lionel?—had caught him. He stood there, cradling the smaller man in his arms, just breathing. After a beat or two, the bigger man put the smaller one down on the ground with incredible gentleness. "Are you all right, David?" he asked.

David nodded, sitting on the floor. "That was a close one. Thank God you were here. I saw…"

Jessica was sure he didn't want to say what he thought he had seen. She could also see that this David wasn't really okay. He was visibly shaking, and his voice was not steady. Jessica felt guilty for having frightened him.

The larger man bent over David then, putting his large hands on David's shoulders. He ran his hands over David's body, as if he had to check and make sure he was still all there. Finding no injury, he laid a hand on David's cheek and then leaned in to kiss him, pulling him to his chest in a possessive, protective gesture that spoke of long years together. Jessica suddenly felt like an interloper in her own home, witnessing their private moment. She also felt strangely jealous.

Jessica wedged her hand into the corner where the ceiling met the wall and pushed down, fighting the buoyancy that urged her upward. It was like trying to force a beach ball beneath the surface of the water. Her slender arms shook with the effort. She cleared her throat. "Could you help me?" Both men turned and looked at her, David grabbing the elbow of the larger man, who stood. He was startlingly tall, but his face as he moved toward her was gentle and kind. She didn't hesitate to reach for his hand when he offered it.

HELEN PLAYS WITH FIRE

Helen tossed off the covers. She couldn't sleep. It had only been a few hours since Cindy had dropped her off, after yet another all night session testing the limits of her abilities, tipsy on wine and drunk on power. She had stumbled to the bedroom, thrown away her burnt-up clothes, and flopped into bed. She fell into sleep like a diver into a pool.

She hadn't expected to resurface again so soon. She checked the bedside clock. Four-thirty a.m. Too late to be called night and too early to be called morning. But her eyelids were up, and she shook with a restless energy. She knew this feeling. It was excitement.

The round of experiments with Cindy last night had shown her what she could do. And she wanted to do more. It had been a long time since her limits had been stretched, since the world had seemed new and exciting. God, what a rush! It was like being in love.

She sat on the edge of the bed for a moment and then padded to the closet and pulled on a long T-shirt. It had been her husband's and proved more durable than he had. She wondered if it were possible to buy fireproof clothing.

Moving quietly through the apartment, she made her way to the kitchen and to the patio doors at the back. She stepped through into the patch of grass that had sufficed as a yard for Mary's barbecue party a week or so ago.

Helen looked around. The windows of the two apartments above Mary's overlooked the yard, but they were dark. The back of the yard was bordered by some kind of industrial strength hedges, probably to protect the homeowners behind from having to see the seedy, little apartment dwellers smoking their cigarettes and drinking their beer.

Helen willed a ball of fire into her hand and made it roll. She tossed it from one hand to the other, rolling it across her arms and laughing. She balanced it on one finger like Wilt Chamberlain and made it spin, first one direction and then another. She made a second and a third ball and tried to juggle them. Whenever she dropped one in the grass, she stomped out the small fire with her bare foot and made a replacement.

When she tired of fire juggling, she decided to try other shapes. She made a sort of spear, a long thin flame. She bent it around itself until it was a ring. She spun it in the air and then around one wrist, like it was a hula-hoop. She thought about spinning it around her waist, but knew the shirt would never survive it. She didn't want to end up naked in her daughter's backyard.

God, this was fun. She hadn't had this kind of fun in years. She lined up a couple of beer cans and soda bottles in various parts of the yard and, making her finger into a gun, shot them with small blasts of fire, leaving smoking piles of melted tin can and broken glass.

She was trying to decide what to do next, when she froze, stopped by a small squeak. The sliding door squeaked in its track. Helen turned, just in time to see her wide-eyed daughter poking her head out the small opening she had made. Her voice sounded almost child-like, like she was afraid. "Mom?"

It was a truth of life that as a woman aged, Helen thought, people tended to treat her more and more like a child. Salesclerks called older women honey, just like they might a child. Senior food and movie tickets were sold at a reduced price, just like a child's. Discounts and nicknames weren't so bad in the scheme of things, but the assumption of incompetence was hard to take. Helen wasn't sure when she had crossed that line—the magic age that made people treat her like she was old— but she had.

It was especially hard to take from Mary. Even when her daughter's advice was good, it still galled Helen to take it. After all, she was the one with the life experience here. Her daughter ought to be listening to her wisdom. But, as Helen had gotten older, she had often thought the roles were reversing between herself and her daughter. It was Mary who was always trying to tell her how to live her life instead of the other way around. It was Mary who wanted to know where she was and what she up to, like it was her job to keep tabs on her mother. It was Mary who Helen had to explain herself to. Sometimes, it was annoying.

This morning, though, was different. Now, Mary, in the role of mother, was watching as she, in the role of child, said again and again, "Look what I can do!" And she could do amazing things. She demonstrated again all the forms she could make the fire take. She showed her the way she was impervious to harm from fire or smoke, clapping out flames in her hands and stomping them out with her bare feet. Mary's face showed a complicated combination of emotions from fear to excitement and back around with a bit of worry and disbelief mixed in.

"But how is this happening? How can this even be possible?" Mary asked.

Helen considered. Should she tell her daughter about Dr. Liu and the pills? She looked at her daughter. Mary was an open-minded person in a lot of ways, but she was also very sure of what was right and wrong. But, still, if she didn't tell Mary, who was she going to tell? It was all so amazing and exciting. Truthfully, she was dying to tell.

"So, do you remember those pills you got for me?"

JESSICA'S GIRLS' MORNING OUT

When Leonel called the next morning and asked if Jessica would like to get some breakfast, Jessica jumped at the chance. The boys were at their respective schools for the morning, so she was free until it was time to pick up Max at noon.

They had gone to a favorite breakfast place of Jessica's, where she had eaten her usual egg-white only omelet with feta cheese and smoked salmon. Leonel had ordered the steak and eggs with a stack of pancakes on the side and the fruit bowl. Jessica's eyes had goggled at the amount of food surrounding her new friend.

Gesturing at the array of dishes, Leonel shrugged sheepishly. "I'm hungry today." Then he leaned in conspiratorially and whispered, "Maybe I'm pregnant!" He widened his chocolate-brown eyes and covered his generous mouth in a dramatic gesture. Jessica struggled to swallow her orange juice around her laughter, half-choking in the process. It was worth it, though. She hadn't laughed like that in ages.

Leonel and Jessica chatted amiably for several minutes, exchanging stories about their children and husbands. She was surprised to realize that Leonel was a grandparent! He seemed so young.

"David and I married young," he said simply. "I was only eighteen when our first child came to us."

Leonel pulled out a brand new wallet, its newness contrasting with the worn softness of his flannel shirt, and flipped through the pictures in the back to show a picture of their oldest child, Lupita, and their grandchild, Carlitos.

Somewhere in the middle of the meal, a silence fell on the table. Jessica's mind drifted into her problems. Unconsciously, she shifted in her seat, trying to find a comfortable position where the weight belt didn't push into her back. She had hardly dared to remove her weights since the incident the day before. It was only Leonel's quick reaction that had kept her problem from causing grave injury to David. She was a danger to others as well as herself. There had to be something that could be done.

"What are you thinking, *nena?*" Leonel had stopped eating and was looking at Jessica with such open sympathy that she couldn't help but respond.

"I was thinking about the accident yesterday. We were so lucky you were there! I don't know what I would have done if my problem had hurt your David."

Leonel patted Jessica's hand. "It wouldn't have been your fault, *cariño*. But I am glad I was there, too."

A troubled look clouded the handsome man's face, and Jessica was sure he was imagining David seriously injured. Leonel picked up the coffee mug with both hands and sipped from it. Jessica was struck by the gesture. There was something delicate about it, as if he imagined himself so small that he would need both hands to support the sturdy mug. She sipped from her own juice, considering.

"My mother has a friend who has offered to help me."

Leonel looked at her questioningly, taking another sip from his coffee.

"She's an herbalist, some kind of specialist in Chinese medicine."

A flicker of something went across Leonel's face, but he didn't say anything. Jessica went on to tell him about the conversation on Sunday after her disastrous trip to the grocery store on Saturday. Leonel was a good listener, clucking sympathetically at the right moments, but never interrupting, never stopping her to ask questions or offer ideas. Only when she had finished, her words run completely dry, did he comment.

"This woman who says she can help you, what's her name?"

"Liu. Dr. Cindy Liu." In her mind, she added, *Who was no more than two*. Her mother had warned her as a child not to make the Dr. Seuss reference in front of Miss Cindy. She was sensitive about it. But she always thought it.

Leonel nodded and then looked toward the window, resting his chin in the palm of his hand, thoughtfully, one finger tapping against his temple. Jessica noticed the little streaks of gray running into his long hair, which he wore bound into a low ponytail. She was thinking about how his hair might feel in her fingers when he spoke again, startling her.

His tone was soft, but somehow a little stern. "She lives in my neighborhood. I knew her mother." He hesitated and then leaned in closer. "I don't know why, but something about that woman doesn't feel right. Do you know what I mean?"

Jessica did. She bit her lip. "But who else can help me? It's not like I can just go to the doctor for this. They'd think I was crazy. I can't make it happen on cue, you know. What if I can't demonstrate? What if I can?"

Leonel reached across the table and held Jessica's entire forearm in his warm, soft hand. "Be careful, *m'ija*." Catching the eye of the waitress, Leonel pulled out his new wallet again. "Let's go shopping," he said. "I need a new shirt."

Jessica drove them to the mall, leaving Leonel's little car in the restaurant parking lot. She couldn't imagine why such a large man would drive such a small car. Although she had already been inside the restaurant when Leonel had arrived, she could picture him getting out of the car and had to stifle a laugh at the awkwardness of it.

"Where do you want to start?" Jessica asked, parking at the mall entrance.

Leonel looked thoughtful. "How about the beauty shop?"

"Be careful. I'll take you up on that!"

"What? I wasn't kidding. Let's go!"

Heads turned as Leonel strode into the salon at the back of the largest department store. They didn't get a lot of male clients, and certainly few that looked like Leonel, Jessica was guessing. But before the stylist even had him leaning back in the chair, Leonel had her giggling. He was obviously very comfortable in this environment. He even convinced the manicurist to roll her station closer to the hair station so that Jessica could have her nails done while he got a haircut and they could still talk.

"Not too short, now," he warned the stylist. "I like my hair long, but maybe you can help me do something with the front. All these layers were a bad idea. I look like Jennifer Aniston."

Jessica and her manicurist hardly spoke, both of them transfixed by the sight of this man in his dirty work boots and faded flannel shirt getting an upscale haircut. In fact, Jessica had agreed to the first thing the manicurist suggested and was surprised when she looked down at autumn orange nails. She had never gotten anything besides nude or pale pink before. She spread her fingers, looking at them doubtfully.

"Let's see, Jessica." Leonel gestured for her to come toward him. His head was leaning forward so the stylist could get to the long hair falling between his shoulder blades.

Jessica obediently splayed her fingers under his gaze.

"Beautiful!" he declared. "You have lovely hands, and this color suits your skin so well. Good work, Maribel."

The manicurist glowed from the compliment.

When Leonel's haircut was over, he checked himself out from several angles in the mirror. The soft layers around his face had been shaped into jagged locks that emphasized his strong cheekbones. He looked amazing. "I don't know. Do you think I'm too old for this?"

Jessica shook her head wordlessly. Too old? What was he? Forty-five? The stylist gushed about the haircut, even taking a picture with her phone to show her friends. Leonel laughed and posed for the camera like a beauty queen, lips pursed and one hand behind his head.

"Do you have time to help me pick some clothes?" Leonel asked on the way out of the salon, folding Jessica's arm over his. Jessica checked her cell phone for the time. She frowned. There wasn't time before Max's pickup.

"Hold on," she said, taking a few steps away and dialing her mother. Her mother sounded happy to hear that Jessica was having a good time and readily agreed to pick up Max. Jessica turned back to Leonel and grinned. "Let's see what we can do about your shirt," she said.

They stood in front of the mall directory for a moment, trying to choose a likely store. "Where do you usually shop?" Jessica asked, thinking this might give them a starting point.

"I haven't been shopping since—" Leonel stopped speaking suddenly. Jessica would have sworn the man was blushing. He continued, "These clothes came from a thrift store, I think." He looked down at himself, tugging at the sagging jeans. "I'm not even sure what size I wear."

Jessica could tell Leonel didn't want to explain the clothing situation, so she didn't ask. Instead, Jessica looked Leonel up and down, walking around him in a circle and stroking an imaginary goatee. "Let's see, my darling," she said, putting on an atrocious Russian accent. "Vhat kind of makeover shall we give you? Walk with me!" Jessica snapped her fingers in the air above her head and stalked off, snapping her hips from side to side in an exaggerated wiggle.

She could hear Leonel chuckling to himself as he followed her. She stopped in front of a store window and leaned into one heel, her hand flared as if she held a cigarette. Loud music blared from the shop, and the air smelled of musky cologne. The mannequins in the window were skeletally thin and posed with their hands in their pockets and their shoulders in a permanent shrug. Leonel stood in front of one of them and adopted the same pose, raising a doubtful eyebrow at Jessica, who fought to stay in character. "No. This simply will not do. Onward!"

They repeated the scene in front of several storefronts before they found one Jessica deemed worth going inside. Jessica was drawn to a plain black T-shirt made of something very soft and a little bit shiny.

It was quite a contrast to the soft flannel Leonel was wearing, but she thought he'd look good in it.

"Here! Try this one!" she said, pulling an extra large one off the rack and thrusting it into his hands. Jessica spun in a circle looking for some pants to go with the shirt. She found a pair of gray jeans that were neither skinny jeans, nor saggy jeans, but just a sort of straight fit that made her think of cowboys. "With these." She eyed Leonel and made a quick calculation. She picked up three possible sizes. "One of these should fit. Now scoot!" She shooed him to the fitting rooms, ignoring the bemused sales clerk.

Once Leonel was inside, the clerk let out a low whistle. "You're going to have to hold on to this one, honey," she said.

"We're just friends," Jessica said.

The clerk raised an eyebrow.

"He's married," Jessica said.

"All the good ones are." The clerk sighed dramatically. "Or gay."

"Or both," Jessica offered. It was probably best that he was.

A half hour later, they had selected six new shirts and pants for Leonel, as well as a pair of boots in soft black leather, a pair of brown semi-dress shoes, and a couple of belts. Leonel shuffled through the credit cards in his wallet, pulled out a card, and laid it on the counter.

"Linda?" the clerk read, doubtfully.

"Oh, sorry. Wrong card!" Leonel said, pulling out a card with David L. Alvarez inscribed on the front.

Jessica looked at the card on the counter. It was the kind with a photo in the corner. The photo was of a pretty Hispanic woman, about fifty years old. Linda Alvarez, it read. Who was Linda? And why was Leonel using a card with David's name on it instead of his own?

PATRICIA AND CINDY ARE SISTERS UNDER THE SKIN

Patricia had not been able to reach Cindy all weekend. She wondered what the woman had been up to that had her so busy she couldn't return even one of her messages. She had left several, trying everything from text to Facebook. She wanted to know what Cindy had learned from all the samples she had taken the week before. Could she explain yet what was going on with Patricia's skin?

Even several days later, she was still reeling from the testing session and the idea that she was bulletproof. Cindy had taken pictures of the area of impact, and there was no sign of damage to the skin. The skin itself was a sort of gray-green and thick as a turtle shell. Cindy had been excited and seemed to think this was something wonderful. Patricia had felt excited, too, infected by Cindy's enthusiasm when they were in the lab. But it was a different story home alone over the weekend.

The condition was getting stranger all the time. Besides the plates, there were now these bumps that popped up along her shoulders. They were really large, like golf-ball sized. They seemed to rise up when she became agitated and then go back down. Were they some kind of bizarre allergic reaction? Once, when she had rubbed at them, she had felt a sharp edge, like a spine. It had actually cut her finger, but when she tried to find it again, it was gone.

On her pillow that morning, Patricia had found little green shiny pieces she couldn't identify. They resembled nothing so much as scales, like from a fish or a lizard. Or a dragon. She found another one in her hair when she had showered. The scales were in a Ziploc bag in her purse right now. She thought she'd show them to Cindy whenever she managed to get a hold of her.

She had Suzie call off and on all day Monday. If she didn't hear from Cindy by lunch today, Patricia figured she would just go over to the house and pound on the door. It occurred to her that Cindy lived alone and worked with a lot of dangerous things in that basement lab of hers. What if she had been injured or exposed herself to something dangerous?

It had happened before, in the months right after Michael's death. Cindy had been living in Boston at the time. Patricia had flown in to visit her after an especially worrying phone call in which Cindy sounded both violent and despondent. Cindy hadn't shown up to pick her up at the airport, and when Patricia had arrived by taxi and let herself in to Cindy's apartment, she found her passed out on the floor. When she regained consciousness, she admitted it might have been more than two days since she had eaten anything.

She had been studying all the case information on Michael, convinced the doctors had missed something that could have saved him. She had his body frozen and was sure she could bring him back. Patricia had stayed with her for several days, forcing her to take breaks from her research to eat and sleep.

So far as Patricia knew, Cindy didn't have anything going on in her lab that would have her working quite that hard, but she still wanted to hear from her friend and be sure that she was all right. She was just considering driving over there when Suzie came in from the adjoining closet they had transformed into a small office for her.

"She's all right."

Patricia felt relief wash over her. "What did she say?"

Suzie laughed. "She said it was a rough night, and that she is hung over, but she can meet you for lunch at two o'clock."

Hung over? Cindy was not a drinker. In fact, she was usually very careful about what she ate and drank. She was always lecturing Patricia about the toxins in the things she ate and how bad processed foods were for you. She wanted to hear this story. "Make us a reservation at Lupe's," she told Suzie.

At two-fifteen, Cindy walked through the door at Lupe's, wearing a pair of sunglasses even though the day was overcast. She grimaced when the door flopped closed behind her with a smack. Patricia could see she was being honest about the hangover. She was moving like she could hear the air circulating.

Putting aside the desire to tease her friend about behaving like a teenager, she kindly gestured the waiter over and asked for a pot of jasmine tea. Lupe's Restaurant used loose-leaf tea in beautiful ceramic pots. She knew Cindy would approve.

"Don't you have any of the Hangover Relief stuff you used to sell in college?" Patricia asked, keeping her voice soft. When they were in school together, Cindy had financed a trip to Mardi Gras by selling a homeopathic remedy for hangovers. There was a lot of demand for it on a college campus.

Cindy let the glasses slide to the end of her nose, and Patricia could see how red her eyes were. "I can't take it now. It won't work on me."

That was odd. "Won't work on you? Why not?"

"It's a metabolism thing. Let's just say it will interact badly with the other things in my system." Cindy was being evasive, and that was often a bad sign.

Patricia was growing more worried by the moment. Other things in her system? Was her friend polluting her body with drugs? "What are you up to, Cindy?" she asked, keeping her tone light though her thoughts had gone dark.

"No good," she responded. "Like usual. Like you." It was an old joke for them.

Patricia smiled. "Situation normal then?"

Cindy nodded and then gripped her head. The motion must have made her head hurt anew.

Patricia patted her hand. "Were we drinking alone?"

"No, I was celebrating with a new friend."

"What's his name?"

"Ha!" The laugh was loud and made Cindy's face turn green. "Ow! His name is Helen. She's not that kind of friend."

"So, what were we celebrating?"

"Success. She's been participating in one of my experiments, and things are under control and looking promising."

Patricia was quiet for a moment. Her own experiment with Cindy, on the patches on her back, was far less successful, and she really wanted to talk to her about that, but it seemed selfish to bring it up right now when her friend was not feeling well.

"Did I tell you I got another intern?"

"Oh, no. Have you made her cry yet?"

"This one is actually pretty good, though she is awfully blonde and cute."

They chatted happily for an hour or so. The tea seemed to help a little with Cindy's headache. Patricia thought she would just wait for another day to talk to her friend about her skin. Today, she needed to just be a friend.

JESSICA IS BLIND-SIDED BY SCIENCE

W hen Jessica woke the next morning, hovering between the ceiling and her bed, she decided it was time to call Ms. Liu. Regardless of any misgivings she might have about the strangeness of the woman herself, there was no one else she could call on for help.

Rolling around like an astronaut, she tumbled in mid air until she managed to work herself over to the closet and then down to the floor. She grabbed the plush pile of the carpet with her fingers and tugged herself forward one handful at a time, her legs floating above her. Her arms were quaking from the effort by the time she crawled back to the bedside table where she'd left her weights.

Clasping on her ankle weights, Jessica blessed herself for insisting that Nathan sleep in the guest room the night before. She hadn't been sleeping well, and he had agreed, after some cajoling, to deliver the boys to preschool and let her sleep in.

Nathan was still avoiding the whole subject of how he'd gotten hurt. Every time she tried to bring it up, he got this look on his face, and all the color washed out of him until he looked like a grimacing corpse. On the upside, this made him more amenable to handling some of the day-to-day household tasks, especially if those tasks involved not being at home. She had no idea what it was going to mean in the long run. He was going to have to face up to her situation sooner or later. They couldn't keep living like this.

Avoidance was becoming Nathan's M.O., though. During the cancer year, she'd been through the biopsy and testing and had her surgery scheduled before he would even say the C word. He kept calling her cancer by euphemisms like "you know" or "the problem." Jessica understood why he might want to avoid talking about it in front of their boys. But when they were alone?

She had been so frustrated with him. All her so-called friends, who were really his friends from work and business contacts or the wives of those contacts, kept talking about how lucky she was to have a man like Nathan. Jessica didn't feel lucky, but she thought she could see why they would think so, observing from the outside.

On the surface, Nathan did seem really supportive. He pushed his way through hospital bureaucracy to make sure she got the best care. Then he bragged about it at cocktail parties, deaf to the bullying disrespect to the hospital staff and the needs of other patients the story portrayed. He arranged for his company to sponsor cancer related charity events and never missed an opportunity to let people know his wife was fighting the disease. He even teared up, giving the speech at the big charity ball he had arranged.

In big, abstract, public ways, Nathan offered a lot of support, and that's what these women saw when they told Jessica she was fortunate. But in private? When she was fighting to keep down Jell-O and crying over the clumps of her hair coming out in the brush, he had disappeared into the woodwork. Once, he had literally backed out of the bathroom rather than help soothe her. She had seen him in the mirror. Later, they'd both pretended he'd not been there at all.

In a way, it felt like her cancer had become part of him. Not that he had taken on the sickness itself, but he had somehow taken on the public sympathy. The very personal loss of her ovaries and all the implications to her health and well-being, even the emotional toll; all of this had been co-opted by Nathan, made into part of his networking persona. It felt as flat and insincere as the flair waiters were required to wear at party restaurants. It didn't really reveal anything of the heart. Jessica felt empty, even invisible.

She'd always known Nathan was a little self-absorbed. It was part of what made him so successful: the confidence and assurance he exuded. People listened when he spoke. Jessica had liked being a partner to that, when she had been a partner. It had felt like, together, they could rule the world, or at least the boardroom. Once upon a time, they had plotted together how best to work the room and get the grunts, as they called them, to do what they wanted. Jessica had been good at it, too. She wasn't without her own charms and ability to influence people. She had qualms from time to time about the manipulative maneuvers, but trusted the work was important and that success would give them the opportunity to do a lot of good in the world.

But once she had fallen ill, that all ended. He hadn't even told her about the year-end party last winter. He had just donned his suit and left. True, Jessica had still been a little weak, but she could have handled sitting at a banquet and listening to speeches. It stung that he didn't even ask. She'd been his partner, but he had left her behind when life had made her unable to keep up. Now that she was able to run again, she found she wasn't even invited to the race.

Thank God she had her mother. Eva Roark was a realist and a fighter. She'd come through her sudden widowhood with grace and calm, and she'd been fully confident her daughter could do the same with cancer. *"My daughter, beaten by the uncontrolled division of abnormal cells? I think not!"*

Eva had found a support group for family members and sought advice for how best to help her daughter. She'd hired the temporary nanny and arranged for the preschool and day care programs her boys would need. She'd been the one to talk to Frankie when he realized his mother was sick. They'd looked at books together about cancer and about women's bodies. Jessica remembered the relief on Frankie's face when he'd understood Jessica's cancer had been caught at Stage I. "That's good, right?" he'd asked. Yes, that had been good.

She owed it to her mother to figure this out. As for Nathan, well, she'd figure that out another day.

Weights in place, Jessica sat on the edge of the bed for a moment, running over her day in her head. It was surprisingly empty. She checked the clock and was not that surprised to find out it was ten-thirty. She'd obviously needed the extra rest. It was still early enough to see Ms. Liu and probably pick up the boys herself. She picked up her phone and texted her mother, who quickly responded that she could pick up the boys so Jessica didn't have to rush her visit with Cindy. "I hope she can help, darling," was all she said. She didn't push for information, trusting, as always, that her daughter would share when she was ready. Jessica pushed down the guilt of not yet having told her mother what was wrong, telling herself she was protecting her from unnecessary worry, that it was better to tell her when she understood it better herself.

Jessica texted her thanks and padded to the bathroom, smoothing the tufted carpet back down with her feet and picking up her soft pink track suit on the way. She always wore soft stretchy clothes when she had to see a doctor. It had become a habit when she'd gone through her cancer treatments. If you avoided tight, restrictive garments and didn't wear any metal, sometimes, the doctors could let you wear normal clothing while they worked. She didn't know what kinds of tests Ms. Liu might have in mind, but figured it was better to be prepared for anything.

Once downstairs, Jessica stood in front of the refrigerator for a long time, thinking. Everything in the fridge was pre-packaged and already prepared. She grabbed a peeled, boiled egg from its grocery store package and a container of strawberry yogurt, taking them to the dining room table with her and setting them next to her iPad. Then she went back to the kitchen and brewed a cup of tea.

While she waited for the few minutes it took to steep, she called Ms. Liu, who sounded delighted to hear from her. They agreed to meet at twelve-thirty at Ms. Liu's house. Ms. Liu said she'd have lunch for them. Jessica settled with her breakfast and started reading her e-mail and checking in on the socials, feeling good that she was taking action to solve her problem.

$\sim$

At a quarter past noon, Jessica found her way to Ms. Liu's house. It was on a pleasant street in an older neighborhood. The houses probably weren't that old, but compared to Jessica's neighborhood, where everything still had sales stickers on it, it felt old. At least the trees were fully grown in. You got the feeling that more than one generation had grown up here.

Slowing to peer at the house numbers, Jessica remembered Leonel had said he was Ms. Liu's neighbor. She wondered which of the houses belonged to him and David. She'd had a wonderful day with Leonel the day before. Things felt so easy with him. It was good to have a friend, a real one. The relaxed, natural, open conversation she had with Leonel contrasted strongly with the shallow, image-conscious conversations she had held with so many wives of Nathan's co-workers and moms of other boys that knew her boys.

She liked those women, but it wasn't the same as having a friend who was drawn to you for yourself rather than thrown in with you by circumstance. Women she had grown up with were still in her social circles, but they weren't close enough to matter when the chips were down. They weren't the kind of women she could call to keep her company at the hospital or to talk heart to heart about her worries about her family and her marriage.

Leonel cared about her. It was strange to feel so close to someone she had so recently met, but she did. She had talked with Leonel more freely than she had talked with anyone in years. Leonel had seemed to enjoy talking with her, too. Jessica felt like he had been lonely recently, and he needed a new friend as badly as she did.

She'd been surprised to learn David and Leonel had raised three daughters. The oldest was twenty-five, only a few years younger than Jessica herself. She hadn't realized it was possible for a gay couple to adopt so long ago. She thought that was a much more recent development. Leonel talked of his daughters with a mix of exasperation and admiration that was a pleasure to listen to. He glowed with pride, showing pictures of his five grandchildren. Jessica hoped she could be half the parent he was.

His relationship with David was obviously very strong as well. She hadn't seen them together since the day of the ladder incident, but she could feel that they were strong in their faith in each other. They definitely had each other's backs.

Leonel didn't complain, but Jessica gathered that there had recently been some tough times, and they were getting through it. Leonel so obviously loved David and cherished him. Jessica wished she felt cherished by her husband in that way. She tried to have faith that they were going through a tough time right now and things would get better. Watching Leonel and David, though, she wondered if her own marriage had that kind of strength. Comparing her marriage to theirs seemed like comparing a raspberry bush to an oak tree.

Parking in front of Ms. Liu's house, Jessica sat with her hands on the wheel, thinking. She should sit in the car and wait. It would be rude to arrive so early. She pulled out her phone to play with and looked out the window at the house.

Ms. Liu's house was surrounded by a variety of trees. From her car, Jessica could only make out a corner of the porch and an upstairs window, but it looked like the house was the same style as many others on the street: one story, in that bungalow sort of shape that had been popular in the fifties. There was a large garden area in the front yard. Everything in the garden was very tall and had a wild and unkempt look that made Jessica nervous. The HOA would never allow such a garden in Hollow Oaks. Jessica wondered if it would be rude to offer Ms. Liu the contact information of her gardening company. They weren't that expensive and kept things really nice.

As she sat waiting, Jessica grew more anxious. She had a bad feeling. It was vague, but nagging, this little voice telling her not to go inside. She chided herself for being xenophobic and ridiculous. Ms. Liu had been her mother's friend as long as she could remember. She had been nothing but kind and solicitous. There was no reason to think ill of her.

Tired of stalling, Jessica stepped out of Nathan's car and let herself in through the old-fashioned wrought-iron gate. Expecting it to stick, she pulled it harder than necessary, and it bounced against the fence and nearly smacked her in the shoulder on the way back. *Calm down*, Jessica told herself again.

As she stepped into the yard, she began to hear music. It was something bold and classical. There was a vocalist, but Jessica couldn't understand what she was singing. It grew louder as she approached the door, and billowed out of the house when Ms. Liu answered. Ms. Liu gestured for her to come in and then ran to the stereo to turn it down. "Sorry. I listen to it loud when I am alone. Come in! Come in!"

Jessica stepped into the dark living room. She had to stop and wait for her eyes to adjust. "Thanks for seeing me, Ms. Liu."

"Call me Cindy, please. There's no need to be so formal. Come on into the kitchen. I've made us some sandwiches. Would you like some tea?" Ms. Liu talked very quickly and almost fluttered as she moved. She seemed nervous, like Jessica's good opinion mattered a great deal. Knowing Ms. Liu was nervous too made Jessica feel a little better. Maybe it was just that they'd never dealt with each other this way before. Maybe all her bad feelings could be chalked up to discomfort and embarrassment.

Relaxing a little, Jessica followed where Ms. Liu had gone and sat down at the diner style table, with a scarred, red Formica top and a silver band around the outer edge. The band had come unglued on one side and stuck up like a bad haircut. Jessica's grandmother had owned a similar table, with little chairs with fluffy cushions that made a whoosh sound when you sat on them. Ms. Liu's chairs did not match the table. They were hardwood and un-cushioned. They were also a little tall. Jessica found that surprising, given that Ms. Liu was only an inch or two taller than her. She'd have thought such a small woman living alone would have small furniture.

Ms. Liu set a plate of sandwiches on the table next to a tea set and took the seat opposite Jessica. She immediately picked up the small stone pot and poured them both a cup of tea. It was the licorice and ginseng smelling tea that Jessica had been drinking. It was nice of Ms. Liu to serve her favorite. Jessica pulled a sandwich off the platter and held it in her hand. Ms. Liu had neglected to provide any plates to set it down on, so she just held it in her hand between bites. It was peanut butter and jelly.

Cindy immediately apologized for the sandwiches. "I planned to make a nice chicken salad, but found that I don't have a thing in the house. Living alone, I often forget to grocery shop. It's easy just to pick something up, you know."

Jessica nodded, sympathetically. She knew her own refrigerator was often bare or stocked with prepackaged kid-pleasing foods only. She didn't have half the excuse Ms. Liu did, given that she was at home most days, but she guessed she was one of those women with no interest in cooking. It didn't come automatically with the kitchen, after all.

Ms. Liu was a fast eater and downed her sandwich in a few quick bites. While Jessica was still chewing, Ms. Liu pulled out a small computer and began clicking around. "Do you mind if I ask some questions while you eat?"

Jessica nodded, her mouth glued shut with peanut butter. She set her half-eaten sandwich on the edge of the platter and picked up her tea. She wasn't that hungry, anyway. "Shoot!"

Ms. Liu ran through a barrage of questions. Some of it seemed unrelated at first. She asked about Jessica's sleeping and eating patterns. She examined Jessica's tongue and announced that it was "Pinkish with a thin white coating. Normal." She'd sounded disappointed.

She asked about Jessica's bowel movements. She took her pulse and said it was "wiry" and wondered if that was its usual state. She asked about her relationship with Nathan and the boys, how often she was having sex, and about her cancer treatments. She wanted to know how recent her last x-ray was and what her most recent levels of CA-125 were. It wasn't like any other doctor's appointment Jessica had ever been to. Though Jessica felt embarrassed by some of the questions, Ms. Liu took every answer in stride, and Jessica began to feel it was impossible to surprise her.

She wanted the exact details of what Jessica had been doing in the hours before the first incident, even what she had been watching on television and what position she had been sitting in. She asked a lot of questions about what had changed when she went from floating to falling the day of Nathan's accident.

Jessica told her everything she could think of. She described the tickling sensation in her belly, the difficulty of moving herself through the air with any speed or directional control, the feeling that she would just keep on floating higher and higher if she ran into no barriers to stop her. She talked about the grocery store incident and waking up floating above her bed that morning. She showed Ms. Liu the weights she had taken to wearing throughout her waking hours, just in case.

Ms. Liu typed away on her small computer as she listened, making small, excited sounds, and talking to herself as she typed. "Eructation associated with loss of buoyancy."

Jessica translated in her head. Burping associated with falling. Interesting. She hadn't thought of that, but, yes, burping did seem to happen as she came back to earth. Maybe she was like a balloon and was filling up with something lighter than air. It was ridiculous, but it kind of made sense. So, where was this lighter-than-air gas coming from? It wasn't like she was sitting around taking hits off a helium tank.

"I'd like to analyze your breath," Ms. Liu announced. She flung back her chair and scurried out of the room. She came back with a little, gray box with a hard plastic straw sticking out of the side. Jessica recognized it as some kind of breathalyzer, though it looked more complex than any device she'd ever seen at a roadside check. Ms. Liu punched some buttons on it and held it out to Jessica. "Please breathe into the straw."

Jessica did as she was asked, and Ms. Liu grabbed the machine when it beeped, clicking some more buttons. The machine rolled out a piece of paper like a cash register receipt. Ms. Liu read the list quickly, muttering. "Nothing out of the ordinary." Again, she sounded disappointed.

She looked sharply at Jessica. "We'll need to get a reading when you are floating, to see what's different."

Jessica looked at the small red clock above the sink. It was nearly three o'clock. "I'm going to have to go, Ms. Liu. I have to pick up my boys. Maybe we can talk again tomorrow?" There was no need to tell Ms. Liu that her mother was going to pick up the children. She could use the time-honored approach of letting her children help her make a graceful exit. Jessica stood and picked up her purse. She couldn't explain it, but she had a strong feeling it would be a mistake to go down to the lab.

Ms. Liu grabbed her wrist. Her hand seemed very strong. Jessica looked up in surprise. "I must insist you stay until we finish the testing," Ms. Liu said, her voice icy and her face emotionless, a frightening intensity in her eyes. She removed a hypodermic needle from her jacket pocket and stuck Jessica with it in a sudden darting movement.

Jessica had no time to react or protest. She grabbed her arm where she'd been stuck through her thin sweater. "What are you doing?" she yelped and then hit the floor.

JESSICA UNDER GLASS

essica woke in a glass tube. She thought she must still be asleep and was having some kind of science fiction dream about long-term space travel. If it were a movie, she would sit up and frantically ask someone what year it was. But this wasn't a movie, and Jessica was confused.

Her head felt fuzzy, and the inside of her mouth was cottony and dry. She turned her head and groaned. The little movement revealed a massive headache. She raised her arms to pull at her hair. She had read somewhere that headaches came from lack of blood flow and pulling your hair could stimulate the circulation. But when Jessica bent her elbows, a pain shot up her arm into her shoulder. She looked down at her right elbow and saw that there was an IV needle affixed at the bend with white medical tape.

The pain helped Jessica focus through the strange grogginess. She tried to remember what had happened. She had gone to visit Dr. Liu, who was going to help her with her problem. Feeling uneasy, she looked down. Her feet were bare and weren't touching the bottom of the tube. Her ankle weights had been removed.

What had happened? Dr. Liu had asked a bunch of questions, but then it was time to go. She'd try to leave. Then what? It flashed into her memory: Dr. Liu's grim and unyielding face and the needle in her hand.

Fully awake now, Jessica pushed against the walls of what she was starting to realize was her cage, but met with only resistance. Fighting down her panic, Jessica looked for a way out. The glass right in front of her face was a little cloudy, probably from her own heavy breathing. She raised the arm that wasn't impaled on a needle and wiped the steam away with her hand.

Through the smeary window, she could see a large room, lined in white and chrome. Where was she? Leaning forward, she pressed her forehead against the glass, trying to see into the wider room. The window felt cool against her head, and there was a soothing vibration. Jessica took a slow breath, ignoring the hitches in it, and then another and another. If she was going to get out of here, wherever here was, she was going to have to get it together.

A flurry of movement caught her eye. Along one wall, there was a line of wire box cages. Jessica could see the animals inside jumping and hurling themselves at the bars. That was when she realized she couldn't hear anything, not a bark, whimper, or cry of any of the animals, not the cages shaking. She realized the tube must block out sound. She heard an airy whirring sort of sound, and that was all.

A moment later, she saw what had caused the animals to react. Dr. Liu had entered the room. Jessica fought down another attack of panic at the sight of the woman. She pushed her body downward and leaned to the side of the tube, trying to get a better look at Cindy Liu.

Dr. Liu was standing at a work table in front of the wall of animal cages. She was dressed in a lab coat that swirled to mid-calf. Her back was to Jessica, her attention focused on a rack of vials in front of her. From this angle, it was impossible to see her face, but Jessica could see her movements. She appeared to be completing some sort of complicated process.

Dr. Liu picked up a long green stone and then dropped it into a small machine. After a moment or two, she dumped a powder out of the machine into a small bowl. She added something from a triangular flask on the table to the powder and stirred it, making a bright green liquid. Using a syringe, Dr. Liu added drops of the liquid to each of the vials in the rack on the table.

After each addition, she held the vial up to the light, swirling it and examining it. Then she placed the vial back on the rack and typed some notes into the same small laptop she had been using when she interviewed Jessica.

The procedure took a long time, and Jessica watched with interest, watching for anything she could use against her captor. She seethed with anger that this woman had trapped her like this when she had come to her for help. An opportunity would come, and when it did, Jessica intended to be ready for it. She'd see Dr. Liu pay.

After Dr. Liu finished mixing the various vials and making her notes, the horrible part came. She removed a rabbit from a cage first. She inserted a hypodermic needle into the first of the vials, drawing up the green liquid inside and then injecting the animal. The creature went into convulsions of obvious pain. Dr. Liu was barely able to keep hold of it as it pushed with its back legs and twisted in her arms.

Jessica felt sick watching but also couldn't look away. The animal was in such pain. When the convulsions stopped, the rabbit was put back into its cage, where it lay on its side, panting visibly. Jessica was sure Dr. Liu was some kind of sadist or madwoman. Her fear skyrocketed again. She began pounding on the sides of the tube, praying that she might find a weak spot.

As her anxiety rose, so did her body. Before long, her head was pressed up against the top of the tube, her body bent awkwardly as it tried to rise in an area too confined to allow that to happen. It was hard to breathe.

Then she heard Dr. Liu's voice telling her to relax. "It will be easier if you relax, Jessica. Take a deep breath."

There was a hissing sound, and Jessica suddenly felt sleepy. As she slipped into unconsciousness, the last thing she saw was Dr. Liu's face staring back at her through the glass. The doctor had her head tilted to the side and was examining her with an expression of excitement. That was more frightening than anything else she had seen.

~

When Jessica woke again, there was a new bandage on her forearm, her throat was raw, and she had a killer headache. The headache was so strong Jessica was seeing a bright white light that seemed to sear into her brain. Only when she was able to block out the light with her hand did Jessica realize the light was external. It was some kind of shop light, she guessed. It was incredibly bright and made it impossible to see anything else.

Pulling her knees into her chest, Jessica sank down into the bottom of the tube. Since most of the tube was made of a hard, clear material, Jessica had a only partially blocked view of the rest of the room.

Resting her head against the tube, she tried to see out. The now-familiar humming thrummed at a different frequency than her headache. The combination of vibrations made her teeth hurt, but she didn't move her head. She wanted to see what her captor was doing. She didn't know how she was going to get out of this, but she would, and when she did, she was going to hurt that woman.

A pair of legs walked past Jessica's view. They were bare, and the feet were wearing simple, black ballet-style shoes. A long white lab coat flapped against the back of the knees. So, the doctor was still working, or was working, again. Jessica didn't know how long she had been unconscious. That thought gave her hope. Her mother would have picked up the boys hours ago. She knew that Jessica was coming to Dr. Liu's. Help might be on the way right now.

There wasn't much to see from down in the bottom of the tube, but it was easier to think without that horribly bright light shining in her face. After a moment or two, Jessica realized she could hear the sounds of Dr. Liu moving around the lab. When the crazy bitch had turned on the speaker to communicate with Jessica, before she gassed her into unconsciousness, Dr. Liu must have left it on.

At first, Jessica couldn't make much sense of what she was hearing. There were some clatters and thuds, a few animal noises, which made Jessica remember the poor animals in the cages. Had any of the rest of them suffered like the rabbit? She heard a machine making a whirring sound.

Then the feet returned. This time, they were raised off the ground slightly and tucked around a metal bar. Jessica realized Dr. Liu must have been sitting on a stool right outside her prison. She closed her eyes, mimicking sleep. Maybe she would hear something.

At first, all she heard was keys clattering as the woman typed on her computer. She started to doze a little. But she startled awake when she heard Dr. Liu's voice. Luckily, the doctor's attention was not turned on her but on the little computer again, so Jessica could still observe her unnoticed.

The voice was very loud, like an announcement, and Jessica didn't understand why Dr. Liu would be speaking so loudly to herself. Then there was a click, and the same words repeated. Jessica realized the doctor must have been listening to a recording and making notes. Jessica let her head droop, so her hair would hide her expression more fully, and focused her attention on the words.

A lot of it didn't make sense to her, but she could tell she was hearing experiment notes.

"Subject seven had an adverse reaction to the serum," she said.

Jessica wondered if that had been the rabbit. While subject three "had not aged," its "regression had slowed." Jessica wondered what subject number she was. Having seen how the doctor had treated the animals in her experiments, she worried for her own safety.

"Must obtain additional supply of emeralds," Dr. Liu's clipped recorded voice reported. Dr. Liu stepped down from the stool, and Jessica watched her feet cross the lab to the work table lined with all the herbs and minerals. She closed her eyes again when she saw the feet come back, in case Dr. Liu decided to check on her captive.

She heard a phone ringing and was confused by the sound at first, until she realized Dr. Liu was using the speaker phone. There was a series of recorded menus in a language Jessica didn't know and assumed was Chinese. The conversation with what seemed to be a saleswoman was also in Chinese, but Jessica could tell Dr. Liu was not happy about the order from the anger in her voice. When she hung up, she muttered something like, "Three to six weeks? Ridiculous! There has to be a way to get more sooner."

Jessica peered out through her hair one last time, anxious to see what the woman was up to. Dr. Liu was standing just outside the tube, holding something in her hand that she was counting. As she turned to put the objects into a small plastic bag, she dropped one. Jessica saw it glinting on the floor. It was a beautiful green stone, cut into a long shard. It seemed almost alive somehow. If she had been able to, Jessica would have picked it up. She wanted to know what it felt like, if it would be cool or warm against her skin, rough or smooth. Lost in contemplating the gem, Jessica didn't notice when Dr. Liu left the lab, until the whole room went suddenly dark.

PATRICIA LETS GO

Once the nearly-weeping former employee, Marcie, had left, Patricia spun her desk chair in a circle and stretched her arms out wide. "That, my girl, was a great morning! A promotion and a firing." Suzie grinned at the compliment, which, unfortunately, made her look about thirteen years old. But Patricia was getting past that. Suzie might be young, but she was Patricia's kind of woman: capable, analytical, forward-thinking.

Patricia was energized by the easy flow of the morning. She really loved a kick-ass-and-take-no-prisoners kind of day, and she saw too few of them in the corporate world where everyone was so damn politic all the time. She tired of how her co-workers were always pussyfooting around. They thought conflict was something to avoid. You couldn't ever just move in a straight line from point A to point B.

A day like today was a rare treat. It was good to lose herself in the work and not think about her skin for a while. Her brain was still buzzing from her phone conversation with Cindy the night before. Cindy went on about what the skin looked like under the microscope and how it was a breakthrough. She hadn't said anything about how to get Patricia's skin back to normal. Patricia had hardly slept; she was so worried about what it meant. Would she be this way forever? But

GOING THROUGH THE CHANGE

after the morning's work, she felt strong and excited, ready to take on the next mountain.

"And good timing, too! You'll have time to take a breather before your next appointment arrives," Suzie said, clearing away the files and charts and settling them into their cabinets and folders. Suzie had been great during the meeting, anticipating what document Patricia would want and having it right there in her hand at the right moment.

The positive glow fading quickly, Patricia said, "I didn't ask for another appointment." She frowned. Forward-thinking was one thing, but she was in charge of her own day, and Suzie had overstepped her bounds if she scheduled something without getting the go-ahead from her.

"It's a doctor I found who will come to the office and see to your shoulders. He's very discreet. No one will even know he's here."

"What?" Patricia stood, feeling her face flush with rage. She drew up to her full height and loomed over the smaller woman. "Who asked you to get involved in my personal affairs?"

Suzie stepped back but didn't break Patricia's gaze. "I am your assistant, Ms. O'Neill. I am responsible for making sure you have everything you need. That includes your health and well-being."

Patricia stepped around the desk, closing the few steps that separated them in a single long stride. "What makes you think I can't take care of my own medical needs?" It wasn't like she wasn't seeking help. She'd gone to Cindy's and submitted to her testing. She would call her again this afternoon to talk about the results in more detail and about how to deal with this. What good was another doctor going to be? She was growing armor plating, not suffering from simple eczema! Patricia's chest felt tight. She tugged at the neckline of her blouse impatiently.

Suzie looked up into Patricia's face, unflinchingly. "It's not that you can't. But you won't. You don't think it's important, but I'm telling you"—Suzie grabbed Patricia's arm and dragged her over to the closet mirror, pointing at the bulges visible through the suddenly tight sleeves of her blouse—"this is not normal!"

Patricia flung out an arm, catching the mirror with the back of her hand. The mirror shattered, and Suzie squealed and threw herself back, away from the flying shards.

Patricia whirled on Suzie. Her voice seemed to have thickened in her throat. She sounded raspy, like a pack-a-day smoker with a cold. "You think I don't know that? Of course I know. But it's not your place, missy. My life and my body are my business!"

Suzie gasped, covering her mouth with her hands. "Ms. O'Neill!" She reached a hand toward Patricia's extended arm. The look on her face was strange: part panic and fear, part concern, and part something that might have been fascination. "The glass!"

Patricia looked down at her forearm and found a thick shard of the mirror sticking into the flesh. She couldn't feel it and wondered if that meant she had severed a nerve. Then she noticed there was no blood. The shard might as well have been stuck into the sheetrock. She stopped, fascinated and appalled at the same time. She grabbed at the shard with her other hand, which was looking distinctly claw-like, and plucked it out. She didn't feel a thing.

Patricia felt as though she couldn't breathe. Suzie was leaning against the desk, holding on to it like she might need its support to keep her from falling onto the floor. Patricia dropped to her knees, wrapping her claw hands over her head, like the danger was falling from the ceiling. In the scattered shards on the floor, she saw pieces of her reflection—the gray-green scales that covered her neck and cheeks, the yellowish spikes sticking out of her shoulders through her white silk blouse, now shredded and hanging in pieces from her shoulders. If it weren't for her red hair, she wouldn't believe it was herself she saw in the reflections. She was a monster.

She ran from the office, ignoring her intern's calls behind her. She had to get to Cindy. She had to get help.

LINDA SAVES THE DAY

L inda had tried all day yesterday to reach Jessica. She was worried about the younger woman. She so obviously needed a friend and not just because of her gravity problems. Whether she knew it or not, her marriage was in trouble as well.

Once she and David had gotten her off the ceiling and back into her weights, she and Jessica had talked the afternoon away while David finished fixing the light fixture. David had even made a comment about how this was a job and not a hen party.

The breakfast and shopping expedition the next day had cemented Linda's affection for the young woman. In many ways, she reminded Linda of her baby sister, the one they had not been able to save. It made Linda want to help her that much more.

Her mind circled back to the strangeness of finding out that they both used Dr. Liu's products. She hadn't yet told Jessica about her transformation. The woman had enough to deal with in her own problems. The coincidence was too much to ignore, and Linda wanted to talk to Jessica about it. It might have been time to be more forthcoming about her own issues.

Linda rolled over and patted David on the shoulder. "David?" He murmured something in his half-sleep that sounded distinctly like "*gallinas chocolates.*" Linda smiled. Chocolate chickens? That couldn't be right. "David, *despiértate*. Wake up, my love." Finally, he rolled onto his back, and she could look at his slightly puffy, sleep-smooshed face. It was wonderful to have him back in their bed.

Last night, their fumbles had finally turned into something that had worked for both of them. David had been patient night after night, assuring her that they would find a way. She didn't understand how he could be so sure, until he had finally confessed he had a male lover in his youth. She knew it had been hard for him to admit that out loud. It was one of those things that happened a lot, but no one spoke of. David had blushed when he told her and refused to look her in the eye. Linda had to laugh, given that she was sitting naked in their bed in the body of a man. Obviously, she didn't have a problem with the concept of men loving men.

It hadn't been perfect last night, but it had been good. She had been able to make David's eyes fall closed and his breathing shift into the pattern that told her she had found the right touch. When he had used his mouth on her, she had almost broken the bedpost. At last, she understood what the fuss had been about.

It gave Linda hope they could learn to please each other again. Her heart full, she pushed David's hair back from his forehead and kissed him. He smiled groggily and reached up to pull her closer to him for an embrace. They could talk later, Linda decided, folding into her husband's arms, her *pinga* already responding to his touch.

Once they had disentangled from each other's limbs, Linda went to the kitchen to make a nice warm chocolate to start their slow morning. While David took a shower, Linda lovingly set the table with wide-mouthed cups of thick chocolate and churros and strawberries for dipping. She frowned at the vase of flowers. They were browning.

Dumping the water into the sink, she stepped out onto the back patio, looking around self-consciously to make sure none of her neighbors were up and about. Seeing no one, she padded over to the compost boxes and dropped the flowers in. Then she pulled her garden shears from the little tool bin her daughters had bought her last Mother's Day and walked to cut a few blossoms for their breakfast table.

Bending to cut the flowers, Linda realized she was becoming accustomed to her new body. She was no longer startled by the sight of her own hands when she performed small tasks, no longer knocking things over or breaking fragile things by misjudging her strength and size. And after her weekend with David, she knew that he, too, was making his peace with her changes.

Her penis stirred a little against her new bathrobe as she remembered the pleasures of the night and the morning. He could still be hers, and she could still be his. They were the same people, even if she was housed differently now.

David was sitting at the table when she came back in, his hair still curling and damp after his shower. She brushed his shoulder as she walked by, and he grabbed her fingers and kissed them just as he always used to do. She noticed the hand-shaped bruise on David's shoulder and flexed her fingers guiltily. She'd have to be more careful with her strength.

"Viviana called while you were in the yard," David said quietly, like it was no big deal.

But Linda knew how hard it was on him that their youngest daughter refused to accept Linda was still her mother.

Linda sighed. "I don't know what to tell her."

David dipped a churro and nibbled at it thoughtfully. "*Mi amor*, we have already told her the truth. I guess she just needs more time to accept it. I'm going to try to get her to come to dinner with the rest of us this Sunday."

Linda leaned across and kissed her husband on the top of his head. "If anyone can get her to listen, it is you." She said a silent prayer that their daughter would indeed listen to her father. David loved all his daughters. He wouldn't be truly happy until they were all together again.

Changing the topic, Linda said, "I would like to visit Jessica today."

"Señora Roark? *Por qué?*"

"I'm worried about her. She hasn't responded to any of my calls."

"Maybe she's embarrassed. Maybe she doesn't want to see you."

"It's just a feeling, *corazón*. Something isn't right."

After lunch, Linda drove to Jessica's house and knocked on the door. A small woman with a perfect ash-blonde coif answered the door. She had to be Jessica's mother. Linda could see her new friend's delicate features echoed in the older woman's face. She smiled in the formal way women smile when they don't mean it. "Yes?"

Linda twisted her husband's baseball cap in her hands and asked if Jessica was there. The woman's face remained guarded, and Linda remembered she was now a large man. She rushed to reassure the woman she meant no harm. "My name is Leonel. I helped to install the new chandelier a couple of days ago?"

"Oh, Leonel! Yes, she told me about you. How is your, um, partner?" The woman relaxed a little, changing her hold on the door so she was no longer poised to slam it shut.

"David is well, thank you. May I speak with Jessica?" Linda felt oddly like a child asking if a friend could come out to play.

"She's not in right now." The woman's voice was tense and quavered a bit. There was definitely something wrong.

Linda considered. She rubbed the back of her neck and shuffled her feet uncomfortably. This part would have been so much easier as a woman. She could only hope Jessica had said something to her mother that would let the woman trust her enough to tell her what was going on. When they'd last talked, Jessica had said she had not yet told her mother what was going on with her. Her children had seen it, but they were very young. No one believed them. "Jessica was supposed to meet me yesterday to discuss some remodeling, but she did not come. She has not answered her phone, either, and I am worried about her. Is everything okay?"

The woman still looked hesitant, but she also looked like she wanted to say something. Linda asked gently, "Do you know where she is?" Linda tried to look small and nonthreatening. "I just really want to help. Is there anything I can do?"

The woman looked back over her shoulder, like she thought someone might be listening. Suddenly, she seemed to come to a decision. She stepped out onto the stoop, pulling the door closed behind her and taking Linda's arm. Linda let the petite woman lead her back to the truck.

"She went out yesterday afternoon and hasn't come home yet. She sent a text and said everything is fine, but she's not responding to my calls and messages. This is just not like her. I'm worried. She hadn't even made arrangements for the boys. I had to come over so Nathan could go to work." There was a strange emphasis on the word "work" that told Linda Nathan was not the son-in-law of the year.

Linda nodded thoughtfully. "Do you know where she went when she went out? That would be a good place to start, I think."

"She said she was going to see a family friend, Cindy Liu. But Cindy says that she never heard from her."

Linda wrinkled her forehead. "Have you called the police?"

Jessica's mother nodded. "They say they can't do anything. She hasn't been gone for forty-eight hours yet, and there's no sign of violence. They act like my baby would just walk away from her family." She lifted her hand to her mouth, covering it like she could keep the words from spilling out.

Linda patted her shoulder, reassuringly. "She would never do that. Of course, she wouldn't." She leaned against the truck. There had to be something she could do to help. Cindy Liu's name kept coming up. Much too frequently to be mere coincidence. Maybe Ms. Liu didn't know anything, but Linda was going to check.

She pulled a business card out of a little holder affixed to the dashboard of the truck and pulled a pen out of her pocket. She circled her husband's phone number and wrote "Leonel" and her cell phone number on the back of the card. "This is my partner's card. But you can reach me at the same number or at the cell phone number on the back. If you hear from Jessica, or if you need anything, please call me."

The woman looked down at the card. "Thank you, Mr. Alvarez. I'm Eva. Eva Roark." She turned to walk back to the house, clutching the small card with both hands, like it was vital to keep it flat. She stopped halfway up the walk and turned back. "She'll be all right, won't she, Mr. Alvarez?"

Linda nodded and did her best to look confident. "I'm sure she will be."

Linda took the short drive back to her neighborhood and parked the truck in her driveway. She pocketed the keys but didn't bother to go inside. David wasn't home. Their other car was missing. He'd probably gone to the office to talk with *el jefe* about the chandelier job at Jessica's house. She paused for a moment, realizing that, as a woman, she would have left a note saying where she was going, "just in case." As a man, she didn't feel the need. She could look out for herself. It was freeing.

Linda walked three houses down to the Liu house. She remembered when old Mrs. Liu had lived there. She was the kind of person who kept you standing on the stoop for an hour talking if you stopped by to share your extra cookies. Linda had liked her and had been saddened by her death.

She'd only met the younger Ms. Liu a few times, buying her products at the farmer's market. "Younger" was a kindness. Cindy Liu was at least twenty years Linda's senior. She didn't have her mother's friendly air, though she had come a long way from the surly young woman who had frightened the girls when they were children. And she did make lovely skin products. Linda had tried to be welcoming when Cindy had moved into her mother's old home.

Linda approached the house. The garden had become quite overgrown. It was pretty in a way, wild and untamed, but also, somehow, a little threatening. The elder Mrs. Liu had always kept the garden so well. Linda had enjoyed sitting in it with her on warm evenings and listening as her neighbor poked fun at the younger people in the neighborhood. In a way, it had been like sitting with her own mother, had she lived to old age.

The house didn't appear to have changed much in spite of the constant stream of workmen she had seen at the place. The changes must have been all inside. The same rattan furniture sat on the porch, the cushions now torn and water-soaked. The birdhouse still sat on its pole in the middle of the garden. Even through the shoulder high plants, Linda could see no one was putting bird seed in the tray any longer. If this was how Ms. Liu was keeping the yard, it would go to seed in another year or two. Linda clucked her tongue at the waste.

Looking toward the house, Linda noticed that the basement windows were soaped over, like they did at factories. It gave the house an abandoned look. Linda knew Cindy Liu still lived there. She and the other neighborhood ladies had often whispered together about the strange deliveries at odd hours and the crazy way that woman drove. Her car wasn't in the driveway. Maybe she wasn't home.

Pausing on the front porch, Linda listened, trying to decide if she should knock or not. At first, she didn't hear anything. Then she thought she heard sobbing. She knocked. "Ms. Liu? Are you there? It's me-Lin, uh, Leonel, your neighbor?"

She listened again. The sobbing stopped. She thought she heard a voice, but it sounded far away, and she couldn't understand what it was saying. "Ms. Liu?" Linda bumped the door open, wincing at the cracking wood sound that meant she had probably broken something. She leaned her head inside. "Ms. Liu? Are you all right? Can I come in?"

No one answered. Linda stepped inside. It was very dim in the living room. The blinds were pulled and blackout curtains had replaced the white lace that had once covered the windows. Waiting for her eyes to adjust, she stopped just inside the door and stood very still, listening. Nothing. Then a distant yell, "Hello!" The location was hard to guess. The voice echoed strangely, like a bad phone connection.

She called back, "Hello? Ms. Liu?"

"Basement!" The voice called.

Linda guessed that was an invitation. The hairs on the back of her neck were standing up, and she felt suddenly very awake, very aware. She didn't know yet what was wrong, but she had a bad feeling about this. She walked forward, anyway, unconsciously flexing her muscles.

She remembered where the basement was. She used to help the elder Mrs. Liu haul her laundry up and down the stairs when it got too difficult for her to manage alone. She strode through the living room and opened the door that led down to the cellar.

The stairwell was unchanged, though Linda now had to duck to avoid bumping her head on the dangling bare light bulb as she worked her way down. She called out again, not wanting to frighten anyone, "Hello! It's me, your neighbor, Leonel! Is everything okay?" Linda realized that Ms. Liu had not yet met her as Leonel, but explaining who she really was could wait for another time. Given that Ms. Liu had not attempted to include herself in the neighborhood, that probably wouldn't make any difference.

When she rounded the corner at the foot of the stairs, she stopped in her tracks. There was a huge metal door, like the kind you see on giant walk-in freezers in restaurants. That was definitely new. Not sure what to do, she knocked on the door. The rapping of her knuckles, though gentle, reverberated eerily. She heard it again: the voice. "Leonel!" This time she understood why the voice sounded so strange. She was hearing it through the ventilation system. The silver boxes ran above her head in the close ceiling.

"Yes, it's Leonel. Can I come in?" Even though Ms. Liu had never met Linda's alter ego, the voice sounded welcoming, happy that it was her. That raised the hairs on the back of Linda's neck again.

The voice was muffled, but she caught a few words. Linda tilted her head toward the vents above her. She heard three words. Locked. Trapped. Help.

Help? That was good enough for her. She grabbed the handle of the door. It resisted. Locked. So, she pushed harder. The entire mechanism pulled off. She dropped it and pushed the door open.

She burst into the room, trying to look everywhere at the same time. Her eyes glanced over the racks of beakers and test tubes, the animal cages, the table with a mortar and pestle and some mysterious-looking roots. What she didn't see was a person needing her help. Had she imagined the voice?

She heard knocking and turned to look at the wall behind her. There was Jessica, banging with all her might on the walls of some kind of metal and glass tube. Linda could see that she was screaming, but only the smallest of sounds was escaping.

Linda looked over the capsule, trying to figure out how it opened. There was a keypad on the front and a small dial. She turned the knob a few times, but it quickly became obvious you had to know the code to open the capsule this way.

She stood in front of the window and yelled, "Cover your face!" Just in case the soundproofing worked both ways, she used her arms to demonstrate. Jessica nodded and turned away from the door. Linda took off her outer shirt and wrapped her right elbow in the cloth and then thrust her arm through the glass side panel, shattering it. There was a whooshing sound, and the tube shuddered.

Linda gently knocked the small shards still attached away with her fingers. The opening was small, but so was Jessica. Linda leaned her head in. Jessica was pulling an IV out of her arm. Her hair was wild around her head, but her eyes were clear. "Can you fit through here?"

"Yes, I think I can!" Jessica crouched and maneuvered through the opening carefully.

Linda supported her as she stepped over the pile of broken glass, protecting her bare feet. Free, she threw herself into Linda's arms and began to sob. "Thank God you found me!"

Linda lifted Jessica as easily as a child. "Let's get you out of here."

"Wait!" Jessica slipped back down to the floor and bent down, examining the glass. She picked up a small object and grasped it in her hand. She pointed at the orange bag on the small desk. "That's my bag."

Linda grabbed the orange purse and flung it over a shoulder. She bent to gather Jessica back into her arms and took the stairs three at a time. She didn't understand what was happening here, but she knew it wasn't good. She didn't know what Cindy Liu had to do with it but didn't think she'd stick around to hear her side of the story. She'd get Jessica to safety and then figure out what to do from there.

They had just made it to the porch when Linda halted mid-stride, stopped by a strange figure dressed in a black hooded cape. The figure spoke. "Who are you? Where's Cindy?" The voice had a strange quality, like sandpaper or maybe the scrape of a match being lit. The person advanced toward them.

Linda couldn't tell if the person was male or female, but the person was tall and hiding his or her face. Linda felt instinctively that the person could be dangerous. She turned, shifting Jessica's weight to her left side so she could free her right arm in case she had to fight their way free.

"Is she back?" Jessica twisted in Linda's arms, panic clear on her face and in her voice. "Don't let her hurt me!" Jessica's body grew light in Linda's arms, and she knew her friend was losing her hold on gravity. Jessica grasped fiercely at Linda's shirt, and Linda heard the cotton tear slightly.

Linda shifted to hold her more securely and whispered assurances in her calmest voice. "I won't let you go, Jessica. It's going to be all right." She guessed Jessica believed her, because she loosened her death grip on Linda's shirt sleeve. She looked at the person standing in their way with narrowed eyes. Linda didn't know how much use Jessica would be in a fight, but the will to use whatever strength she had was definitely there in the set of her jaw. It was impressive, even if her pink tracksuit and tousled ponytail didn't make her look very imposing.

The hooded figure retreated the couple of steps it had taken toward the pair. One hand snaked out of a sleeve and scratched at the other wrist. The fingers were claw-like, and Linda was sure she saw scales on the exposed forearm. The figure spoke again. "She hurt you? Why would she hurt you?"

"Listen, I don't know who you are, or what you want, but I need to get my friend to safety, and we'd rather not be here when Ms. Liu returns. So, if you'll just move aside, friend, we'll be on our way." Linda pulled herself to her full height and tried to bring a little threat into the word friend, like she had heard her brothers do when they wanted someone to back down. She felt more worried than intimidating but tried not to let it show.

It must have worked, because the figure took another step back. Linda pushed past the person and walked down the porch steps. She felt eyes on her back, but she didn't turn around. She just kept striding straight for the safety of her own kitchen three doors down.

Once inside, she gently sat Jessica in a chair. She watched as Jessica dug through the orange bag and put on her weights, then she handed her the phone. "Call your mother, Jessica. She's frantic over you."

Jessica nodded and obeyed, big, fat, silent tears running down her cheeks. Linda put a box of tissues on the table next to her friend.

Trying not to eavesdrop, Linda busied herself at the stove, brewing a nice cup of tea and preparing a little tray of milk, sugar, lemon, and a few cookies. She was filled with a strange restless energy, a mix of emotions hard to define. She was relieved to have found Jessica, but it didn't feel like it was over. Not by a long shot. She had this powerful urge to hit something. It wasn't like her, this violence. But she was angry. It vibrated through her like the energy of a train when you stand too close to the tracks. The surprising thing was how the anger felt good, felt right.

PATRICIA'S OLD FRIEND AND
NEW ENEMY

Patricia watched them leave. The man strode down the street still cradling the woman in his arms. It was like a scene from an action movie. Patricia made note when they entered a small white cottage three houses down. She'd have Suzie look up the address later and see what she could find out, that is, if Suzie would even talk to her after the way she ran out. She knew she'd have to make it up to her intern when she came back.

The man and woman had been a strange pair, indeed. The woman had been frightened of even the mention of Cindy, and the very handsome man seemed to be on a rescue mission. The woman had obviously been through something awful. She had clung to the man with a naked panic that was painful to watch.

The woman was very small, barely five foot tall, probably not more than ninety pounds, what Patricia's mother might have called "a slip of a girl," but the large, muscular man with the soft brown eyes seemed to have some trouble holding her. Strangely, it wasn't like he was going to drop her, but more like she was going to fly out of his arms. He seemed to be helping to hold her down. That couldn't be right.

Patricia was very confused about what she had just seen but didn't know where else to go. She'd come here looking for help from her friend and unofficial doctor, but she'd walked in on something that gave her a hollow feeling in her gut. She decided to stay, anyway. She and Cindy went way back. She'd wait and find out Cindy's side of things.

Cindy was unconventional, to say the least. After all, a silenced gun had been one of the lab instruments she'd used with Patricia, and without asking her permission first. Patricia had just about ripped the good doctor a new one about the risk she had taken, but Cindy had been very reassuring. "There was no doubt what the result would be, Patricia. I was just gathering the final evidence." Patricia had eventually calmed down. No harm had been done after all, and they'd learned something important about her condition. Extraordinary circumstances called for extraordinary action. Maybe what was going on with Blondie and He-Man was just a misunderstanding, an overstepping of bounds.

Of course, giving Cindy the benefit of the doubt didn't mean Patricia wouldn't snoop around while she was waiting. It was good to see things for yourself and draw your own conclusions.

A quick walk around the rooms of the first floor didn't reveal much. There was a lot that didn't seem very much like her old friend at all. Like Patricia had noticed on her previous visits, there was lots of lace and chintz and other materials that must still be there from when she had inherited the house from her mother. If Cindy had decorated herself, the house would have been all modern and glossy. Chrome and glass, maybe. Not florals and lace, certainly.

There were some oddities, but nothing Patricia could learn anything from. There was a strange pattern of dirt on the rug in front of the sofa that almost looked like burns in the shape of feet. There was a bird perch sitting by the window, but no bird, just a series of small leather straps dangling. The bird must have escaped. The windows had very heavy draperies that blocked out all light. Patricia wondered if Cindy had become very paranoid about her privacy or if she was having vision problems that made her light sensitive, perhaps migraines.

All this conjecture was just making Patricia even more impatient. She flipped the curtains closed again and stalked away. The huge yellow spikes that had destroyed her blouse had finally gone down, but her skin was still scaly and bumpy. Where was that woman? When Patricia had fled her office, she had driven almost straight here, taking a moment to throw the cape around herself, happy she had neglected to take it back inside after the charity gala the weekend before. She had been sure Cindy was the one person who could help her. It hadn't occurred to her that Cindy might not be home, or that she might really be up to no good. Counseling herself to wait and see, Patricia went back to examining the house.

The books on the shelves were science volumes interspersed with romance novels with covers that made Patricia smile to herself, and other books with titles Patricia couldn't parse because they were written in Chinese. She pulled down one of the Chinese ones and tried to flip through the pages, but couldn't manage with her claw hands. She tore a page when she tried to catch the book as it slipped from her fingers. It showed a diagram of a person's tongue with arrows pointing at different parts of it. It made Patricia think of old pseudoscience trends like phrenology, one step removed from the truly absurd things like astrology and palm reading.

Cindy had often tried to convince Patricia to be more open-minded over the years, but Patricia reminded her that she was from Illinois. She was familiar with the smell of bullshit. Had Cindy stepped fully over into nutter-land? Was she going to offer to read Patricia's star chart when she finally returned home? The tests the other night had felt scientific, using tools Patricia could respect, like petri dishes and microscopes, blood samples and chemistry. She hoped her friend was still the rational and reliable woman Patricia believed her to be.

On the table in the kitchen was a small stone tea set just like the one she remembered from when she and Cindy had been college roommates. Patricia thought the tea smelled terrible, preferring her coffee, but seeing the tea set gave her some small reassurance that the woman she knew was still here. She felt calmer. At least until she went downstairs to the lab and found the broken door and shattered tube. Had the blonde been inside the tube? Had that man done this to the door? She didn't see any signs of tools, and the handle was completely squashed. He must have been amazingly strong.

What was her old friend up to? Cindy was going to be furious about the mess. She had always been a freak about her workspace.

Patricia had just returned to the living room when she heard the sound of a car door closing and voices. She retreated to the window area behind the couch, and peeked through the blinds. She pulled up the deep hood of her opera cloak, hiding her still-scaly face. Cindy was not alone.

Patricia watched as Dr. Cindy Liu walked into the living room, laughing. Another woman followed her three steps behind, her arms full of packages labeled "Scientific Svc. Co." and "Medicines and Herbs" and bolts of cloth. They were having an odd conversation that seemed to be about alcoholic beverages and extremely hot temperatures. Cindy's companion was a rather rotund woman around their age, with beauty shop hair, the kind so perfect it almost appears to be a wig.

When Cindy turned to say something to the other woman, Patricia got a look at her face. She was flabbergasted. Cindy looked like a woman in her twenties. She didn't look much older than Patricia's intern. Patricia knew Cindy was nine years older than her. It had been a sore spot when they went out together in college and Cindy, age thirty, would get carded, but Patricia, barely twenty-one, wouldn't. To look at her now, you would think no time had passed. This was getting stranger by the moment.

If anyone could help her, it was Cindy. So, checking to make sure her cowl was in place, Patricia cleared her throat to get the attention of Cindy and her unknown companion. The chubby stranger gasped dramatically, and Cindy turned to see what was the matter. She stood looking at Patricia for long seconds, unblinking, and then stepped toward her. "Patricia? Is that you?"

Not wanting to speak, Patricia inclined her neck, trying to nod without knocking the hood loose from her head and revealing her hideous face.

"Helen, can you give us a moment? Just take the packages into the kitchen for now." The woman, who was apparently named Helen—presumably the same Helen Cindy had gotten drunk with—didn't like the imperious tone, nor being sent away, Patricia could tell. She got a strange feeling, looking at her. The woman certainly didn't look threatening, all soft edges and dimples, but Patricia had good instincts for danger, and this woman was danger-ous. Not a direct sort of dangerous, either, but the stealthy, stab-you-in-the-back sort of dangerous. Patricia had seen her kind before. She would bear watching.

Once Helen was out of the room, Patricia pushed back the hood of her opera cape with one clawed hand. Cindy didn't gasp or cry out, but her eyes grew wide. She rushed to Patricia, grabbing her taloned hands and pulling her to sit on the sofa. When Patricia sat, she felt a leg of the couch give and knock the sofa off kilter, but Cindy didn't even seem to notice. She was running her hands over the scales on Patricia's neck and face, examining the area around her ears. "When did this happen?" Patricia was glad she had come. Her friend would help her. She was obviously concerned.

"A few hours ago. In my office." She shuddered at the sound of her own voice. It was so thick. Her tongue felt strange in her mouth. Her anxiety leaped again.

"And you came straight here?" Cindy asked, her tone flat.

Patricia's ears perked up. She knew Cindy was never more inter-ested in something than when she affected an air of unconcern. If she sounded bored, it was probably because she was fascinated. Cindy was extremely interested in what was going on with Patricia, and Patricia was no longer sure if that was a good thing. She'd come here for help, but now, she wasn't so sure help was what she would find. Not after what she'd seen in the basement laboratory.

Patricia nodded warily. Cindy pulled a small flashlight from a pocket somewhere and shined it in Patricia's eyes. Patricia grimaced and felt an odd fluttering sensation move up her cheeks. She knew it was the scales thickening like they had done in the office. She opened her eyes and looked into her friend's face. It was rapt.

"What is it about you, my friend? Why does it do this to you and not to the others?" Cindy seemed to be muttering to herself as much as talking to Patricia. Patricia was used to Cindy's habit of talking to herself when she was thinking, but the mention of "do this to you" and "others" had her internal alarm bells clanging, especially in light of the apparent rescue she had interrupted.

"Why does what do this to me? What are you talking about, Cindy?" Patricia pulled back from Cindy's touch. "Do you know what's happening to me?"

"Could it have to do with your red hair? The mutation in your genes? Come. Let's go down to my lab. I need to get some more samples."

Patricia didn't rise, letting her weight hold them there. "Wait, Cindy. What's going on here? When I arrived, there was a man here with a woman." Patricia paused, trying to find a way to say what she had seen without sounding like she was attacking her friend. "The woman said you hurt her."

Cindy spun, the color high in her face and the pitch of her voice rising. "What did she look like?" Her tone was accusatory, and the shift in her mood sudden and shocking. There was something hawk-like in Cindy's face that worried Patricia. She answered softly, not sure if the answer was going to make Cindy explode or calm her down.

"Little, blonde."

"Jessica!" Cindy ran from the room, flinging open the door to the basement and running down the stairs like a woman half her age. Patricia knew when her friend saw the broken capsule, because she heard Cindy howl with rage. It was an animal noise, frightening and ferocious. She shuddered, unconsciously gathering her cape around her. The spikes on her back and neck rose again, pushing the cloak out around her.

Helen came running from the kitchen, a box of Borax in one hand and a ball of fire in the other. Patricia sprang to her feet, poised to dodge or hit back, whatever was necessary. The two women stood sizing each other up. The ball of fire in Helen's hand grew, and Patricia bent her knees and moved her balance to the balls of her feet.

They could both hear Cindy in the basement. It sounded like she was having a temper tantrum, throwing things to the ground. They both heard crashes and cursing. Helen dropped the Borax on the small table at her side and clasped her hands together, extinguishing the fire between them. She glared accusingly at Patricia one last time, and then turned and hurried down to the basement, her lumbering steps making the old stairs creak.

Gathering her opera cloak around her once more, Patricia left. She knew now. Her friend was quite mad. The woman she'd called her friend had kidnapped someone. Worse yet, she suspected what was happening to her was somehow Cindy Liu's fault. She had to get back to her assistant, to Suzie. They could figure this out together.

CINDY LIU FLIRTS WITH DISASTER

Helen hung the final swath of cloth, labeled "7", over the improvised clothesline in Cindy Liu's front yard. This one was coated in a sodium silicate formula. The sixth piece had been dipped in a mixture that included borax, the others in ammonium chloride, alum, and several concoctions Helen couldn't remember the details about. After the samples had a chance to dry, she and Dr. Liu were going to try them out against her flames. Helen was hopeful they could find a formula that would allow her clothing to survive when she used her power.

Dr. Liu had given strict directions, including proper glove use and how to keep from contaminating one sample with another, but left Helen to do the tedious work of dipping each piece, labeling it, and hanging it to dry. She herself was cleaning up the mess in the lab the ungrateful girl, Jessica, and the mysterious man had left the day before. Once she'd calmed down, Cindy had explained how she was trying to help the poor girl regain her hold on gravity, and how she was worried Jessica might be mentally ill. She didn't know who the mysterious man was that had made such a mess of the lab. Part of Helen hoped the man would come back. She'd burn the truth out of him for Cindy. Her fingertips twitched imagining the scene.

She wouldn't mind scorching that lizard-woman, Patricia, for her, either. She had a bad feeling about her. Cindy insisted she was an old friend, but old friends have more hold over you, which makes them dangerous. History isn't always a good thing. Even before she'd seen her demon-face, she'd hesitated to leave Cindy alone with her. Cindy was too trusting. She needed someone to watch out for her. Helen could be that person. She was getting really good at manipulating her new power. She'd gladly use it to protect her new friend.

Just as Helen hung the last piece of cloth, Cindy stepped onto the porch, a cardboard box of broken glass in her arms. Her dark hair was pulled up into a jaunty ponytail on top her head. Dressed for cleaning, she wore a simple soft, purple T-shirt over gray capri pants with plain black sneakers. She looked all of twenty-seven years old. Helen looked down at her own billowing pink T-shirt and green cargo pants and sighed over her own girth. How did Cindy do it?

Helen suspected Cindy must have been experimenting on herself with some kind of aging reversal formula. It made sense from the woman who invented Surge Protector and who had a flying rat in her living room. Cindy was some kind of genius. Helen suspected Cindy was also a little crazy, but it wasn't such a bad thing, having a crazy genius in your corner. She was certain crazy was better than boring, which is what her life had been up till now.

The crazy genius brought the box to the rubbish bin at the end of the garden path and was walking back to Helen just as a police car pulled up. Helen looked at Cindy, raising a small ball of fire in one hand and a questioning eyebrow. Dr. Liu shook her head, a small quick motion that somehow still seemed imperious. "That won't be necessary. I've got this."

Helen was disappointed, but she dropped the ball of fire and stomped it out with her foot. She stepped closer to the house, staying just out of view in the eaves of the porch.

Cindy turned gracefully, bringing her hands to her chest in a decidedly girlish gesture. "Oh, officer! You startled me."

"Pardon me, miss. I'm investigating a complaint this morning." The officer pulled a fancy cell phone from his chest pocket and pushed some buttons on it. "Are you Cindy Liu?"

Cindy giggled. Helen was astonished. The officer looked up from his phone, a puzzled expression on his young face.

"Oh, I'm sorry, officer," Cindy said, resting her long fingers lightly on his bicep. "It's just funny that you would mistake me for my Auntie Cindy." She gestured at his phone. "How old is the woman you are looking for?"

The officer looked at his device again. He actually blushed. "Sixty-seven." He grinned sheepishly. "I see your point."

Cindy leaned back on one foot, thrusting a hip forward and tilting her head up at the officer, emphasizing her small size. Helen had to give her credit. She was good. She decided to sit on the porch steps and watch the show.

"I'm Chen-tao Zhang," she lied smoothly. "Cindy is my Auntie. How can I help you, Officer?"

"There's been a complaint against your aunt," the officer said, again consulting his notes on his phone. "I've been asked to investigate."

"Investigate what?"

Was Cindy actually pouting? Helen had to put her hand over her mouth to stifle the laughter.

"I can't say, miss." The officer stiffened his posture, and Helen could see he was fighting to hold onto his professionalism. "Can I come in and look around?"

Cindy put a finger against her lips, apparently thinking, and, at the same time, making sure the young man noticed her mouth. "Well, I don't know. Auntie's not home right now. I'm here to help run her errands. I don't think I should let someone in her house without talking to her first. She's a very private woman."

Suddenly, she gasped a little. "Wait! Is she in trouble? Are you here with a warrant?" She placed her hand over her heart in a theatrical gesture that also drew the young man's eyes to her breasts.

Helen couldn't see Cindy's face from her angle on the porch, but from the officer's reaction, she was sure Cindy had gone all doe-eyed and frightened looking. This young man didn't have a chance. He was faced with a seemingly twenty-something girl, with all the craft and knowledge of her sixty-seven years. Helen wanted to cheer aloud.

"No," he said, hesitating. "I don't have a warrant."

Cindy looped her arm through the officer's elbow, turning his bulk toward his car and walking him down the paving stone path. "Do you have a card I can give my Auntie when she comes back? I'll have her call when she gets home, and you can come back and talk to her then."

The officer stopped, obviously not happy with this turn of events. But he fished out a business card and handed it to Cindy.

The flirtatious smile fell off of Cindy's face as soon as she had her back to the officer. It was replaced with a stony expression of resolve. She walked back to Helen on the porch and sat down next to her. "I think we'd better go, my friend. He'll likely be back with that warrant in a few hours."

Helen nodded. Pushing with her arms, she heaved herself up and walked over to the hanging cloth samples. "How do I pack these up?"

LINDA GETS A PARTNER IN CRIME-FIGHTING

Linda was stretched out on the sofa, watching her *telenovelas* on the DVR, when the doorbell rang. When she peeked out the small window beside the door, there was a woman she didn't recognize standing there. She didn't look like a saleswoman. She was nicely dressed in an expensive suit, and her short red hair was professionally coiffed. She wasn't holding anything in her hands. Linda opened the door and stepped onto the porch. "Can I help you?" she asked.

The woman looked uncomfortable. She looked down the street toward Dr. Liu's house and then back to Linda. She leaned in to speak like someone could be listening. "I need to talk to you. It's about your neighbor."

Linda was curious but cautious. She sized up the person standing on her porch. She was probably around sixty years old, in good shape, athletic. Her clothes bespoke money and work in an office. She was tall, nearly as tall as Linda was now. When she was female, Linda would have found her intimidating. Besides her height, the woman was also built strongly and had a serious and severe face. Something in her expression said she was not to be messed with. This could be very interesting. She'd listen. Linda leaned against the doorframe, crossing her arms over her chest in what she hoped was a tough-looking pose. "Yes?"

The woman paced a few steps back and forth, running her hand up the back of her short hair in an agitated manner. Then she stopped and turned to face Linda with a quick sidestep. She threw out her words quickly. "My name is Patricia O'Neill. Your neighbor, Cindy Liu, is an old friend of mine." She paused, seeming to consider how to go on. She looked frustrated. "I don't know where to begin." She paused again. Linda waited, keeping her face impassive. "This is really a long story. Let me cut to the important part. That was me in the cape. When you rescued the blonde girl, the one who seemed to be floating out of your arms?"

Linda stared at the ordinary looking woman before her and thought about the mysterious figure in a black cape with lizard-like claws poking through the sleeves. It could be true. The woman shared height and build with the figure. She hadn't been sure at the time if the person inside was male or female. Other than the person with taloned hands, who else would even have known she was there?

Silently, Linda pushed the door open behind her and gestured for the woman to come in. The woman entered and stood uncertainly in the small entrance hall. Linda closed the door, turned the deadbolt, and pulled the side curtains closed. She pointed to the living room. "Please, sit down." The woman glanced around the room and then picked the big brown chair by the door and sat perched forward, both feet on the floor like she might have to take action.

Linda picked up the remote and turned off the television. She sat at the end of the couch nearest the woman and waited, tucking one foot up under her own bottom and leaning her face on her hand, elbow resting on the cushioned armrest. They sat in awkward silence for a few beats and then the lady blew out a big breath. "How should I begin?" she asked.

"Let's start with how you found me," Linda suggested.

"I just watched where you went when you left," Patricia said. "My assistant looked you up based on your address. I know that this is the house of Linda and David Alvarez, and you've lived here for twenty-eight years. I assume you must be David?"

Linda didn't correct her. She didn't like the idea that this woman had been looking up things about her and her family. She untangled her legs and put both feet on the floor, leaning forward with her elbows on her knees, flexing her fingers and cracking the knuckles. "And what do you want with me?"

"I want to know what you know. I think we might be of use to one another."

Linda looked into the other woman's face for a good long while, searching her eyes for signs of trustworthiness. The woman met her gaze levelly, her ice blue eyes calm and focused. Linda was a great believer in the feeling you get from a person, the sense of whether they possess a good heart. What she once would have called her women's intuition. She didn't get a bad feeling from this woman. But she also didn't get a good feeling. "You first," she said.

Over the next half hour, Linda listened as Patricia O'Neill laid out her concerns about Cindy Liu. They had been friends since college, it seemed. Cindy had always been brilliant, a ground-breaking researcher and inventor. She had won grants and awards. There had been an article about her last summer, detailing her work with bio-luminescent insects.

Linda could hear in her voice how much Patricia admired and respected her friend. She could also hear how worried she sounded. "I just keep coming back to what she has done, and I can't explain it. It's not like her. I want to understand what could have driven her to act like this. I want to understand where you and that blonde come in." It was stated as a command.

Linda could easily picture Patricia seated upon a throne and issuing the decree. But there was also a note of panic there, and of sadness.

Linda couldn't quite sympathize. Cindy had always struck her as strange. She'd seen her many times over the years, whenever she came home to visit. Every time she was in town, her mother would go into a tizzy, wanting to make everything perfect for her demanding daughter. But Cindy didn't seem to notice. She didn't even remember Linda, whom she had met on multiple occasions, when Linda stopped by with a casserole to offer her condolences when Cindy's mother died. Linda liked to believe the best about people. She wanted to think anyone could be good. She just had her doubts Cindy would make that choice.

Kidnapping didn't seem so far-fetched to Linda. But Patricia had won her over. She was a hard woman, but her concern and need for help were genuine. Linda might not buy her theory of a Cindy in need of rescue, but she felt she could trust Patricia to try and do what was right.

She stood. They'd been talking a long time. She stretched her arms over her head, cracking her back. When she turned back to her, Patricia was staring at her strangely. "Come on," Linda said, walking toward the kitchen. "I want something to eat."

Patricia seemed a little hesitant, but she followed Linda and took a seat on one of the high stools by the window. Her legs still reached the floor easily. Linda turned around, pulled a blue glass pitcher from the refrigerator, and grabbed a plate of cookies from the counter. In the couple of minutes it had taken her to grab the snack, Patricia had pulled out a phone and seemed to be checking her e-mail.

Linda ignored her rudeness and poured two cups of horchata, placing one in front of her guest, along with the plate. Without looking away from her phone, Patricia picked up a cookie and nibbled at the edges. Then she smiled and took a larger bite, setting the phone aside. "These are wonderful. Your wife must be an excellent cook."

Linda laughed, a short bark that almost sounded like a sneeze. Wife, indeed. "Thank you," she said and sat opposite Patricia at the tall table, stirring her drink with the cinnamon stick, waiting for the woman to begin.

When she didn't, Linda stood and walked to the window, glass in hand. She reached up and idly tugged a small cobweb from the upper corner of the window and then washed her hands at the sink. "You should know that I think your Cindy Liu is crazy, Patricia. She kidnapped my friend. And the things she makes..."

"Are dangerous," Patricia finished for her. "We've got to stop her."

Linda sat back down and leaned toward Patricia. "There's no delicate way to ask this, so I'll just be blunt. What has she done to you?"

Patricia stood up and removed her suit jacket. She pointed at the large patches of what looked like extremely dry skin on her upper arms. Linda must not have looked impressed, so Patricia explained. "This is what it looks like when I'm calm. When I get upset or worked up, it's worse. There are scales and spikes."

"When we ran into you on the porch, I thought I saw claws," Linda said.

Patricia nodded. "When I had skin troubles, I went to see her, and she gave me a cream. I think that cream is what did this to me."

Linda sipped her drink and sat thoughtfully and then got up and left the room. She came back with the soap, sloppily re-wrapped in its paper wrapper. "I bought this from Ms. Liu at the neighborhood farmer's market."

Patricia picked it up and looked at it. "What did it do?" she asked.

Linda turned red, suddenly embarrassed. Her answer was a mumble. "It made me into a man."

Patricia laughed. "What?"

"It's no joke." Linda grabbed a picture off the refrigerator and flung it on the table between them. It showed a large family: two grandparents, three young couples, and five grandchildren, all grinning at the photographer. Linda gestured at the woman in the center, a forty-something woman with dark hair surrounding her face in gentle waves. "That's me, a matter of weeks ago."

Patricia's smile died on her face. She picked up the photo, looking back and forth between the woman's face and Linda, sitting across from her. "Dear God. Cindy's soap did that to you?"

Linda nodded, replacing the photograph carefully and affixing it with small round magnets her favorite grandson had made for her.

"And your friend? The one you rescued?"

"She floats, like a balloon."

Patricia nodded. "That's why you were having trouble holding her on the porch. Cindy kidnapped her?"

Linda explained how Jessica had come to see Dr. Liu for help but had changed her mind and tried to leave, and then woke up inside some kind of glass tube in the basement. "We've told the police, at least about the kidnapping part. That was her rescue you walked in on."

Patricia pulled her feet up onto the rung at the bottom of the stool and peered out the window. She seemed to be trying to see Cindy's house, but Linda knew it wasn't visible from the kitchen window. "Do you think they'll do anything?" Patricia asked, turning back for another cookie.

Linda had her doubts. Police were not used to things like this, things that should be impossible. Women becoming men. People who float like balloons or become dragons. "They'll check out the kidnapping, but I don't know what they can do about the rest. Even proving it would be crazy. They'd laugh us out of the station."

Patricia set her glass down. "We need a plan. We'll have to take care of this ourselves."

Both women pulled out their phones at the same time. "We can meet here," Linda offered and then stepped out the room to make her calls from the living room.

HELEN'S DRIVING MISS CINDY

Helen watched Cindy pace around the hotel room she had rented for them. The woman had hardly sat down since they arrived. Helen didn't know what to do with her friend's nervous energy. Wasn't she tired? It had taken all the previous day to set up the truckload of stuff from Cindy's lab in a storage unit, rented in Helen's name since the police were likely looking for Cindy Liu.

As soon as she was awake, a good two hours before Helen would have preferred to rise, Cindy had wakened Helen and rushed her back over to the storage unit so she could select the items she needed for the experiments this afternoon. Cindy had been a flurry of activity all afternoon, running back and forth between three stations she'd set up in the kitchen area like a hamster on a diet of espresso beans. Helen had clicked through channels, nursing her sore muscles, bored out of her mind. You would think hiding from the police would be more exciting.

Still, progress was being made. Helen's new fireproof clothes were hanging to dry in the shower. The counter was covered in powdered varieties of different things, roots and bones and stones. Cindy had tested them all afternoon, refusing to say anything about what she was looking for.

For a while, Helen watched. It was all intriguing, but since Cindy wouldn't talk about what she was doing, Helen didn't really understand it. Plus, Cindy kept snapping her chewing gum, an adolescent habit Helen had always found particularly annoying.

Helen had read magazines and played with her phone, tempted to leave, but also wanting to linger nearby in case something happened. She hated to admit it, but she didn't really have anywhere else to go. They had effectively shuffled her out of this month's rotation at the realty offices. Her daughter was probably at work, and if she went home to Mary's apartment and found her there, Mary would want to talk about their feelings. Helen didn't feel up to more of that.

She was growing restless. She wanted to be able to do something. While the results of Cindy's experiments were wondrous and exciting, the process was boring as shit.

She thought some more about the situation. It seemed that Dr. Liu's products had interesting effects on others, not just her. When she'd been able to get Cindy to talk over the past few days, she learned Jessica had been drinking a tea designed to help with depression. Cindy thought the floating response had something to do with the girl's survival of cancer. Maybe her body chemistry was altered in a way that caused a unique reaction, or maybe it had to do with the parts of her body the western doctors had hacked out of her. Cindy had all but spat on the floor when she said "western doctors." Helen was willing to bet there was a juicy story behind that attitude.

Patricia, the lizard lady, had been using a cream developed for skin conditions like eczema and psoriasis. Cindy had used it on several test cases, but Patricia was the only one to respond so strangely. Helen wasn't surprised Patricia would be the strange one. There was something off about that woman. She hoped she'd get the chance to do something about her for Cindy.

Even her own condition was an anomaly. Other users had described the same tingling and cooling sensation, but no one else could turn the heat into actual fire. Cindy hadn't yet identified what it was in Helen's makeup that made her react so differently. She thought it might have something to do with the amount of the product Helen had been taking, or maybe it was Helen's ability to visualize so powerfully. Helen figured she'd stock up on more Surge Protector just in case. She was enjoying her new-found powers and didn't want to take the chance that they might go away.

Helen wished they were still in Cindy's lab. She would have liked to go back into the fireproof booth and try out what she could do. She had played around in the bathroom a little, but she had to be careful, so she didn't set the hotel on fire. They didn't need to call any attention to themselves. No one was looking for Helen yet, and they hadn't figured out Cindy Liu looked more than a little youthful for her age, but a fire would definitely attract unwanted attention.

Finally, Helen couldn't take Cindy's pacing anymore. She caught her arm before Cindy could start another loop. "Cindy! Stop it. Sit down."

Cindy scowled and threw herself onto the high backed stool at the breakfast bar in the kitchenette. She immediately began drumming her fingers on the countertop. She hadn't been seated five minutes when she jumped out of her seat again and moved to the window. She yanked back the curtains with a ferocious energy.

Helen blew out the small flames she had lit over each of her fingers and walked to look out the window with Cindy Liu. "Great view, huh?" she joked, gesturing out at the sea of SUVs filling the parking lot. Cindy grunted, crossing her arms over her narrow chest. Good grief. She was behaving like a teenager. At least there was a nice sunset.

Helen's phone made a beeping sound, and she saw that her daughter had acknowledged her text about having a girl's night out with some friends. "Don't do anything I wouldn't do," read the response. Helen was glad to see the attempt at humor. Mary had been really frightened by Helen's fire play in the backyard the other night.

Even with Mary's willingness to believe in impossible things, it had taken the rest of that night and the following morning to calm her down and convince her it would be okay. Helen was really enjoying her flames now. But she understood how strange it must have seemed to her daughter. It would take time to help her see how exciting it really was, being able to do something like this.

She texted back. "Guess that leaves me a lot of leeway then. LOL. Good night." She slid the phone into the pocket of her jeans and grabbed Cindy's arm. "Let's go somewhere. Your pacing is wearing me out. You hungry?"

Cindy blew out a breath, pushing her hair straight upward out of her eyes. "Yeah, okay. Anything has got to be better than hanging out here with nothing to do."

Helen shook her head. Just like a teenager, frantic to bored in thirty seconds flat.

A few minutes later, the pair was cruising downtown with the top down in the little red convertible Helen had rented. Cindy was pouting because Helen wouldn't let her drive. "Hey, it's not my fault the rental place didn't believe you were twenty-five. Besides, you drive like a crazy person. You'd get us pulled over." Helen turned the corner to an area with more restaurants. She hoped Cindy couldn't see her smiling with her head turned away.

It had been something else when Cindy had presented a driver's license for a sixty-seven year old woman. The clerk had lectured her about basic common sense and told her if she was going to use a fake ID, she should at least get a believable one. She threatened to cut up the license and call the police right there, but Cindy snatched it back and ran away.

Helen, approaching the desk afterward, had pretended she didn't even know her and asked if she could rent the convertible, since the girl wouldn't be taking it. The clerk and she had wagged their heads together over kids these days. Helen decided not to tell Cindy any of that. She probably wouldn't have picked a fire-red convertible as the getaway car, but she had to admit it was fun driving it. It was a shame that by the time in life you could afford a car like this, you no longer looked good driving it.

"What kind of food do you want?" Helen asked.

"I don't care. Just find someplace with a little life. I'm so bored!"

Helen laughed to herself. The younger Dr. Liu appeared, the

younger she behaved. This beauty treatment must have been more than skin deep. Still, Helen felt she could go for a little liveliness herself.

Helen pulled up to the valet stand in front of a promising-looking bar and restaurant called "Cuba Libre." She liked the music coming from inside, and the valet boys were good-looking. "Let's try this one."

Cindy got out of the car, and stood leaning into one hip impatiently while Helen handed over her keys and got her ticket. Cindy's sullen expression brightened when they stepped inside. The place was busy but not yet packed. Helen was looking around at the Andy Warhol style canvas prints of Che Guevara and Marilyn Monroe when the hostess came to seat them.

"Taking your mother out tonight?" the hostess asked Cindy.

Now, it was Cindy's turn to laugh, and Helen's turn to look stern.

They took seats at the corner of the bar, where they could watch the room and easily get the attention of the bartender. Luckily, the bartender didn't card Cindy. They were going to have to get her a fake ID. No one was going to buy her real one at the rate she was going.

Helen was getting worried about how quickly Cindy seemed to be getting younger. When they met, just a few days ago, Cindy looked like she might be forty-five. Helen knew now that she was sixty-seven. By the time the police came yesterday, she looked like she was in her later twenties. Now, she was having trouble passing for twenty-five.

She looked at her friend. Cindy was sipping something fruity through a straw and scanning the room. She had one foot hooked into the barstool and was leaning on her elbow. If she had snapped her chewing gum just then, Helen would have sworn she was seventeen.

She leaned in to her friend and whispered, "I think we're going to have to get you a fake ID."

Cindy nodded. "I've ordered one. We can pick it up tomorrow. But buying drinks and renting a car are the least of my worries. The process is accelerating. I need to get back into my lab and find a way to slow this down. At this rate, I'm going to be a teenager by Friday night."

Helen had driven by the house that afternoon to check on things and found it wreathed in crime scene tape. Getting back in wasn't going to be simple. "Can you work somewhere else?" she asked. She wondered if the foreclosure on Wild Oaks was still sitting empty. They could probably squat there unnoticed a good long while.

Just then, a young man popped up at Cindy's shoulder, swaying a little unsteadily on his flip-flop clad feet. "I'm Dennis," he yelled into Cindy's ear.

Cindy made an annoyed face. "I'm busy," she yelled over her shoulder before turning back to her conversation with Helen.

Helen thought Cindy might be passing up an opportunity. College boys were eager and easy to direct. It had been a long time since Helen had garnered attention from a man that young, but she remembered it fondly.

The boy dropped a heavy hand onto Cindy's shoulder, pulling her blouse to the side with his clumsy fingers. Cindy picked up the hand and took it between hers, pinched the nerve between his fingers painfully, and then turned back to Helen and smiled sweetly.

The boy pulled back his hand and waved it around. "Ow! You don't have to be a bitch about it," he whined.

Cindy's eyes narrowed. She might have struck the boy, but Helen caught her eye and shook a finger subtly. "Wait," she mouthed.

Helen returned her gaze to the boy, or more specifically to the glass in his hand. She stretched out the finger holding her own glass, aiming it casually at the boy's beverage. She concentrated briefly on the liquid inside, and then on the container itself. That was when the glass shattered, spilling surprisingly hot beer down the boy's arm.

He shook his arm in dismay, yelling, "Fuck! What the fuck just happened?" until the bartender came around and led him toward the entrance and out into the street.

Cindy covered her mouth as if she was upset, but Helen saw her laughter when she made eye contact. She lifted her glass in a little salute, which Cindy returned.

PATRICIA SAVES THE BEAUTY QUEEN

I t had been an eye-opening weekend. Patricia never would have suspected what a valuable ally Suzie could be. When she'd returned from the disastrous visit to Cindy, Suzie had been waiting for her, pacing in front of her condo. "I was so worried about you. Don't you ever run off like that on me again!"

Suzie stopped short of hugging her, but Patricia thought that was as much due to uncertainty about the scales as it was to any reticence. She was also surprised to find she would have welcomed the hug.

Patricia had always taken the attitude that the only person she could rely on was herself, so she was shocked to find how grateful she felt that Suzie was there and cared about where she had been. She wasn't sure, but she thought she felt tears in her eyes. Patricia never cried.

In the condo's living room, sprawled on the floor to avoid damaging her leather furniture, she told Suzie the whole story: the eczema problem, the cream her friend had given her, the gunshot test, the discovery of what Cindy had done. She'd never told one person so much about herself in her life. It felt good. It calmed her. And as she calmed, she felt the scales retreat. By the time they finished talking,

Patricia almost looked like herself again. The plates on her chest and back remained, but the scales and talons had retracted.

Suzie listened. When Patricia's words finally ran dry, the two women sat there together on the floor, staring out the large windows that overlooked the city, and thinking. After a while, Suzie pulled a legal pad out of her messenger bag and began writing. When she was finished, she held it out for Patricia to see.

It was a sort of bubble map. In the middle was a circle that said "Cindy Liu." There were lots of small bubbles around it with adjectives and questions. Patricia scanned over them, bouncing from "crazy" and "dangerous" to "police?" Other circles on the paper said "the cream" and "Patricia's condition." She couldn't read all the notations in Suzie's scrawling handwriting, but she could see the girl definitely was brewing a plan.

Finished reading, Patricia looked at Suzie questioningly. The younger woman chewed the eraser of her black Ticonderoga pencil thoughtfully. Then she said, "I think we should start with the cream and some clothes that will work for you. Let's go to the mall."

Patricia laughed. "That's your big idea? The mall?"

Suzie joined in the laughter. "I'm serious, though. There's a chem lab just around the corner from Holly Hills where we can get the cream analyzed to find out what's in it. There's an REI in the mall where we can get you some durable, flexible clothes that can handle your transformations. Plus, I want a smoothie."

"What about Cindy?"

"We'll need more time to think about that one and decide what to do. Involving the police is complicated. Our story isn't all that believable, and I don't know how deeply we want to be drawn into this. Let's work on the other problems first and take time to think about Cindy."

Patricia nodded. She was starting to think Suzie was a woman after her own heart. She was eminently practical and obviously a woman of action. If only she weren't so damned young and cute.

A few hours later, they were sitting by the fountain in the center of the mall, drinking smoothies and trying to ignore the teen beauty pageant on the stage behind them. Several large shopping bags filled with yoga pants and different kinds of athletic wear sat at their feet.

Patricia gestured behind her with her empty smoothie cup. "God, I hate these things."

Suzie nodded, slurping something pink through her straw. She wiped her mouth on the back of her hand and said, "I don't know what's worse: the old men ogling not-yet legal girls or the girls themselves, pinning all their hopes on push-up bras and makeup."

Patricia stared at her. "I'm surprised to hear you say that."

Suzie said, "I'm just blonde, Patricia. Not stupid."

Patricia cringed a little. "I know you're not stupid. At least, I know that now. But look at you."

Suzie looked down at her bright blue skirt and pink platform sandals. "I like bright colors." She turned to face her boss. "Listen, Patricia. This is how I look. I can't help that any more than you can choose how you look. I was born this way. But how I look is not who I am."

"I really underestimated you."

"Of course you did. Everyone does. That's part of what makes me so awesome. I'm a secret weapon."

Patricia laughed.

Just then, a gunshot rang out. The crowds of people milling about transformed into a panic of pushing and screaming lunatics instantaneously. Patricia and Suzie crouched on the floor, using the bench as shelter as people streamed past them. Patricia saw the source of the gunfire first. The gunman was a twenty-something white kid with black emo hair hanging in his face, wearing an army coat over a black T-shirt that said, she was sure, something hip and ironic. He was holding a big black machine gun of some sort. Patricia guessed he was modeling himself after one of the hundreds of other skinny white boys who'd taken guns in hand in the past few years to fight their feelings of inadequacy and invisibility.

He was still standing on the stage, holding a bony little blonde girl by her up-do. The girl's strapless blue sparkly dress stayed, amazingly, perfectly in place. Beauty queen duct tape, Patricia guessed. Her makeup, however, was running in black streaks down her cheeks as she sobbed and yelled, "Somebody help!"

The mall cops who weren't pushing customers to the exits, were gathered in a small, sad clump a few hundred feet from the stage, talking to each other and consulting their various devices. They were not equipped to deal with this sort of thing, and it would take the real police too long to get here. The girl was in serious danger.

Suzie pulled Patricia's shoulder, and Patricia crouched down lower to listen. "You've got to do something, Patricia."

"Me? What the hell could I do?"

"You're bulletproof. You can get that girl away from him. You can save her."

"Again, I say, why should I?"

"Because you can." Suzie's face was bright with something Patricia couldn't read. Excitement? Sureness? Faith?

Patricia peeked over the bench again. There was a short chubby woman standing just below the stage, howling and sobbing. She had to be the girl's mother. Her blonde helmet of hair didn't move as she lunged at the stage, or when the mall cops pulled her to safety. Patricia turned back to her intern and friend. "Suzie, I'm not Peter Parker. I don't buy the whole 'great power comes with great responsibility' racket. I didn't ask for this, and I don't owe anyone anything."

"Everything happens for a reason, Patricia. That girl might be foolish, but she doesn't deserve this. You can do something about it."

Damn it. She was right. Breathing in deeply, Patricia took off her jacket and laid it on the bench neatly. She took off her low-heeled slides and slid them beneath. Then she took a deep breath and stretched her arms in a wide circle around her. She hadn't tried to make the transformation happen on purpose before, but she figured it must be the opposite of making it go away. She needed to get herself worked up.

As she pushed out her breath through her nose in fast, snorting breaths, she thought about what Cindy had done to her. Used her. Like a lab rat. Her anger building, she flexed her arms and upper back and felt the spikes pop out. It didn't hurt. Very little could hurt her these days, at least physically, but it felt strange, sort of like feeling the rumble of thunder through your feet or chest; Patricia could feel it, but it was distant and vague. If it weren't for the additional weight the plates put on her frame, she might have thought she imagined the prickly sort of feeling as they sprang up.

It was stranger still when she rotated her head and felt the scales spread up her neck and onto her cheeks. Those she could feel. It was like they slipped out from secret compartments in her skull and slid into place, forming a protective mask. There was a rustling sound as they configured themselves under her hair and around her eyes and ears. She'd never get used to that.

She heard Suzie gasp and turned to grin at her. "Guess my reputation as an old battle-axe is truer than they know, huh?"

Suzie grinned back. "Go get 'em, Tiger," she quipped, and then crouched behind the bench again to watch.

It was hard to sneak up on people when you were a six-foot-tall lizard woman, but Patricia tried to creep around the potted plants to approach the stage platform from the back. The mall was empty now. Even the mall cops had retreated, dragging the poor beauty queen's mother with them.

Patricia caught a glimpse of herself in the reflective glass of the darkened Bible bookstore. The creature she saw there was broad and fierce, covered in gray-green scales with spikes sticking out of the back and shoulders. Her white tank top was stretched to its maximum and now had holes up the back where the back plates had sprouted bumps and then spikes. The black yoga pants were similarly strained. The only thing that still looked like her was the shock of red hair she paid her stylist to maintain. It looked very red against the scales.

Otherwise, she looked like some kind of alien, or maybe a bipedal dinosaur, one wearing yoga clothes from North Face.

She walked through the deserted mall as quietly as she could, but her heavy footsteps seemed to echo against the glass storefronts. Some of the storefront windows and pull-down security cages shook as she walked by. She hadn't weighed herself yet fully armored, but she had a feeling she wouldn't like the number.

She saw the moment when the boy spotted her. He was pacing the stage, dragging the poor girl around by her hair. The girl was trying to get her feet back under herself so she could move with him, but he wouldn't give her a moment's pause. The spindly high-heeled shoes weren't helping.

The boy must have heard Patricia's thudding steps, because he turned in her direction, a defiant sneer on his face. The sneer melted when he spotted her, and, for a moment, his naked panic was clearly visible. If the beauty queen had looked up just then, she might have felt less afraid. She would have seen her captor was just a scared boy, probably not any older than her. The boy recovered from his fear quickly, though, and grabbed the girl more strongly, pulling her up and wrapping one arm around her waist so she was held against his chest. If not for the struggling, the weaponry, and her tears, they could have been posing for a couple's portrait. The girl squeaked, like some kind of mouse or rabbit. As Patricia approached, the boy moved the gun back and forth between her and the girl a few times before deciding to keep it trained on Patricia. "St-st-stay back!" he stammered. "I'll shoot you!"

"Go ahead, honey. If it makes you feel better," Patricia said, stepping onto the stage. There was a groaning sound as she progressed, and the panels of the floor flexed under her heavy steps, but it seemed like the platform would hold.

Patricia could see the terror in the boy's eyes, but he brought the gun level. "I mean it!" His voice shook, but she gave him credit for the steadiness of his hand. Surely, none of the scenarios he had imagined had featured anything like her. He'd envisioned himself fighting police officers and ordinary people, not science fiction creatures.

"I'm sure you do." Patricia didn't stop walking. The boy loosened his hold on the girl, who fell like a dropped handkerchief at his feet. He gripped the weapon with both hands and opened fire. Patricia was sure the bullets had hit her. How could he miss at this distance, after all? But she didn't feel a thing. Behind the boy's left shoulder, a stage light shattered. *Ricochet*, Patricia thought.

She closed the remaining space between them in two steps, pulled the gun from his grip with one of her hands, and slapped him with the other. His head snapped back, and he fell like a scarecrow, boneless, out cold. Things like jaws didn't hold up very well against her armored skin, even when she didn't use much force. It was probably like being slapped by a rock. His jaw was probably broken. She'd been feeling kind of cranky when she slapped him.

Patricia turned to the young woman, still laying there playing damsel in distress. "Girl," she hissed, "Get up." The girl got to her feet, shaking, her arms wrapped around her slender body, her eyes darting between Patricia and her erstwhile captor, unconscious at her feet. "See what pretty gets you? Try for smart next time." The girl stood wide-eyed, immobile. "Go, girl. Go home!" At last, the girl slid off the stage and ran sobbing toward the exit, leaving both of her ridiculous shoes behind.

Suzie jumped up from her hiding spot behind the bench, squealing and clapping. "You were great!"

Patricia smiled, saluted Suzie with two fingers, and bounded off the stage, stalking away with a confident stride, moving as quickly as her bulk allowed. As she walked, she began her calming breathing. She thought about the sound of the ocean, pictured wide calm water stretching to the horizon. She didn't feel the scales retracting exactly, but she could tell that her steps were becoming lighter. She could move more quickly.

A few steps farther, and she was at the bench. Suzie was holding out Patricia's new green jacket, and she quickly shrugged it on and slid into her shoes. "Let's get out of here!" she said. Suzie handed her half the bags, and they walked off, looking for all the world like two friends who had just been shopping.

NOT JESSICA'S CUP OF TEA

essica held onto the newly installed safety bar in her shower, letting the water run over her. Billows of steam filled the bathroom. She thought she was done crying now. She hoped so.

A gentle knocking came at the door. Her mother's voice called out, "Everything okay, sweetheart?"

"I'm fine, Mom. Just enjoying the heat." Jessica heard her walk away. Her steps were quiet and slow, not at all like the usual fast pace of heels clicking that she associated with her mother. Jessica turned off the water and stepped out in a cloud of steam, choosing a fluffy yellow towel off the rack to wrap herself in and a smaller purple towel to wrap her hair in. Her hair wasn't really long enough to necessitate a second towel yet, but she had clung to the habit, even when she'd been bald.

She wiped a swath of mirror clean with the palm of her hand and looked at her eyes in the mirror. They looked surprisingly calm and clear. She didn't feel that calm inside. She laid a hand on her heart and rubbed the skin as if she could slow the frantic beating with the touch. She sat down on the closed toilet and wrapped her arms around herself. She felt nauseated.

It had been difficult, but she'd told her mother the whole story. How she'd tripped and not fallen, floating around her house until she fell on Nathan, resulting in his trip to the hospital. The grocery store. The weights. Meeting Leonel and David. How Cindy had been waiting for her when she arrived to pick up the children. The ladder incident. Her decision to take Cindy up on her offer to help. What happened when she tried to leave. Waking up in the laboratory. Her rescue by Leonel.

Her mother had listened carefully, her expression growing ever more severe. She sat with her hands clasped over her mouth in horror when Jessica demonstrated her problem. Her hands shook as she helped strap the weights back on to pull her daughter back down to earth. At the end, she had drawn Jessica into her arms and held her like she was a small child again. When Jessica looked into her face, she was shocked by how old and tired her mother looked. She had never looked like that, not even visiting Jessica in the hospital as she fought ovarian cancer.

"How could she do that to you? To my baby?" she said, anger putting a quaver in her voice. "I thought she was my friend."

At her insistence, they called the police. As they tried to explain the situation to the officers who came by, Jessica could see them making eye contact occasionally and wondered what they were communicating silently. She had spotted one of the two writing "domestic" in his small notebook, and wondered if that meant he was writing this off as not a real crime.

There was an awkward silence when one of the officers asked why Ms. Liu would want to kidnap Jessica. They couldn't really explain her motivation without explaining Jessica's entire situation, and they had agreed to leave that part of the story out. Eventually, Eva just shook her head and said, "I don't know, Officer. I really just don't know." His face softened then. Eva had a way of bringing out the protective nature of men.

Jessica glossed over how she escaped as well, just saying she was lucky, that she saw her opportunity and ran for it. She could see that the officers thought her story sounded a little fishy, but she didn't want to get Leonel involved unless she had to. The last thing she wanted was to send trouble to her one true friend.

The officers left, promising an investigation would be opened. Jessica's car was still missing, so, if they could find it, that would help the credibility of her story. She understood they needed evidence. They had taken the clothing she had been wearing, but Jessica doubted they would find anything to help them on it. Jessica hoped they'd find something all the same. Ms. Liu needed to be locked up before she hurt someone.

Still wrapped in a towel, Jessica strapped the new weights her mother had purchased for her around her ankles. They were padded and covered in tan cloth. They weren't as heavy as her father's old scuba weights, but, so far, it seemed like they would do the job, and they didn't hurt nearly as much to wear. She padded to the bedroom and sat on the bed, staring at the closet.

Nathan's side of the closet was open. He never remembered to close doors behind himself. Staring at the line of his suit jackets hanging there, she suddenly felt angry again. Nathan had not worried about her. Instead, he'd actually yelled at her when she came back, like she was a teenager who had just been on an irresponsible joy ride. "What were you thinking? Leaving us in the lurch like that? Your mother had to come and take care of the boys so I could go to work!"

He had stormed out the door with his overnight suitcase packed and gone straight to the airport, never once asking where she'd been or if she was all right. She hadn't been able to get a word of explanation in. He didn't seem to notice the disarray of her appearance. The fact that he was gone when the police arrived probably raised the wrong sorts of red flags for the officers, too. She felt strangely satisfied at the idea of him being pulled out of his board meetings to talk to the police about what had happened to her. It would serve him right.

She closed Nathan's side of the closet and opened hers, choosing a soft pair of sweatpants and a comfortable T-shirt that read "Soccer Mom" across the chest and "No, really!" across the back. All the moms on Frankie's team had gotten them last spring. When another set of burbles lightened her belly, she grabbed the new handle by the closet and waited it out. The feeling was short lived this time. The ankle weights held. She hovered only inches from the floor. Thinking about her conversation with Ms. Liu, she forced herself to burp and then fell softly back to the carpet. *Loss of buoyancy associated with eructation,* she thought. So much for table manners.

When Leonel had brought her home, he'd also brought David and his tools along, and the two of them had installed a variety of handles and safety bars all over the house while Jessica and her mother talked. Jessica couldn't believe how kind the couple had been to her.

The boys seemed to be unaware that anything had been amiss. They were just excited about having company and about all the cool tools in David's kit. Max kept quoting all the Spanish he knew, mostly words he'd picked up from Dora or Diego cartoons. Both boys took to Leonel right away, especially when they found out that he could lift them over his head and fly them around like airplanes. Stretching his arms out like Superman, Frankie giggled like mad. It had been more than a year since Jessica was able to pick him up and play with him like that. He was just too big now. And Nathan wasn't the sort to play roughhouse games with the boys.

Leonel had even made dinner. He'd had a lot of fun trying out the dual ovens and moveable plates in the stove top. Jessica didn't know what half the stuff was on the table, but it was all delicious and had filled the house with wonderful smells all day. The boys kept running through and asking for bites, and Leonel kept shooing them away with a wooden spoon and a smile. It was the liveliest and tastiest dinner the house had seen yet.

After Jessica and Eva had seen the boys to bed, the adults sat at the table together. David, Leonel, and Eva sipped the chocolate Leonel had made, but Jessica went and made herself a cup of tea. When she sat down and began to sip, Leonel suddenly reached across the table and took Jessica's hand. "Jessica? May I look at the box for that tea?"

Jessica nodded and retrieved it for her friend. Leonel pursed his lips as he tried to read the list of ingredients printed in small type on the side of the box. He held his head at an odd angle, and David silently reached into his chest pocket and passed the other man a pair of glasses. Leonel smiled at him and put on the glasses, studying the box more easily now. "I don't see anything unusual in this ingredients list, but I think you should stop drinking the tea. I think it might be causing your gravity problems."

Jessica laughed. "It's just tea, Leonel."

Leonel and David exchanged a look, and David nodded and then stood behind Leonel's chair, resting a hand on his shoulder. Leonel reached across the table and took one of Jessica's hands. "My name is really Linda."

Jessica was confused. Was it a joke? Or was Leonel trying to tell them he preferred to be called Linda? Was he a man who would rather be a woman? "What do you mean, Leonel?"

"Until a few months ago, I was a woman."

Eva and Jessica listened as Leonel recounted his tale of transformation. When he—no, when she—talked about her feats of strength, the mother and daughter moved closer to one another, looking to each other for reassurance. Two weeks before, they might have called the police to remove the crazy person from their house. But two weeks ago, Jessica had not broken the bounds of gravity. Impossible things seemed much more possible now.

"And you think Cindy's soap made this happen?" Eva asked, incredulous.

Leonel spread his—her—hands out and shrugged. "I don't know, but it seems more than a coincidence that both of us have had such strange things happen to us and both of us use Cindy Liu's products."

Eva said, "But I drink this tea, too. And nothing bizarre has happened to me."

David jumped in. "Maybe it doesn't do it to everyone. Maybe it's just if there's something about the person using the stuff. Like when you have an allergy? It's fine for everyone else, but not for you.

Remember when we found out that Estela's stomach problems were from the milk?"

Everyone nodded and Leonel squeezed his husband's hand and smiled at him.

Jessica pushed her cup of tea away forcefully enough to cause the cup to clatter in its saucer. "Is there any more of that chocolate?" she asked.

JESSICA BREAKS IN

Jessica was accustomed to feeling short. But standing between Leonel and Patricia, she felt like Gulliver among the giants, watching carefully to make sure she wasn't accidentally crushed. Patricia, in particular, moved with a briskness that required others to be on their guard. Jessica knew now that Leonel was so considerate in part because he really did know firsthand what it was like to be a small woman.

Jessica turned and looked up at her friend. He was easily a foot taller than her. He was a very handsome man, too. Well-muscled without being bulky. He wore his long hair tied in a low ponytail. She could give in to a crush on him very easily. He wore a soft white T-shirt that clung to his muscular chest and jeans that accentuated his rounded ass. His face was gently lined around the eyes in a way that suggested a person who laughed a lot. Looking at him, she had trouble believing he had once been a woman called Linda. To her, he would always be Leonel, her rescuer and friend.

She felt a little guilty, ogling him that way, but the truth was the spark had been gone with Nathan for a long time now. Nathan had been so charming when he was pursuing her. They'd met through a friend. She had found him handsome but maybe a little shallow. He always said, though, he'd fallen head over heels for her from the moment he first saw her.

His attention was like a spotlight. He'd won her over with extravagant surprises and exciting opportunities. She'd missed half of her last semester of college because Nathan would just show up and whisk her away. It hadn't seemed important at the time that she wouldn't graduate. She wasn't going to need a degree in physical therapy for the life she would lead with Nathan.

The first five years of their marriage had been full of tickets and trips. She'd worn a cocktail dress at least every other week. True, she was bored at most of the events, but she felt proud of Nathan and enjoyed watching him work a room. He was certainly a man who was going places, and she guessed she was lucky to be the woman who would go with him.

These days, she wasn't so sure she'd call herself lucky. It had been a long time since Nathan had taken her anywhere. He certainly wouldn't like where she was now, standing with Leonel and Patricia, waiting to help break into Dr. Liu's house.

Turning her head the other way, Jessica could see Patricia, her other partner in crime. Patricia looked to be in her late fifties or early sixties. She had this really intense way of looking at a person that made Jessica want to hide. She was obviously not someone you wanted to cross. Ever. Despite the softness of her yoga pants and tank top, she looked hard and mean. When she had shown them her scalier self earlier that evening at Leonel's house, Jessica had quite nearly peed her pants. When fully transformed, Patricia looked like some kind of lizard or dinosaur or maybe a crocodile, but with spikes. Even Leonel had taken a step back, resting a hand on his chest and murmuring something in Spanish.

In fact, the two of them seemed so strong and skilled that she wondered why she was there at all. Leonel was incredibly strong. Patricia was impervious to harm. Even bullets couldn't get through her armor! What good was she? A former gymnast who floated like a balloon? She felt strangely jealous. None of them had asked for this, but the other women had gotten amazing and useful powers. She didn't get a super power; she got a disability.

The original plan had been to go in through the lab window. There was a tree right outside the window that blocked the view, and would help make sure no neighbors saw them breaking in. They didn't want to explain themselves to the police, after all. But when they got there, they realized only Jessica was small enough to fit through the space. They'd circled the house, examining windows and doors, and finally decided the back door was the best bet. It was difficult to see from the street or the neighboring porches, and the light seemed to be out. Jessica would climb through the old-fashioned transom at the top of the door, drop to the floor inside, and let the other two in.

Flicking his flashlight to catch the attention of the other women, Leonel gestured to the transom above the back door. It was tilted in slightly. Leonel knelt down, holding his hands in an obvious sign that he intended for Jessica to step into his hands and be lifted to the window. She stepped into his hands and tried to keep her body still as he moved to a standing position. When she stretched her hands up, she almost got the giggles. The position was an awful lot like a free liberty cheerleading stunt. She had a sudden image of herself, Patricia, and Leonel in cheerleading sweaters and had to fight her own laughter again. She scolded herself internally to get it together. This was no time for hysteria. They were trying to get in quietly and look around without attracting unwanted attention.

Jessica could just reach the top of the transom with her fingers. She tugged, and the window made a horrid screeching sound. All three women froze, looking around anxiously. After a few seconds, it seemed the sound had not attracted any attention, so Jessica grabbed onto the edges of the window frame and pulled herself upward. Her upper body strength hadn't been this impressive since she won the state meet back when she was a tween, before she hurt her knee.

Holding onto the trim around the window, Jessica tucked her body into a rolled up position. She didn't want to end up falling face first into the foyer. Once inside the window opening, she twisted, unrolling her lower half on the other side of the door. Changing her hand holds, she went through the window backward, hanging briefly from her hands before she dropped to the floor inside. Without thinking, she found she had landed with one foot in the front of the other and her hands above her head. She could almost hear her old coach's voice calling out, "Way to stick it!" Muscle memory was incredible.

Wiping her gloved hands on her pants, Jessica hissed through the doorframe, "I'm in." She turned the four locks one at a time, jumping a little as the noise seemed to echo in the empty house. She was relieved when the door swung open and her larger companions could enter. It was creepy in there. There were strange rustling sounds.

The women didn't bother with the main house but headed straight for the laboratory. Anything that was going to help them was going to be in there. As they'd agreed, Patricia headed straight for the charts and notebooks, Leonel stood lookout, a baseball bat in his hands, and Jessica waited. She'd done her part getting them in, but waiting was boring. After a few minutes swinging her feet back and forth as she sat on a stool, she hopped down and started looking around the lab.

Someone had cleaned up the glass from her rescue, but the tube was still there. Had she really been inside it? It was bizarre looking, somewhere between a canister jar and a bug holder. It looked like something from a science fiction movie, the kind of thing an alien might be enclosed in, floating in yellow liquid. The lock that had given Leonel such trouble was still closed, and a red light was blinking on the display screen. She could see all kinds of readout screens along the side of the tube and was creeped out to see a clipboard with notes about her on it. "Subject 17: Jessica Roark: 32, Spontaneous Buoyancy." Now she knew what number subject she was, she supposed. Thinking about the rabbit she had watched Dr. Liu test, she felt sick about the other sixteen subjects and anxious about what might have happened to her if Leonel hadn't gotten her out. Would she have been howling in the same kind of pain while Dr. Liu took notes about her reaction?

On impulse, she released the clip, rolled the papers together into a sheaf, and shoved them into her back pocket. The police would probably miss it eventually, but she was sure the information would do her more good than them. She wondered if the police had been in the lab yet. There wasn't any crime scene tape, but maybe they only put that on the outside of the house. Jessica was sure Cindy Liu would have a plan in place to hide her actions from the authorities.

Looking for a distraction, Jessica checked on her companions. Patricia was still digging through the papers and files. She had booted up the desktop computer and was moving files onto a small hard drive. She moved quickly like she knew exactly what she was doing. Jessica admired her confidence. She bet Patricia never second-guessed herself.

Leonel was standing just outside the door, watching the stairs. He smiled in her direction when Jessica poked her head out, but turned his concentration back to the task at hand. He looked very intimidating standing there with the baseball bat. You could watch his muscles work when he moved it in his hands. He seemed a little tense and jumpy. Jessica would definitely think twice about coming down those stairs if she were an intruder here.

Jumpy, restless, and fighting a growing feeling of unease, Jessica wandered to a table off to the side of the lab. When she'd been held prisoner, she hadn't been able to see this table well, but she knew it was where Dr. Liu kept the green gems she had been so intent on. She reached in her pocket and touched the one she had stolen. It was warm to the touch, and Jessica could have sworn it vibrated in her hand. Maybe she was just nervous.

The wall above the table had a series of pictures pinned to it. They featured different views of the inside of the body, focusing on different systems. They were rather like the illustrations in an anatomy textbook. Jessica couldn't glean anything from them. She was getting tired of not understanding what was in front of her or even what was happening to her.

She had almost turned away when something glinted on the worktable, catching her eye. She moved a pestle and mortar to one side and revealed a small stash of the greenish crystals. Jessica picked up the stone and held it to the light. It was beautiful, translucent, and almost glowing. There were three large pieces of it on the worktable. Jessica pocketed them. Something about them just appealed to her. Besides, Cindy Liu owed her.

LINDA STANDS GUARD

Linda shifted again. Guard duty was turning out to be pretty dull. But she knew Patricia was right. Of the three of them, Patricia was the best suited to dig through the papers and files and find the useful stuff quickly.

But still, watching the spiders spin webs on the creaky old staircase was growing old quickly. Linda almost wished someone would come, just so she'd have something to do. She was restless. Plus, she was hungry. Her new body seemed to require a lot more food than her old one. The salad she'd prepared for dinner had been delicious, but now, her stomach was growling like a bear. Linda remembered how hungry her brothers had always been growing up. Her mother used to fuss about how it was like feeding an army, even as she hummed her way through the hours of baking and cooking. Linda had inherited a love of cooking from her.

Linda was pulled out of her daydream about *ropa vieja* and fresh homemade tortillas by a squeak in the floorboards above. She leaned her head into the lab, whistling softly. Jessica jumped but then nodded and moved to Patricia's side. When Linda turned back, she was face-to-face with a very young Asian woman who had to be Cindy Liu.

The girl jumped back at the sight of Linda. "Who are you?" she asked. "What are you doing in my laboratory?"

Linda gulped and then stood up taller, showing her full height. "We don't want any trouble."

"We?" Dr. Liu stretched her neck, trying to peer past Linda into the open door behind her. Linda moved to fill the gap. "Who else is with you?" Dr. Liu's tone was demanding and shrill.

Maybe it was a trick of the light, but Linda would have sworn Cindy Liu now looked as young as one of her own daughters. She knew Cindy Liu was twenty years her senior, but the woman on the staircase, staring her down, looked twenty-five at the oldest. Patricia hadn't been kidding.

Just then, Patricia stepped up behind Linda and cleared her throat, cuing Linda to move. She tried to position herself so she could watch Patricia and Dr. Liu at the same time. She didn't see Jessica. She wanted to go look but didn't want to leave Patricia unprotected, either. She stayed where she was.

"Patricia! Where did you go the other day? I was so worried about you!" Cindy's voice was solicitous, but the kindness didn't touch her calculating eyes. She moved down two more stairs, stretching out her arms like she might embrace Patricia, but Linda stepped up and moved the bat in her hand just enough to call attention to it.

"That's close enough," Linda said.

Patricia didn't acknowledge Cindy. She put a hand on Linda's shoulder. "We've got what we need. Let's go."

"You heard the lady. Go back up the stairs." Linda poked Cindy with the bat. It was a gentle touch, but she still reacted like it was painful. The flash of rage in her dark eyes worried Linda, but she wasn't going to let it show. She jabbed the bat toward the top of the stairs. "Go," she said, pushing her voice low to sound more threatening.

Cindy Liu compressed her mouth into a thin line. But she obeyed. In her stiff back, Linda could see the angry and difficult woman who had upset the elder Mrs. Liu all those years. Linda remembered the worry in the old woman's face whenever she talked about her Cindy.

She was worried her daughter might do something really awful one day. *"She just doesn't understand that other people are people,"* she'd said, wringing her hands in her lap. *"She is like her father that way. Heartless."*

At the time, Linda had written it off as an anxious mother venting, but now, she wondered if the old woman had been right. After all, Cindy seemed to think it was okay to inject Jessica with something that knocked her out and then confine her to a glass tube in the basement to run tests without permission. Who knew what she would do to the rest of them given the opportunity?

Linda still wanted to ask about Jessica, but something told her to keep her mouth shut. She would just have to trust that Patricia had taken care of her. As if she could hear Linda's thoughts, Patricia silently held out her hand for Linda to see when Dr. Liu was not looking. In it was a tan weight band—one of Jessica's ankle weights. Linda nearly gasped aloud. Patricia narrowed her eyes and shook her head to silence her, and then pulled out the other ankle weight before handing both to Linda. Linda shoved them into the pockets of her jeans for safekeeping and said a silent prayer that the other two women knew what they were doing. Jessica was untethered.

Linda pictured Jessica hovering in the rafters of the lab behind them and wondered what plan Patricia had made for getting her out of there. They couldn't just leave her. She wished she felt a little more sure that she could trust Patricia to act in everyone's best interest.

At the top of the stairs, just as Dr. Liu stepped around the corner, Patricia suddenly shoved Linda forward. "Get down," she shouted.

Linda, startled, toppled forward, the baseball bat skittering away across the hardwood floor. She caught herself on her hands and knees, just as a burst of fire scorched the wall where she had been standing, leaving it charcoaled. Linda felt a wave of heat go past her in a burst of wind that ruffled her hair.

Quickly moving into a crouch, Linda threw herself into the living room, aiming for a large, flowered armchair she remembered. Her aim was good. She landed behind the chair, which immediately burst into flame. She shoved at the chair with her boots, pushing it away from her and trying to stay hidden behind it at the same time. Where was the fire coming from? The chair was smoking now, a horrible black smoke that made Linda want to gag. She crawled on her belly toward the window.

"Call off your watchdog, Cindy," a voice demanded.

The voice sounded strange, but Linda knew it had to be Patricia. Was the smoke getting to her? If she had to, she could carry Patricia out of there, she was sure. After all, she had carried a piano. Linda crouched on her toes behind the couch, trying to see what was going on.

The sight on the other side of the room would have knocked her over if she weren't already on the floor. Patricia had transformed into her dinosaur shape. Linda thought she looked even larger than she had when she had shown what she could do in Linda's garden.

Patricia was facing a woman Linda didn't recognize. She was short and round, probably in her early sixties, with stiff blonde hair that stood out around her head like it wasn't actually hers. She wore a pair of black capri pants and a billowing white blouse with pink high top sneakers. That wasn't the strangest part, though. The woman was standing with her hands out to her side like a waitress balancing trays. In each of her hands was a rotating ball of fire. Her face was a mask of mad glee that made Linda sick to her stomach. That woman wanted to hurt someone.

Cindy Liu stood behind the fire-juggling woman, coolly examining her nails, as if she couldn't be bothered by the chaos happening around her, as if it were all commonplace.

"What are you doing in my house?" she asked, her voice quiet, calm, and somehow threatening. She might not look scary, but Linda knew looks could be deceiving. Cindy was definitely scary. She wasn't concerned about who might get hurt so long as she got what she wanted.

Watching her, Linda had the feeling Cindy might well want to hurt someone, too. Patricia was so sure Cindy was good at heart. Linda didn't know about her heart, but, outwardly at least, Cindy was the gasoline to the other woman's fire.

Patricia spread her hands in a gesture of supplication. It was less

195

than convincing, given that her hands looked more like claws, and her fingers ended in talons that could eviscerate anyone who got too close. "I was just looking for information about this." She gestured to her own body. "I want to know what you did to me." Linda thought Patricia had growled as she spoke. The fire-woman must have thought so, too, because the balls of flames in her hands grew larger.

Linda decided it was time to make her move. As quietly as she could, she moved to the end of the couch, where she had a clear shot at the fire-wielding woman. She moved into a crouch like a football player. Before she could talk herself out of it, she ran toward Cindy and the fire lady, yelling, "Get out of here, Patricia!"

PATRICIA FIGHTS FIRE WITH CLAW

Patricia didn't move. She stood there open-mouthed watching Leonel hurtle himself at Helen. What was he thinking? The woman could throw fire! He was going to get himself burned. Idiot!

Acting quickly, she leaped into the air, lunging toward Cindy and Helen. She cleared the short end table easily, but knocked over the other armchair with her elbow. The chair landed in Leonel's path, and he tripped, flying straight toward Patricia.

The next thing she knew, Patricia was sprawled out on the ground. She sat up. The room was becoming thick with smoke. They had to get out of there before the police and firefighters arrived. "Leonel!" she called.

"Here!" He was behind her. She moved to his side and helped him sit up. His forehead was bleeding. He wiped the blood from his eyes, leaving a grisly smear across his cheek and coughed. "Where are they?" he asked.

"There, by the wall. I think Helen is knocked out. We have to get out of here before she wakes up and tries to torch us again!" Patricia tugged at Leonel's arm, but he remained stubbornly seated.

"Where's Jessica?"

"She's fine! I sent her out the window. She'll be waiting in the tree outside the lab, around back." Leonel was still sitting on the floor. Patricia stood and reached to tug him to his feet. "Come on! The fire is spreading. We've got to get out."

Leonel coughed into his sleeve and then pointed at Cindy and Helen's limp bodies. "We can't just leave them here. They'll die!"

Patricia hated it when she had to admit someone else was right, but Leonel was right. She took a deep breath and ran over to Helen's inert body. The smoke was thicker over there. She struggled to move the fat woman, but she was just too heavy. Patricia could see Cindy trapped beneath the large woman's body. "A little help?" she yelled.

Leonel appeared at her side. He knelt and scooped up Helen easily. "Where?" He coughed, eyes streaming.

"Outside!" Patricia's lungs were starting to burn. She thrust her arm out toward the door. Oddly, her vision stayed clear. She wondered if her scales had come with some kind of protection for her eyes as well. That could be handy.

Leonel moved quickly toward the front door. It was closed, and his hands were full, so he kicked the heavy wooden door with one booted foot. To Patricia's surprise, the door fell forward, pulling the police tape with it as it fell onto the front porch like a drawbridge.

Patricia tossed the limp body of Cindy Liu over her shoulder in a fireman's carry, leaning forward to avoid spearing her on one of her back spikes, and followed Linda and Helen out of the hole where the door used to be. They staggered down the steps and collapsed at the edge of the lawn. Patricia flopped Cindy down, resting her head against Helen's prone form. Both of the unconscious women seemed to be breathing.

Patricia sat on her haunches, looking out at the street in front of them. She could hear distant sirens. Neighbors were starting to come out of their homes. Leonel was throwing up into the garden bed. Patricia tried to calm herself down. She hadn't worn the opera cape. There was no way to hide her condition. She needed to calm herself so her scales could retract, or the sight of her was going to start a mass panic.

When he finished throwing up, Leonel sat back on his heels. "Jessica!"

Patricia's eyes flew open. She had entirely forgotten the other woman. Leonel was on his feet with astonishing alacrity. He was already running around the side of the house by the time Patricia found her feet and pursued him.

She found her partners in the backyard. Leonel had just pulled Jessica down into his arms. It was hard to tell if the tears streaming down his face were from relief or from smoke damage. They left sooty tracks down his cheeks. Glancing back at Patricia, he pulled the ankle weights from his pockets, strapped them onto Jessica, and then gently lowered her to the ground.

"What took you so long?" Jessica asked, rubbing her arms. They were visibly shaking.

Patricia felt guilty for leaving her to cling to the tree so long. The smoke hadn't harmed her. She could have gotten to her sooner.

"We ran into some trouble," Leonel said, shooting another meaningful look at Patricia.

Patricia snorted. "I'll say." Trouble in the form of an inept and uncooperative man named Linda-Leonel. She kept the thought to herself for the moment. Right now, the important thing was to get away from there without having to confront the authorities. "We've got to get out of here. I don't want to explain to the police and fire department what we've been up to tonight."

The three women quietly joined the perimeter of neighbors and gawkers gathering. Though Patricia's feet were bare, her clothing torn, and Leonel's face was bloodied, they managed not to attract much attention. There were others with injuries, and most people focused on the rising flames in front of them. Patricia's head swiveled. No one seemed to be paying attention to them. That was good.

A quick glance at the yard revealed an empty lawn. Helen and Cindy must have regained consciousness and slipped away. That was probably bad. At least they had gotten what they came for. Jessica still had the small backpack Patricia had filled with papers and the hard drive she had stolen.

Jessica tugged at Patricia's arm. "Is there anything in Dr. Liu's lab that might explode?" Her eyes were wide and fearful. Patricia reviewed the lab in her mind's eye quickly. There were tanks along the east wall. Of what, she didn't know. Who knew what was on her lab shelves? She nodded to the other two.

"We've got to get these people away from here!" Jessica shouted.

All three women stood, still thinking.

Suddenly, Patricia grinned. "I've got this one." She turned away from the crowd for a moment, her body a strange ripple in the darkness. Her reptilian face fully on view, she thrust her claws at Jessica and said, "Now scream!"

HELEN NURSES HER WOUNDS, AND A GRUDGE

Helen crouched in the bushes of the house across the street, the still unconscious body of Dr. Liu beside her. The homeowners were out in the street, gawking like all the other neighbors. They should be safe for a few minutes. There was time to catch her breath and figure out what the next step should be.

Helen was fuming. In fact, her palms were still red as coals, and her entire body was putting off steam. When she moved her hands, she saw she had burned handprints into the grass they were resting in. She burned a wider swath of grass and patted it out with her hands, trying to make it less obvious.

She checked Cindy again. She was breathing, though she sounded asthmatic. Helen, of course, was unharmed by the smoke and fire, but she worried Cindy would suffer lung damage. She knew better than to seek medical attention, which came with other kinds of attention as well. Attention they didn't need. She would wait for Cindy to wake and find out what she needed.

Patricia O'Neill. Helen had known she was trouble when she first laid eyes on her. She'd been right. If only Cindy would have listened to her, they might have avoided all this. Cindy had insisted Patricia was an old friend and would do them no harm, that there was no need to seek her out. Helen had bowed to her wishes. After all, Cindy was the genius.

Old friend, indeed. Old was right—that woman had to be at least sixty-five—but she was no friend to Cindy. Helen itched to get back out there and fight, but she knew Cindy was in no shape to take them on. She knew she herself would be bruised and sore as well when the adrenaline wore off. So, she sat down and waited, watching the chaos through the shrubberies that shielded them from view.

She saw it when Patricia and the man reappeared at the side of the house. They both had protective arms around a small blonde that had to be Jessica Roark. The big guy had been calling her name when he got back up after the fight. Patricia had told him Jessica was all right. Jessica, she remembered, was the blonde girl who had come to Dr. Liu for help and then left the lab in a mess and called the cops, claiming she'd been kidnapped. Cindy had just been trying to help. Jessica hadn't even let her explain.

She watched the large man with special interest. Patricia had called him Leonel. This had to be the same man who had broken the stasis tube in the basement laboratory and taken Jessica away the day she had first laid eyes on Patricia. Who was he? Cindy said she had no idea. Jessica had a husband, but clearly, this wasn't a marketing executive stalking across the lawn, hair flowing behind him like some kind of god. Cindy had said Jessica was an only child, so he couldn't be her brother, either. Could he be her lover? How had he tracked Jessica down to break her from the tube?

The tube had been made of industrial polymers. Cindy said it could have withstood explosive charges, yet, he had broken the glass, and they didn't find any evidence he had used anything other than his bare hands. Not to mention what he had done to the door, the door that was as heavy as a bank vault seal. What gave this man such incredible strength?

He had carried Helen effortlessly, and Helen knew she was no lightweight. Most men would have struggled to move her, but this man had lifted her up and carried her as though she were a mere doll. Helen had struggled not to gasp aloud and reveal that she was conscious when he kicked down the front door. She touched her rib cage, below her breasts where his hands had cradled her. Even rushing from the burning building, he had carried her with such gentleness, laid her in the grass with such care.

Helen shook her head. This was no time to go all mutton-headed over a man, no matter how attractive he might be. If this man was working against Cindy Liu, then this man was her enemy. He had come to the lab with Patricia and Jessica to... to do what? That was the question of the night, wasn't it? What had they been after?

Helen thought about what she'd heard Patricia say when they thought she was unconscious. Those two had brought Jessica with them, and she had gone out the window. That meant she'd been in the laboratory, rifling through Dr. Liu's supplies and notes, taking who-knows-what. Were they looking for evidence? Surely, the police had already taken anything that would help their case. Were they looking for blackmail?

If Jessica had gone out the window, then whatever they wanted had been in the lab. And chances were they had gotten it. Helen watched the fire engulf the front of the house. Black smoke filled the night sky, which had turned a dark and ominous orange. Cindy had not been able to get the materials she had come for. She hadn't even made it into the lab, and now, her supplies were going up in smoke.

Damn those three troublemakers. If they had simply had a little faith in Cindy, Helen knew Cindy could have helped them all, and herself. Now, what was to keep Cindy from just getting younger and younger until she reverted to infancy? Where would Helen get what she needed? Dr. Liu had been evasive about whether Helen needed to keep taking the pills to maintain her power. But Helen suspected she did. It made sense, didn't it? If the pills triggered the gift, lack of pills would take it away. And she needed Cindy to provide the pills.

She couldn't go back to being ordinary after this. Now that she had tasted power, knew what it was like to wield fire, how could she go back to being a realtor, living a boring life like anyone else's? She turned to Cindy, who was now coughing and beginning to regain consciousness. She would protect this woman no matter what. Cindy Liu was her ticket to a life worth living. And a life worth living was worth fighting for. And if she had to push her way through a lizard, a hulk, and a bubble, so be it. She would.

WHAT JESSICA BRINGS TO
THE TABLE

J essica stepped into her dining room, having seen her boys to
bed. Her husband was still on his business trip. His text said he
wouldn't have time to call tonight. That was probably for the
best. He was still angry about the police officer who had pulled him
from his meeting with the implication he had harmed his wife. She'd
listened to the accusatory voicemail he'd left when she decided to
ignore his earlier call.

She had a feeling this was it, the crisis moment that had been
building in her marriage. Now that it was here, she was taking a page
from Nathan's book and avoiding it, at least for now. She needed to
decide what she wanted before she'd be able to fight for it. Did she
still want Nathan? She honestly wasn't sure.

Standing in the doorway, she looked around at the war council.
That was what it was, after all. They were there to plan strategy, to
figure out how to stop Dr. Liu and Helen before they hurt someone.
Her eyes ranged around the table.

Leonel and David sat together at the far end of the table, talking
quietly to each other in Spanish. David checked the bandage on
Leonel's head again, and Leonel patted his hand reassuringly. He

gestured at Patricia and seemed to be explaining how the injury had happened.

Patricia and Suzie had taken positions opposite each other in the middle, the papers spread out in neat piles between them. They were shifting papers from one pile to another and referring to a chart sketched out on some graph paper. Suzie had her laptop open and clicked away. Her portable scanner made quiet electronic sounds as she processed all the documents they had found that weren't already digital.

Jessica's mother, Eva, hovered at the side buffet, fussing over the coffeepot. Her hands shook. Jessica felt guilty, putting her mother through so much stress. She went to her and rubbed her shoulder gently. "Would you like to go lie down? I can fill you in later."

Eva smiled at her daughter and nodded. "It has been rather overwhelming." She hugged Jessica tightly before she left the room. "I'm so glad you made it home safely."

"Me, too. What would we do without me?" Jessica grinned. She was pleased to see that her mother smiled at the weak attempt at humor. They'd make it through this.

Looking around at the other four people at the table, Jessica wondered what she was doing there. The others seemed to think she should be there, but she couldn't for the life of her imagine what use she could be, other than maybe having a ready supply of coffee and a large dining room table. She had no idea what they should do from here. Nothing in her life had prepared her to make sense of the lab notes they had stolen or to guess what a madwoman might do next. She was in way over her depth.

She poured herself a cup of coffee, wishing it tasted as good as Ms. Liu's tea had, and sat down at the head of the table, sipping and waiting for someone to start the discussion. For at least the third time since this had all began, Jessica felt invisible and useless.

As she waited, Jessica played with the green stones she picked up from Dr. Liu's lab. She had put them in a little silk bag hung on a long chain and wore them around her neck inside her shirt. She found she was already developing a habit of pulling them out to play with whenever she was idle. She liked how they felt in her hand. Running her finger along the bumps and hard smooth edges was soothing. They were always cool to the touch, even when they'd been against her skin.

She wasn't entirely sure why she had taken them. She knew they were important to Dr. Liu, so that was part of it. After all, Dr. Liu had kidnapped her and kept her in a space age tube in the basement. The woman had offered help and given harm instead. The gems were the first of the payments Jessica intended to extract for her trouble. But now that she had them, she knew there was more to it than that. She was drawn to the gems themselves. She wanted them because she wanted them.

Eventually, Patricia sat back and looked around at all of them. "Okay. Here's what we have. Suzie?"

Jessica turned her attention to the presentation and to the young woman that had come with Patricia, her intern, apparently. Jessica wondered idly what else there was to their relationship. She was certainly very pretty and obviously worshiped Patricia. Patricia seemed a little less frightening when Suzie was around, too. Softer somehow.

Suzie turned her laptop around so that it faced the center of the table. Jessica and Leonel obligingly scooted their chairs around so everyone could see. "All of you used Dr. Liu's products. Jessica drank her tea. Leonel used her soap. Patricia used her skin cream. I took some of Patricia's skin cream to a chem lab yesterday for analysis. If you will share some of your tea and soap with me, I can have them analyzed as well."

The other women nodded their assents, and Suzie continued, "The interesting thing, so far, is the complexity of the product. It was all I could do to get back out of the lab this afternoon. The tech was so excited. He said he'd never seen anything like it. There were ingredients in it he hadn't been able to identify."

Leonel chimed in, "I bet the fire lady used something, too."

Patricia grunted agreement. "And Cindy has been doing something to herself as well. Did you see how young she looked? She's almost ten years older than me!"

Suzie added Helen and Cindy's names to her graphic with question marks for product information. Leonel raised his hand, like he was at school, and Patricia waved for him to speak. "Ms. Liu sold her soap at the farmer's market in my neighborhood. I know I wasn't the only woman to use it. You are also probably not the only people who are using her tea and her skin cream. So, why us? Why did it change us and not others?"

Suzie frowned. "That's been puzzling me as well. I can't find a common demographic among you. You have different ethnic origins, different ages, different home addresses, different ways of life in just about every way. At first, I thought maybe it had something to do with hormones associated with menopause, because that's what started Patricia's complaint, but Jessica is much too young for that to be a factor."

"No, I'm not," Jessica said, blushing a deep red when all eyes turned to her. She tried to keep her voice even and act like it was no big deal, even though she was shaking inside. "I'm a survivor," she said. Everyone looked at her blankly, and she knew they didn't understand. She took a deep breath. "Cancer. Ovarian cancer. I lost my ovaries about a year ago. It sent me into early menopause. I was drinking Dr. Liu's tea to help with the depression."

Leonel shoved back her chair and rushed to Jessica's side. Hugging her, he cried, "Oh, you poor girl!"

Suzie had a thoughtful look on her face. "And you, Leonel? You are also a little young."

Leonel shrugged. "It happens early in my *familia*. My grandmother was only forty-five. I am forty-eight. I stopped—*Lo siento*, David—six months ago—the bleeding." Leonel dropped his voice and whispered the last two words, like they were a secret. Jessica noted that David had turned his careful attention to the window behind him. She smiled. Men could be so delicate about the female body.

Patricia waved her hand in a gesture that said none of this was important. "What happened to us isn't what matters now. We need to figure out what Cindy is going to do next. One of the folders I found was her reports on herself. They show a series of tests for reversal of effects of aging. At first, the change was gradual, but here, lately, it has accelerated. She was trying a variety of compounds to slow it down. I think that's why she was at the lab last night: to find something she needed to slow down the process. In the space of a week, she has easily lost ten years in appearance."

Leonel jumped in. "We should find out more about her friend as well. Cindy may be the crazy one, but this Helen is dangerous. We need to watch out for her, find out how to stop her."

Patricia seemed annoyed. "I had it under control, Leonel. If you hadn't thrown yourself at her, we could have gotten out of there without burning the whole place down."

"Under control?" Leonel stood, bumping his head on the chandelier as he did. "That's what you call control? She would have killed you. I was saving you!"

"I didn't need saving." Patricia leaned across the table, growling. Scales moved across her cheeks, and David and Suzie both leaped back, alarmed.

"How was I supposed to know that? You didn't even see fit to warn me that our little adventure might end with a fireball hurtling at my head!"

"I didn't know she would be there!"

"That's not the point, Patricia." Leonel's voice was calm and steady. Jessica recognized the tone as the one you use when you're talking to an unruly child and are worried you might just start screaming. A smart child figures out when Mommy is that kind of calm, you'd better shape up. "You knew that was possible, and you didn't even tell us. What happened to working together?" Leonel reached out an arm and touched Patricia's elbow.

"If you had just done what I said, we wouldn't have been in that mess. I had a plan, and you ruined it."

Leonel drew back his hand, his face stiffening. "What plan? How was I supposed to know what your plan was? What made you think we would all just follow you blindly?"

Patricia's face turned a frightening shade of purple. "I know Cindy. That made me the best person to handle her. What? You think we should follow you just because you're a man?"

Stricken, Leonel gasped like he'd been physically slapped. His lips trembled, and silent tears began to run down his cheeks. Jessica and David grabbed Leonel's arms and soothed him, shooting twin accusing glares at Patricia, who threw her arms into the air and growled at the ceiling. "Women!"

Suzie stepped up. "Please sit down, everyone. We can work this out."

Just then, Eva came clattering into the room on her heeled slides, her eyes wide. "Jessica! You've got to see this!"

They all followed Eva into the family room where the TV news was playing. Eva clicked rewind to start the segment over again. As the images ran backward, they all saw a close up of Patricia in her dinosaur shape, chasing people away from the scene of the fire. Her scales appeared to almost glow in the strange light of the street. When Eva pressed play, they saw Patricia thrust her claws out in front of her and bellow. The group gathered, fascinated.

As they all watched, Eva grabbed her daughter's arm and looked pointedly at Patricia. Jessica nodded. Yes, the lizard lady was Patricia. Her intentions were good, but the bedside manner could have used some work. She had gotten the people away from the danger of the burning house full of potentially explosive things, but she had also scared the hell out of them. Jessica was beginning to understand that Patricia was an "ends justify the means" sort of person.

The clip ended when the video went all topsy-turvy as the photographer changed his mind about standing his ground and ran away. The news reporter said the footage had been taken earlier that evening just outside a house fire in midtown. The cause of the fire was as yet unknown, and no injuries or deaths had been reported. The image changed on the screen behind the reporter's head and showed a still picture of a fiery cloud engulfing the back of the house. Jessica couldn't believe how close they had all come to being blown up.

The house, another reporter said, speaking from in front of the burned out shell that had once been Ms. Liu's laboratory, belonged to a sixty-seven year old woman who was not on the scene and had not yet been located. The image of Cindy Liu must have come from her driver's license. The greenish cast of the photograph added to the appearance of a madwoman. Police were at the house just days before to investigate a possible kidnapping.

Jessica squeezed her mother's hand, reassuringly. "We'll find her," she said. "Don't worry." Jessica could tell by her mother's face that worry wasn't something she'd be able to turn off, but she seemed to appreciate the attempt at reassurance, anyway. Eva smiled wanly and turned back to the television.

This was the second sighting of the strange lizard woman. She had been seen at the shopping mall during a hostage standoff a few days earlier. Grainy security camera footage was shown, including the moment when the boy with the gun hit the stage like a sack of potatoes. The women watched in stunned silence as it was announced that authorities wanted to question this mysterious woman and were offering a reward for information.

The anchorwoman tried to laugh it off as a prank, but no one in Jessica's family room was laughing. All eyes turned to Patricia, who shrugged. "So much for working in secret," she said.

HELEN AND CINDY'S SECOND CHILDHOOD

Helen sat on the bed bewildered, listening to Cindy sobbing in the bathroom. What had happened to the strong woman she'd met at The Market? Where was the scientist? The visionary? Now, Helen was worried she had saddled herself with an infant, blubbering all the time. This was getting old fast. She wanted to leave but needed to keep Cindy on her side. No Cindy, no pills. No pills, no powers. Besides, the woman couldn't even take care of herself in this state.

At last, Cindy came out of the bathroom, rubbing her face with a hotel washcloth. "I'm sorry. I don't know what's wrong with me." She tossed the washcloth over her shoulder in the general direction of the bathroom and threw herself on the bed, sprawling there on her belly.

"I do," Helen said. "Puberty."

Cindy laughed, but then gasped, smacking herself in the forehead. "Shit. You could be right. I've got to be—what do you think? Fifteen?"

Helen nodded. Cindy had that lanky half-unformed look girls in their early teens develop. Legs as long as horses with torsos still slender as a child's. When her daughter had been at that stage, they called her The Gazelle. Mary had cried for what seemed like three years straight. Helen had strongly considered child abuse. "Think about it," she said. "You've been a mess these past few days. The younger you look, the worse you get."

Cindy looked thoughtful, picking out a small pimple on her chin. "I've got to get some more emerald powder. It slows the process. It'll give me time to figure out how to reverse it, or at least stop it from going further."

Helen frowned. "But your lab is up in smoke now. Where can we get more?"

"I've got a source, but it takes weeks. Technically, it's illegal to export to the United States." Cindy was starting to sound like she might cry again. That hitch was in her voice again, that whine that drove Helen crazy.

Helen stood up and paced the small living room area of the hotel suite. She set each of her fingertips aflame in turn and extinguished them by popping them into her mouth. It tickled the inside of her cheeks. Suddenly, she stopped. "Could your supply have survived the fire?"

Helen hadn't mentioned the fire since it happened, feeling guilty that she had destroyed her friend's home, even if she had done it defending them both from intruders and thieves. Luckily, Cindy didn't see it that way. She seemed to think it had been lucky Helen was there to defend her from her erstwhile friend and the mysterious brute that had attacked them in the living room.

Cindy rolled over onto her back, facing the ceiling. She ran her fingers through her hair, apparently considering. "Yes. Maybe. It's not flammable itself or explosive. If the fire didn't burn too hot…yes!"

"Then we've got to go back."

Cindy agreed. "Yes, as soon as it is dark."

A few hours later, Helen and Cindy were exiting the rented little red sports car parked three blocks over from Cindy's wreckage of a house and skirting through backyards and tree-lines to get there. It was three in the morning. They had agreed it was better to go during the sweet spot after the night owls had gone to sleep and while the early birds were still sleeping.

Both women were dressed all in black, Helen's clothes now fire-proof, she hoped. They had made it through a quick round of experimentation in a quiet corner of the park, anyway. Helen felt sore and tired after the adventures of the past few days. She wasn't built for being thrown across rooms by angry men or running away from the police.

Just for a moment, she thought longingly again of her ex-husband's armchair. But the moment passed quickly. Sore muscles and bruises or not, Helen felt more alive than she could ever remember feeling. If this was the cost, she'd pay it.

There was something thrilling about being a part of all this. Helen had not led a life of adventure. She had married her high school sweetheart, raised their child, and sold real estate. George hadn't liked to travel, and Mary had left as soon as she'd turned eighteen to seek her own adventures. That left Helen. She'd been so bored. Life had brought her none of the joy and excitement she had imagined as a girl. Instead, she felt like she'd wasted her youth on drudgery and then missed the payoff.

Since she'd met Cindy Liu, life hadn't been boring, at least not most of the time. Okay, the time in the hotel room had her crossing her eyes from boredom, but at least there was the promise of something exciting on the horizon, something like sneaking into a burned down laboratory to find illegal gemstones to grind into powder for a secret formula. Take that, George! Helen's adventure was much more exciting than a little cross-country motorcycle trip and a mid-life crisis divorce. She just wished it had come a little sooner, when she was a little younger.

She looked at her new friend, who was skipping down a footpath in someone's garden, her large messenger bag bouncing against her thigh. "Don't you love being out at night?" Cindy grinned. "It feels like anything could happen!"

It did, indeed.

When they arrived at the back of the burned-out house, Helen grabbed Cindy's arm to stop her. Cindy had been just about to stroll across the lawn like there was no reason for caution. They were going to have to get Cindy's brain working right. Helen was not interested in being her babysitter, or in inviting the scrutiny of the authorities. "Wait! Look around first. Let's make sure no one is watching."

At three in the morning, the small neighborhood was tucked up tight. Helen listened carefully, but didn't hear so much as a dog barking. "Don't you have something we could use? Like night-vision glasses or something?" she said to Cindy.

Cindy shrugged. "Nah. I'm not so much interested in machines and gadgets. Biology and chemistry, now that's interesting. Gears and wires? Not so much."

Helen let her Mission Impossible dreams slide away. No gadgets then. When they had gone to the storage unit so Cindy could gather some things, Helen had assumed she'd have something useful. "So, what's in the big bag?" she asked, gesturing at the heavy messenger bag Cindy had lugged along with them.

Crouching in the grass, Cindy opened the bag and pulled out an old fashioned atomizer and sprayed herself with something. Then she pulled out a small cylindrical tank filled with glowing insects, sat it in the grass, and opened the lid. "Our flashlights," she said as the insects gathered around her in a circle. Then she pulled out another tube and laid it on the ground. A long, green snake crawled out, and Cindy affixed a sort of leash to it through a little metal loop that seemed to be embedded in its flesh. "And our tracker."

Helen was not especially pleased to see bugs and reptiles. But then the bugs spread out across the lawn, making a swath of soft green light. She had to admit, it was beautiful. Unlike lightning bugs, these bugs stayed lit. They also stayed close to Cindy. Helen was dying to know how this all worked, but she knew now wasn't the time to ask. She followed Cindy and her menagerie across the lawn.

As the band of light began to encompass the house, Helen saw the extent of the damage. The house was still standing, and recognizably a house, but it looked like it could fall over at any time. Pieces of it were entirely missing. There were danger signs and yellow caution tape surrounding the house at a perimeter. The whole area stunk horribly of chemicals and smoke. Helen remembered the boom they had heard as they fled the scene. It wasn't going to be safe to go back inside the lab. The whole structure could fall down around their ears.

Helen heard Cindy coughing softly. In the hotel room, after their escape, Cindy had mixed up a concoction of pink bubbly liquid and drank it. The stuff had made her vomit what looked like black tar, but her breathing had returned to normal. It was amazing but disgusting. Helen didn't really want to watch that again.

She walked to Cindy's side, intending to offer to go ahead without her. She saw Cindy put on a little cotton mask, the sort you might wear doing home improvement projects. She handed a matching one to Helen. Helen didn't know how it would help, but she slipped it around her head, stretching the band wide over her hair so as not to destroy her hairdo. The mask smelled of something sweet. It must be a kind of filter for the air. Helen didn't need it. She seemed to be immune from the effects of smoke and ash as well as fire. When she had passed out in the testing booth, it had been because it was an enclosed space, and her fire had eaten all the oxygen. Still, it was sweet of Cindy to think of her comfort. Maybe the adult woman was still in there, fighting all those youthful hormones.

Helen had almost forgotten the snake until Cindy hissed at her to slow down or she'd step on it. The snake was zigzagging across the lawn. When they neared the house, it stopped. It raised its head and stuck out its tongue, bowing its head in different directions. Suddenly, it moved quickly toward a tree just outside the basement window. The tree was small with a low-hanging branch that had gotten charcoaled in the fire. Helen figured this must be what Patricia was talking about when she said Jessica would be waiting for them in the tree.

Helen stood and watched as Cindy got down on her hands and knees and began feeling around. She made a low cooing noise, and all the luminescent bugs gathered in a ring around her, lighting the ground beneath the tree.

Cindy squealed and leaped back, putting her hand across her

mouth. She looked apologetically at Helen, whose hands were aflame in preparation to defend them from whatever had startled Cindy.

"Slug," Cindy said, and shuddered.

Helen swatted the flames out against her shirt, happy to see the fireproofing was working, and covered her mouth to hide her laugh. Dr. Cindy Liu, grossed out by slugs? The good doctor didn't let it stop her, though. Wiping her hands on the jeans they had picked up for her at a thrift store, she continued her search, working her way completely around the tree.

Helen actually saw it first, a glitter among some rocks just at the edge of the ring of light. "There," she whispered, pointing.

Cindy grabbed at the green stone and held it in the air triumphantly. Then she threw herself back down and patted the ground in the entire area. After a few minutes, she leaned back on her heels, defeated. "There's only the one piece," she said. "That's not going to be enough. I need the other pieces to make enough of the formula."

Helen leaned against the tree, thinking. As she did, her hand brushed the low hanging branch. Something tickled her fingers. She looked, expecting to find a spider's web. There, hanging from a knot in the tree branch was a clump of long blonde hair.

Pulling at the tuft of hair, Helen met the eye of her new friend and saw her own thoughts reflected there. The tiny blonde, Jessica, the one who refused the good doctor's help and left such a mess in the lab. She'd been the one who escaped the lab and waited in this tree. If anyone had the rest of the gems, it would be her.

"I think I know where we need to start looking," Helen said, raising a hand with all five fingers aflame. "Where does your flighty little blonde live?"

LINDA ANSWERS THE CALL

Linda was just putting the finishing touches on a *Tres Leches* cake when the phone rang. She considered not answering it. The cake was an apology of sorts for David. He was angry with her for putting herself at such risk and not even talking to him about it first. *"Tu vida es mi vida,"* he had said, and he wasn't wrong. She would have been angry with him, too, in the same circumstances. A person with a family should not take such risks with their health and safety. Linda had quite nearly been burned to death, and they didn't even know yet if they had learned anything that justified the danger.

Of course, Linda had not known the extent of the danger she was in. Patricia had not been completely honest with her about what they were walking into. Guard duty against a potentially crazy, but still quite small and physically nonthreatening Asian woman was quite a bit different than guard duty that involved fighting a woman who could throw fire. Patricia's sense of invulnerability made her cocky, perhaps. Or maybe she just didn't think about others with the care she should. Linda still wasn't sure that she liked Patricia.

What she hadn't told David was how exciting she had found the fight, how good it had felt to use her strength that way. Like when she had broken the glass to free Jessica from the tube she was imprisoned in, Linda had felt exhilarated, full, alive in a way that ordinary life didn't often bring. She would like to find a way to help others like that more often. It seemed a waste to have this power and not use it to make the world better somehow. When she had been the small and weak one, how often had she wished that the strong would stand up for her? Now, she was the strong.

But that was a long conversation she wasn't ready to raise with her husband just yet. She was still reeling from her good fortune in keeping him by her side at all. Few husbands in this world would stand by a spouse in her circumstances. She needed him.

So, an apology cake it was. *Tres Leches* cake was also the favorite treat of their youngest daughter, Viviana, and David was going to try and get her to come by that evening to talk about Linda's changes. Linda hoped they might get through to her.

Viviana had still not accepted Linda as a man. While she was no longer denying Linda was Linda, she still insisted the story they had told her could not possibly be true. People didn't just change gender. Not because of soap. Viviana still believed her mother had surgery and was angry at her for not telling the family and letting them talk her out of it.

Never mind that a sex change operation does not make a person eight inches taller. Never mind that a sex change operation involves months of hormone therapy. Never mind that a sex change operation does not make a person any stronger than they were in their previous life. That girl was *terca como una mula*. Linda sighed. Yes, stubborn. Just like her mother.

When the phone persisted in ringing, Linda put down the spatula she was using to ice the cake and took the call. "Hello?" At first, there didn't seem to be anyone there. Just breathing. Was it just a prank call? "Listen you—I don't have time for this—"

"Leonel," a woman's voice sobbed. "Please. You've got to come. They've got my mother!"

"Jessica?" Linda's question went unanswered. The line was already dead.

Staring at the phone in her hand, Linda started out of the room in three different directions, trying to decide where to go, and then ended up standing still in the middle of the kitchen. "They've got my mother," the voice had said. She was sure it had been Jessica. She checked the phone. Yes, it had been Jessica's phone number. "They" would have to be Dr. Liu and her crazy fire-throwing dragon lady, Helen. Why would they want Jessica's mother?

Linda started to call back, but hung up halfway through the call. Jessica might not be able to talk, and if she called, she might be putting her in further danger, letting the bad guys know that Jessica had made the call in the first place. She needed information. She needed a plan. She needed Patricia.

PATRICIA'S BIG IDEA

Patricia pulled up in front of Jessica's house at almost the same time as Leonel, parking her Lexus behind his pale blue work truck. She hurried to join him in the shadow of the large tree across the street from Jessica's house, as they had agreed.

They watched the quiet house together for a few minutes. Patricia had dressed for action in her new knee-length yoga pants and a shirt that Suzie thought would stay in one piece even if spike holes appeared in the back. "Where is she?" Leonel asked. "Do you see anything?"

Patricia narrowed her eyes, searching the block in front of her. The daylight was fading fast. The house was quiet. There was no sign of danger. She didn't even see an unusual car, only Jessica's minivan. "I don't see her." She flexed her shoulders, loosening them, preparing for a fight. "Do you think she got inside?"

"Eva wouldn't have opened the door, and everything looks okay." Leonel looked worried, though. He was chewing his lower lip and tugging his ponytail over his shoulder to play with the strands of hair. At least he was outwardly calm now. He had sounded so panicked on the phone that it had been difficult to figure out what the problem was.

"Let's walk around the outside first," Patricia suggested. "Reconnaissance."

The two walked up to the front door together, both swiveling their heads constantly, looking for trouble, but not knowing which direction it might come from. At the front walk, they split up, each walking up one side of the house.

Patricia's side was quiet. She moved warily, watching for open windows or doors or signs of fire damage. She found she could actually see pretty well in the dark. According to Leonel, Jessica had hung up after her brief warning, like she was worried she'd be caught making the call. Leonel thought Eva and Jessica were being held against their will. Patricia thought she might be right. Cindy was definitely behaving erratically.

She thought back to what Jessica had told them all about Dr. Liu's strange behavior before her kidnapping. Cindy had seemed calm when Jessica first arrived. She was maybe a little nervous, but nothing that set off Jessica's alarm bells. She offered tea and sat with Jessica in the small kitchen, chatting pleasantly. Jessica had answered a lot of questions about the nature of her problem. She was feeling hopeful that Cindy might be able to help her.

To hear Jessica tell it, Cindy had lost it when the younger woman tried to leave. She'd stabbed her with something, imprisoned her in the tube—the same one Patricia had admired during her lab tour, no doubt—and experimented on her. As hard as it was to believe, Patricia had no reason to doubt Jessica's story. She had no reason to lie.

Kidnapping? It was a desperate and impulsive move. It showed no awareness of Jessica as a person, like she didn't matter beyond the information that could be gleaned from studying her. That wasn't like Cindy. Cindy was methodical. She always had a plan ten moves ahead. Surely, she realized kidnapping Jessica was going to be impossible to hide. Jessica had a family that was looking for her. The family knew Cindy and where she lived. Cindy herself knew Jessica. Cindy could be a little cold when it came to other people, but not like this. This was sociopathic. It just didn't add up. What did she have to gain that made such a risk worth it?

Patricia considered. They had all seen how quickly Cindy was getting younger. What if she wasn't able to stop it? That could make a woman desperate. What if, somehow, she thought that Jessica held the key? That could make a woman do things she wouldn't normally do, like kidnapping, threatening an old friend, taking up with strange new people. What if whatever she was doing to herself was affecting her mind?

Patricia was so deep in thought that she didn't hear it when Jessica hissed at her from a small balcony above her head. Only when a marble Jessica had thrown clipped her on the shoulder did she understand what she was hearing and look up. Having caught Patricia's eye, Jessica threw a leg over the railing and lowered herself to hang by her hands. "Catch me!" she called, and let go.

Patricia did her best, but catching Jessica still knocked them both to the ground. Concerned about the noise, Patricia scuttled to her feet ready for action, just in time for Leonel to round the corner at a run and nearly knock her down again. Jessica grabbed both women and tugged them to the back right corner of the house with her.

"This is the blind corner, where the boys go when they don't want me to see what they're up to in the yard. It's not visible from any of the house windows."

Jessica sat down on the ground hard, wiping tears away with the back of her hand. The other women waited for her to calm down and speak. Leonel pulled a wad of tissues from one of his pockets and passed one to Jessica, who blew her nose noisily. "She's in the kitchen with my mother. Mom told her I wasn't home, but her friend just burned the locking mechanism out of the door. She shoved her way in, and now they've got my mother trapped at the table."

"They?" Leonel asked.

"Helen is with her, too. I've been listening through the baby monitor. We still have the two-way system so I can talk Max back into his bed without going upstairs. Mom had turned it on so we could use them to communicate across floors. She was trying to let me get some rest. I was asleep when I started hearing voices in the kitchen through my bedside monitor."

"And your children?"

"At their other grandmother's house. Nathan took them for the day."

"*Gracias a Dios.*"

Patricia tapped her chin thoughtfully. "Leonel, how do you feel about hitting a woman?"

Leonel answered quickly. "To help our Jessica and rescue her mother, I would do this. But I am worried. With my strength, I could kill her."

"I don't want my mother hurt. We've got to find a way to get her out safely. I've put her through too much already." Jessica was near hysteria again.

Patricia had no patience with this sort of thing. Why were young women always so dramatic? Why couldn't Jessica be more sensible, like Suzie? She fought down her angry impatience. Yelling at her wouldn't help. She'd be even more useless if she started blubbering.

"Shut up so I can think!" she growled.

Jessica did her best to comply, slowing her tears to quiet whoops and hiccups.

Linda said, "Maybe we should call the police."

Patricia snapped, "Don't be ridiculous. We'd just get a bunch of officers killed."

"What if we told them it was a bomb? If they came with their special gear, it could protect them from Helen's fire."

"Maybe. If they believed us. If they didn't focus all their attention on the fact that your driver's license says you are a forty-eight-year-old woman and decide to deport you to where they assume you are from."

Leonel pulled another tissue from his pocket and wiped his eyes. When he looked at her again, his eyes were cold fire. Obviously, Patricia had gone too far.

"Then what do you suggest, Patricia?" He pronounced the name as if it were Spanish, all four syllables elongated for emphasis, his eyes glittering with anger.

Jessica glared at her, too. Patricia was getting really tired of people looking at her like that.

"Look," she said, trying to keep her irritation out of her voice, "I just mean—"

Jessica shushed Patricia and grabbed at both women's hands. Cindy Liu had just stepped onto the back deck. There was no place to hide. If she looked in their direction, they'd be seen.

Fortunately, Cindy's attention was on the row of rose bushes along the fence that separated Jessica's yard from that of her neighbor on the other side. The women watched her as she leaned on the rail. She seemed smaller than she had at the fire.

When Cindy turned to light up a cigarette, Patricia got a look at her profile. Her breasts were practically gone. Her pants hung loosely around her waist. Her shirt was too big as well. She was still adult-sized, but she had the build of a middle-school girl. Patricia felt a wave of sympathy for her old friend. If she was smoking again, things were bad. She hadn't smoked since the months after her fiancé's death, more than thirty years ago. She said then that smoking was a slow suicide, and she'd been smoking because she didn't have the nerve to do it quickly.

Patricia looked to her companions. Jessica was clinging to Leonel's arm like some kind of ninny. Pale and trembling, she looked like she might pass out with fear. They had her mother. Sympathy or not, Patricia knew who the real victim was. "Leonel," she whispered. "How do you feel about taking a hostage?"

Wordlessly, Leonel crossed the yard on his hands and knees. Jessica hid behind Patricia, who watched anxiously. Stealth was not one of Leonel's skills. It was like sending a tank on a sniper mission. She prayed he could get close enough before Cindy spotted him.

She needn't have worried.

She lost sight of Leonel as he rounded the deck to the far side, where Cindy was standing. All Patricia could see was two large hands grabbing Cindy around the waist. She was so surprised she didn't even scream. Leonel pulled her over the deck and raced back toward his friends, one large hand over Cindy's mouth, the other holding her curled against his chest. "I got her!"

JESSICA SPRINGS INTO ACTION

J essica looked wide-eyed from Leonel, who was holding a
struggling teenager in her arms, to Patricia, who was grinning
like the Cheshire cat. The plan had worked! They had Dr. Liu.
They could use her to get her mother back.

"Now what?" she asked, breathlessly, grabbing Patricia's arm.
Surely, she had a plan in mind for the next step.

The smile dropped from Patricia's face.

"Where do we take her? How do we get my mother out of there?"

Patricia was silent. Jessica fought an urge to grab the woman and
shake her by the shoulders as the seconds ticked by. Patricia
continued to sit in the grass and fail to explain the plan. Dr. Liu
stopped struggling so hard and joined with Jessica in staring at the
other two women.

"What's the plan, Patricia?" Jessica had a sinking feeling that there
wasn't any more plan.

She was right. Patricia let her head fall into her hands. "I hadn't
gotten any further than this. I need time to think."

Leonel stood, hitching his body so Dr. Liu was folded against his
chest. "Jessica. Get my keys from my pocket."

Jessica obeyed, feeling herself blush as she shoved her hand into

Leonel's front jeans pocket, and fished out the keys. "The small key is to the tool box in the back. The truck is parked across the street under the large elm tree. Bring me the duct tape."

Jessica nodded and started to jog toward the street.

"Don't let her see you!" Leonel called after her in a stage whisper.

Jessica returned to find the women unmoved, crouched in the grass in the blind corner of the house. The tension in the air was thick. She felt like a child walking into the room where her parents had been fighting and only stopped for her benefit. Jessica followed Leonel's directions and duct-taped Dr. Liu's ankles and hands. If she were honest, she'd admit that it gave her great pleasure to do so, and she made it tighter than was strictly necessary. "Now comes the tough part. You've got to be quick. When I let go of her mouth she's going to scream," Leonel said.

"Not if she's unconscious," Patricia snarled, pulling back her suddenly scaly arm and punching the small frightened teen in the jaw right as Leonel let go. There was a snapping sound, and Jessica worried the punch had killed her, but, no, she was breathing. She applied the strip of duct tape to her mouth and collapsed into the grass, automatically checking that her weights were in place in what was becoming a behavioral tic.

"We've got to get inside. Helen is in there with my mother. We've had Dr. Liu out here too long. She's going to notice!"

"She already has, you idiot!" The voice came from the deck above them.

All three women swiveled their heads. Jessica gasped. Helen was standing at the railing above them, holding Eva Roark's elbow with one hand. Her other hand was engulfed in flames.

"Mom!" Jessica yelled, lunging toward the deck.

Leonel caught her around the waist and swung her back to the ground. "Are you crazy? She'll burn you!"

"It's Helen, isn't it?" Patricia said, stepping in front of the other two women, flexing her scaly hands menacingly. "Do you remember me?"

Helen nodded, her eyes glittering in the light of her fire-hand. "I know you, lizard lady. Let her go," she yelled, raising her threatening hand, the flames growing higher.

"You first," Jessica yelled, still trying to fight her way out of Leonel's grasp.

"Everybody calm down," Leonel yelled, sounding anything but calm. "No one has to get hurt here."

"No one has to, but someone is going to if you don't let Cindy go now!" Helen's voice was nearly as dark and thick as Patricia's.

Jessica's panic rose as her mother yelped, pulling at her elbow, which was held firmly in Helen's hand. Jessica was sure she saw her mother's sleeve smoking. In a quick twisting movement, she broke free of Leonel's grasp and somersaulted to land under the deck. She removed her weights and vaulted at the woman, letting her buoyancy give her the extra lift to get from the ground to the deck in a single bound. Climbing onto Helen's back, she looped her arm around her throat and squeezed.

Surprised, Helen let go of Eva's elbow. "Run!" Jessica yelled to her mother who had stumbled a step or two away and stood there looking stunned. "Get my mother out of here," she yelled to Leonel.

Helen flailed around, and Jessica tightened the grip of her arm, hoping her mother and her friends had listened to her. She squeezed Helen's throat as tightly as she could, feeling her legs float into space above them. The woman fell to her knees, leaving a sizzling handprint on the deck flooring as the flames went out. Still, Jessica held on, waiting for her to go slack.

"We've got her!" she heard Leonel yell from somewhere around the side of the house. "Get out of there!"

Jessica let go, and Helen slumped to the deck, coughing and wheezing. Instantly, Jessica shot backward like she'd been the rubber band and the slingshot had let go. She grabbed the deck's shade roof for support as she went by, tucking her body to direct the force around it like a parallel bar and spinning toward the house behind her. Slowing a little, she pulled in until she was crouching against the beam in a gravity-defying sideways hold. Feeling the splinters in her arms, she wished she had opted to have the beams sanded with the rest of the deck, but it hadn't seemed important the supports be smooth this high up.

She looked around frantically for her next handhold. She could hear Helen getting to her feet and knew she didn't have much time before she recovered enough to burn the place down.

Jessica focused on her feet, pulling back against the wooden support beam and aiming her body at the chimney. She pushed off with all her might, but the forward thrust of her movement ended short. She began to drift.

Panicked, she swirled her arms. She had to reach the chimney. It was the only solid thing up here. Her fingertips flailed inches from the brick and metal. Tears streamed down her cheeks. This was it. She was going to float away into outer space. She was going to die.

As she drifted upward, she saw over the roof into the front yard where Leonel was holding her mother's elbow, assisting her toward the minivan. Her mother looked up, shading her eyes against the sun, and Jessica thought it was good that Leonel would take care of her mother if she floated up into the sky until she disappeared.

Then she spotted the small red bicycles under the tall tree. Her boys. She couldn't just let herself drift away. Her boys needed her. She couldn't leave them to Nathan! Newly determined, she focused her thoughts on the chimney, so near, yet, just out of reach. Just go! Damn it. To her great surprise, her body obeyed. She shot forward so quickly she almost missed her chance to grab onto the chimney for support.

Pausing to catch her breath, she became aware of a warm spot between her breasts. She tugged the necklace of Dr. Liu's gemstones out from beneath her shirt. The stones were hot and glowing through the silk bag. She was still staring in amazement at the glowing stones when the first of the fireballs landed on the roof beside her.

Helen was awake.

"Jessica! Get down here!" It was Patricia, yelling from the front yard.

She could see her mother was in the van. Leonel was standing in the driveway, his back to the house. Coming around the house from the far side, where neither of her friends could see, was Helen.

"Leonel! Look out!" she called, aiming herself at Helen and flying through the air like a rocket. She held two fists out straight in front of her, hurtling into the woman with all the force she could muster, and knocked Helen down. The momentum sent Jessica bouncing and rolling across the yard. She came to a stop against the hedges that separated her yard from her neighbor's.

For a moment, her vision was blurred, and she thought she had hit her head. As it cleared, though, she became sure she was merely dizzy. Her whole body buzzed with adrenaline. She had just flown! Not floated uselessly, but flown! She chose a direction and moved through the air. Effortlessly, smoothly. It was the most powerful thing she had ever felt in her life.

As her senses started working again, she realized Leonel was calling to her, and she held up a hand to wave that she was unharmed. In a moment, he was at her side, asking if she was all right.

All right? She was amazing. "Did you see me, Leonel?" she asked, breathlessly. "I flew!"

HELEN, ON THE HUNT

Helen sat up, spitting out mulch, and patted out the flaming plants surrounding her in the garden bed. She wasn't sure how long she'd been unconscious or where everyone had gone. Still seated, she touched her head gingerly. There was a large bump on the back of her head. These things always felt bigger than they were, Helen knew, but it felt like she had an ostrich egg pushing out her hair. Her throat hurt, too. It was probably bruised from being squeezed. Where was Cindy?

She looked back at the house. The shingles were smoking here and there, and the gutters on the front of the house hung askew. But she didn't see any people. She wondered again how long she had been unconscious. Not too long, she guessed, since there wasn't a fire truck or police car here yet. Surely, one of these fine neighbors had called in the fire and the fight in the yard. They'd be worried about their property values if nothing else.

Pulling herself to her feet with difficulty, Helen looked around, thinking. The minivan was gone. It had apparently left with some speed, too. There were black tire marks at the bottom of the driveway and in the street in front of the house. So, they had gone. But where? Where would they take Dr. Liu?

Helen had been so sure this would go smoothly. Grab the girl and her mother. Get the emeralds back. Leave. No one had to get hurt. Not that she cared. She wouldn't have minded hurting someone if it would help Cindy. But it hadn't been easy at all. The pain searing up her leg and across her shoulder, as well as the ostrich egg on her head attested to that. Helen had underestimated their enemies and had paid for it in bruises.

Even Jessica, whom Helen had believed was little more than a blonde balloon, proved dangerous. Her hands were strong. Helen touched the sore skin of her throat again. She owed the little bitch something for that. And where did that powerful flight come from? Dr. Liu had indicated the girl had no control over her direction or speed, but obviously, she did.

Helen tried to wipe some of the garden dirt off her clothes. She was still mad at herself for letting the little twit get the drop on her. It was just so unexpected. She never would've thought the weepy little blonde would just hurl herself at someone wielding fire. Also, obviously, the girl wasn't without friends. That lizard lady was tough, and the man was astonishingly strong. They had snatched the doctor from under Helen's nose and now taken her God knows where. She had failed Cindy.

Distantly, she heard sirens. Maybe it was nothing, but maybe they were coming for her. She couldn't be here when the authorities came. She tried to run toward the little red sports car, but quickly realized that running was out of the question as pain shot up her left leg. She had a massive bruise on the inside of one knee, and the whole calf and ankle were swollen. Between that and the bump on her head, she was going to need medical attention. She was really starting to hate that lizard lady, Patricia.

Cindy said Patricia was an old friend, and that she had a good heart, but Helen thought Cindy was blinded by their old friendship. People changed. That woman was trouble. If they didn't find a way around her to Jessica and those emeralds, Cindy was going to regress to childhood, maybe even infancy. Cindy was sure she'd found the formula that would stop her youthening, if not reverse it. But she needed those Chinese emeralds. Helen was going to make sure she got them.

But first, she had to get out of here. Grimacing, Helen hobbled to the car, wishing they had parked closer. It was four houses down in the driveway of a house for sale. Helen knew the listing. The house was empty.

It was only four houses away, but each lurching step set her teeth on edge with a new wave of pain. When this was all over, she'd have to get Cindy to use that youthening formula on her, too. Getting old sucked. Of course, so did being beaten up by a giant lizard with red hair, and strangled by a cheerleader.

Finally, she got to the car and lowered herself into the driver's seat, silently thankful that it wasn't a stick shift. She whipped the car around and sped out of the neighborhood, right as the fire truck pulled in. Driving toward the city center, Helen punched the radio buttons one after another, but there was no news. Just ads intermixed with the garbage that passed for music these days. Wherever they'd gone, they were lying low.

Helen spotted an Urgent Care center and crossed two lanes of traffic to make a U-turn. Horns honked all around her, but she simply raised her middle finger and kept going. She had to get fixed up and get back to Cindy.

The office was relatively empty. Just a woman on an oxygen tank and a fidgety college boy who kept pulling at the crotch of his shorts. Helen lumbered over to the desk and leaned heavily on the counter, tapping her fingers impatiently. A pasty-faced sausage of a woman wearing bright pink scrubs, as if she ever touched anything dirtier than money, waddled up to the desk with a coffee cup in her hand. She quickly set her doughnut down on a paper napkin next to her keyboard and licked her fingers with a noisy smack.

"Did you sign in?" she asked, gesturing at the lined paper on the clipboard next to the clock.

"No," Helen answered. "We're going to handle this quietly." She didn't have the patience for their procedures. She needed to get patched up and get back out there quickly if she was going to be able to save Cindy Liu.

The woman looked up, confused.

"Get the doc out here," Helen said, coolly, holding up her fingers like a gun and raising a flame where the barrel would be. The woman pushed back her rolling chair so fast she fell on the floor. "Now would be good." Helen grinned. God, she loved this. She was going to have so much fun once she got Cindy back. No one was going to be able to refuse her anything she wanted ever again.

A few moments later, the woman returned, pulling a short Indian man behind her. The man stepped forward, pulling down his coat as if that would make his stature more impressive. "Can I help you?" he asked.

"I sure hope so," Helen said. "I'd hate to have to burn the place down." She stretched out her hand and raised a flame in the flattened palm.

Behind her, Helen heard the automatic doors *shoosh* open. The lady with the oxygen tank was moving with surprising speed through the doors. Helen laughed and then turned to look meaningfully at the college boy. He walked backward to the doors and then almost tripped himself turning to run for the parking lot.

"We don't have much time," Helen said to the doctor and the office clerk, who had grabbed for each other, staring at Helen's flaming hand. "I need you to stabilize this leg for me."

Less than thirty minutes later, Helen was leaving the office, her leg booted. The doctor had tried to stall her with talk of x-rays, alternating with guilt-trips about threatening him and the staff and other patients. Blah blah blah. He didn't appreciate what a favor she'd done him, leaving him and his clinic standing behind her. She'd have Dr. Liu fix her for real later. For now, she just needed to be able to walk. The boot would do nicely. That, and the painkillers she had pocketed.

She stepped into the parking lot fully expecting to have to blow up a police car or something, but no one was there. *The police in this town really need to step up their response time*, Helen thought, pulling back into traffic. The hotel wasn't far. Until she knew where to go, that would do. She needed to gear up and hunt these people down.

LINDA MAKES EVA TURN THIS CAR AROUND

O nce Linda had bundled the inert figure of Dr. Liu into the minivan, Eva had driven them away from the house as quickly as she could. She pulled away so quickly that the women were tossed against the sides of the van, and Cindy Liu slid off the seat and onto the floor. There wasn't even time to think about the unconscious woman they had left in the yard. From the squeal of the tires, Linda knew they'd left a rubber trail at the end of the driveway.

Linda accidentally pulled off the security handle she had grabbed to steady herself and sat staring at it in her hands. She decided she would get David to help her fix it after this was all over, and let it fall into the footwell beside her prisoner.

Her mind was reeling after the fight. She had kidnapped someone! That someone had tried to hurt her friend and had already been responsible for several crimes herself, but it didn't make what they were doing now any less wrong. What had she gotten herself into, following this crazy *gringa*? She glared at Patricia, wondering what had possessed her to do what the woman had asked. She guessed she had just been so happy to have something to do, an action to take, that she had acted without thinking it through. She had no idea what they were going to do next.

Eva had them on the highway and was driving eastward at eighty miles an hour before she called over her shoulder to ask, "Where am I going?"

They all answered at the same time. Patricia said, "the hospital," Jessica, "the police," and Linda, "back home." Then they all started yelling at each other about why their idea was the best.

After a mere minute or two of the bickering, Eva threw up her hands in frustration, swerved violently, and then brought the van to a sudden halt on the side of the road. Punching the button for the emergency lights, she flung off her seatbelt and whirled on the passengers. "Do you even have a plan?" she asked, her voice nearly hysterical.

"It'll be okay, Mom," Jessica said, climbing over the seat to reach her mother. She crouched in the space between the driver's seat and the front passenger seat and hugged her mother awkwardly.

Linda felt instantly chagrined. The woman had just been held prisoner, nearly burned, and rescued in a violent fashion, and they had asked her to drive. What were they thinking?

"We've got to get Cindy to a hospital," Patricia insisted. "We need to find out what is wrong with her."

Jessica turned without letting go of her mother. "Are you crazy? We need the police. This woman is a menace and needs to be locked up before she hurts someone else!"

Patricia's voice reached a new pitch of stridency. "She didn't mean to hurt anyone!"

"Mean it? I don't care what she meant! Have you forgotten that she drugged me and held me prisoner in her basement? Who knows what she would have done to me if Leonel hadn't found me. And she sent her thug after my mother." Jessica's body rose, and she hovered a few inches in the air, ducking her head in the confined space.

There was a pause, and Linda spoke up quickly before either of them could start shrieking again. "We cannot go the police or the hospital," she said. All three women turned to her in surprise. "Think about how this will look to anyone in authority," she said. "Three white women and a Hispanic man walk in holding an Asian teenager bound in duct tape and insist that we are the ones who are in need of help? We'll be locked up before we can get the words out."

"They can't hold us," Patricia said.

"I know that," Linda said, keeping her voice steady and calm, though she longed to scream at Patricia for the trouble she had gotten them into with her cockeyed scheme. "But do you really want to be put in the position of escaping from a cell? Do you really want to have to hurt the men and women who are charged with keeping us locked up?"

Jessica chimed in. "Leonel is right." She didn't sound happy to have to admit it, but Linda was happy for the support. Maybe they would listen to reason after all.

"So, where do we go?" Patricia asked. She sounded defeated. For the first time since she had met her, Linda thought Patricia looked old. The way she pursed her mouth highlighted the wrinkles around her lips.

They all sat silently, just looking at each other, so quiet that the buffeting sounds of cars driving past them on the highway seemed as loud as hurricane winds. Linda felt like she could hear the plans that each of them concocted and dismissed without speaking aloud. They were stuck. Then a phone rang.

Patricia jumped. "That's me," she said, pulling the phone from a side pocket in her pants. She looked at the screen. "It's Suzie." She answered it.

Linda couldn't hear Suzie's words, but she heard the tone and knew Suzie had called to find out what had happened. It had been several hours since Linda had called Patricia at work to bring her in on Jessica's rescue. Suzie must have been on tenterhooks waiting to hear what had happened.

Linda had a guilty start, realizing David didn't yet know what had happened. Pulling out her own phone, she checked the time. He would be home from work by now and should have found her note. She held the phone up and gestured to the outside. Jessica nodded. Linda checked Dr. Liu's bonds and lifted her back onto the seat where

Jessica and Eva could keep an eye on her and then let herself out of the van.

David answered on the first ring. "Are you all right?"

Linda reassured him that she was, starting to tell him what had happened.

David cut her off in mid sentence. "Where are you?" Linda could tell from his voice that he wasn't happy she was out fighting again. "Viviana is supposed to be here soon," he reminded her.

Linda fought down the urge to yell at her husband. She knew his anger came from love. He wanted her safe. He wanted her there, helping to repair the rift with her daughter. But this was important, too. Cindy Liu and Helen were dangerous people, and Linda could help stop them. "I don't think I will be home quite that soon, David," she said softly.

"I see," he said.

Linda thought that maybe he did see, and that he didn't like what he saw. Then the phone was dead, three little beeps announcing the end of the call. David had hung up, without an I love you, without a goodbye. Linda's throat went tight and raw.

"Come on, Leonel," Jessica was calling, leaning out the window of the van and waving. "We're going to the college. Suzie will meet us there!"

PATRICIA IS THE BIG LIZARD ON CAMPUS

Patricia put Suzie on speakerphone. The intern talked Eva through the winds and bends of the college campus to the parking lot where she was waiting. They pulled into an isolated parking place behind the old gymnasium in the dark under a large, old tree. Patricia spotted Suzie sitting at the top of a short staircase and pointed her out to the others. When Suzie spotted the van, she hopped up and waved them down, looking almost elf-like in a bright blue jacket.

When they clambered out of the vehicle, Suzie surprised everyone by greeting Patricia with a hug. "I'm so glad you're all right!" Suzie looked around the circle at everyone, but it was obvious it was really Patricia she had been concerned about. "Where's Dr. Liu?" she asked, her face losing all warmth as she spoke the woman's name.

"Still in the van." Patricia gestured toward the door.

They all peeked around the open door at the seemingly unconscious teenager sprawled across the seat, hanging from the belt Patricia had strapped her into.

"You weren't kidding. She does look like a kid." Suzie turned her back on the doctor and clapped her hands together. "Okay, so Patricia said you need a place to regroup and to keep Dr. Liu confined while you plan your next steps, so we're going to this building."

Everyone gathered obediently to look at the map Suzie had unfurled. Suzie went on. "It's under construction, so should be empty at this time of day. Yes, technically, we're trespassing. But like I said, it should be empty. The work crew leaves by three o'clock each day. However, just in case, I brought you something." At this, Suzie hopped back up the stairs and came down pulling a rolling cart behind her. "Here, you'll need these."

She handed each person a bag. Each contained pieces of costuming. "Patricia, I figured you could just transform, and, as for the rest of you, if you'll put on the masks and costuming, we'll just look like we're having a costume party," she said, settling a pair of white fluffy bunny ears atop her hair and grinning at them.

Leonel laughed when he saw the wolf man mask and flannel shirt she had picked for him. "It's perfect, Suzie. Thank you for your help."

Patricia pursed her lips doubtfully. "A costume party in April?"

"It's college, Patricia. Surely, you remember."

Patricia did remember. She nodded and concentrated, allowing her scales to encase her. Suzie's plan was sounding less harebrained by the moment.

Once everyone was dressed, Suzie said that it would look less suspicious if Jessica and her mother dragged Cindy between them. "You know, like she's your friend, and she just had too much to drink."

Jessica said, "Won't people notice the duct tape?"

"Yeah. I thought of that. I think we'd better remove it."

"Then what's to keep her from yelling out for help?" Jessica asked.

"This," said Suzie, pulling a syringe from her purse.

Jessica's eyes grew wide, and Leonel gasped. Even Patricia felt surprised, and, at the same time, admiring.

"What's in it?"

"Basically injectable ruffies," she said, her tone matter-of-fact. "My roommate is a chemistry major," she added, seeming to realize that the group might want some explanation of how she came by a batch of date-rape drug. "Leonel, can you hold her please? In case she's faking?"

Patricia could see Leonel wasn't sure this was the best course of action, but he complied. Suzie utilized the syringe with surprising facility and then ripped the duct tape from Cindy's face, wrists, and ankles with a look of satisfaction.

"Sometimes you worry me, Suzie," Patricia said.

"I am a woman of hidden talents," Suzie said brightly, putting the cap back on the now-empty syringe and stowing it back in her purse along with the scraps of duct tape.

They walked quietly in a tight group until Suzie told them they were being too suspicious. "Relax," she said. "Try to look like you're on the way to a party."

They spread out a little after that and laughed nervously. It wasn't until they walked past a group of guys sitting on some stairs and smoking that they really fell into their roles. Suzie was the best at it. She laughed and pulled at Leonel. "Come on, baby! We're going to be the last ones there!" She shrieked with laughter and ran ahead of the group.

Leonel shrugged and then chased after her, trying to play along, calling for her to wait. Jessica and Eva swayed convincingly, holding the floppy Cindy Liu between them. They had put a cape on her and a cat woman mask that covered the top half of her face. Jessica was wearing a naughty nurse outfit, and Eva a set of surgical scrubs and a face mask. They talked quietly to each other in a way that really looked like girlfriends conspiring. It was very plausible, Patricia decided.

Patricia herself brought up the rear, just walking silently, ready to act defensively if the situation called for it, but really hoping it wouldn't. When one of the boys called out, "Whoa, nice costume!" she turned to him and grinned. "What costume?" she said. They all laughed. Patricia began to believe the plan would work.

The building was empty, just as Suzie had predicted. Leonel had stepped up when they got to the entrance, planning to break the latch, but found the door behind the "Closed for Renovations" sign was unlocked. So, the group shuffled inside and picked a room to settle into.

There were several small sitting rooms off the main foyer, and Suzie directed them toward one at the back with a couch and a few chairs in it. Jessica and Eva flopped Cindy onto the couch none-too-gently. Watching the way they handled her old friend, Patricia remembered all the cause for anger the Roarks had. Eva had called Cindy a friend. She must have felt betrayed in the same way Patricia did.

The scientist seemed to still be out cold. She lay where she had been dropped. Patricia could see her chest moving in even breaths and felt reassured they hadn't put her into a coma. Eva pulled off the surgical mask that had hid her face and flung it into a nearby chair and then flung herself into it as well, covering her face with her hands.

Patricia noticed Jessica's mother's hands were shaking and felt angry it was her old friend who had brought them to this moment. Cindy would have some explaining to do when she regained consciousness. Jessica knelt in front of the chair her mother had collapsed into and hissed at Leonel, gesturing toward the door with her head. "We've got first watch," she said.

Patricia didn't understand at first, until Leonel grabbed her elbow. "Come on, Godzilla. We should let them talk." He tugged her toward the open door into a second sitting area.

Suzie tried the corner lamp, but the electricity must have been out, because it didn't turn on. So, she opened the blinds to let in a little bit of light from the streetlights and stood looking out the window.

Leonel flopped noisily into the largest chair in the room, dangling his legs over the arm of the chair and letting his head rest against the opposite arm rest. As he moved, he automatically adjusted his hair, and something in the hair-flipping gesture was so feminine that Patricia almost laughed. It was so easy to forget Leonel had not always been a man.

Patricia joined Suzie at the window, looking out onto the darkening college campus. "Thanks," she said, and Suzie's face widened with a surprised smile. Patricia went to pat Suzie on the shoulder and realized that her hands were still covered in scales. She must be more tense than she realized. She concentrated and retracted them.

"So, what's our next move?" It was Leonel who asked, and his voice seemed huge in the quiet room.

Patricia and Suzie both jumped. When they turned to look at him, they found that he had not moved. He had just spoken the words to the ceiling. When they didn't answer, he turned his head to stare at them. "We can't just stay here forever. What happens now?"

Suzie looked at Patricia, too. Patricia stood there feeling frozen. She still didn't have a clear plan, but she didn't want to tell them that, not when they were looking to her to tell them what should be done. "We wait," she said, after a long pause. "When she wakes, I'll talk to her. If anyone can find out what's going on from her, it's me. We go way back."

Suzie pulled out her cell phone to check the time. "She should be coming around in the next hour or so. Right when she awakes, her inhibitions will be lowered. It's probably our best bet to get some straight answers out of her."

"So, the question is," said Leonel, "what are we going to ask her?"

Suzie pulled a tablet computer from her bag and set it up on the end table with a little cordless keyboard. When Suzie gestured for them to do so, Leonel and Patricia pulled chairs up close, so the three of them could all see the screen. Suzie pulled up a document and titled it "What to ask," and sat with her hands on the keyboard, looking questioningly from one of them to the other and back again.

Patricia thought. There was so much she wanted to know, but it was all so hard to put into a list of questions. She wanted to know what Cindy had done to herself that had her looking like a fifteen-year-old child. She wanted to know what she had been thinking when she kidnapped Jessica and brought a crazy woman to threaten her mother. She wanted to understand what had happened to all three of them and what Cindy had to do with that. Mostly, she just felt lost. It was unbelievable to her that her friend had done the things she had.

The cursor blinked on the document accusingly as Patricia struggled to form even a single question. There was a gentle rap on the doorframe, and they looked up to find Eva there. "She's moving," she said.

They all stood and rushed back to the room where Cindy Liu was, indeed, stirring. She stretched like a cat, murmuring, and blinked sleepy eyes. Patricia sat on the edge of the couch and waited. The others stayed a step or two behind her. She could feel the tension radiating from each of them.

"Oh, hey, Patricia," said Cindy. Her words were slurred. "'Izzit time to get up?"

"Tell me what's going on, Cindy," Patricia said.

"Need to get my emeralds," she said. "Can't stop it without them."

Patricia looked significantly at Jessica, who grabbed at the little bag she was wearing under her shirt, bunching up the material. In the car, she had heard Jessica telling her mother about the emeralds she had taken from Cindy's lab and about the effect they had on her flight.

"Stop what, Cindy?"

"Getting too young." Cindy yawned, hugely, ostentatiously.

It hit Patricia how tired she was. In fact, she realized as she looked around the group, they all looked a little haggard and worn. Well, all but Suzie. She cleared her throat. "Why don't you all go find a place to rest and leave me to talk to Cindy? I think she'll talk to me, and then we can decide what to do next."

Leonel stood. "I should call David, anyway," he said and turned to leave the room.

Jessica and Eva looked at each other, and then Jessica spoke up. "I need to call Nathan, too. He and the boys can't go back to our house tonight." Eva drifted after her daughter, pausing in the doorway to glare at Cindy with surprising malice.

Turning to Suzie, Patricia suggested that she arrange for food for the group. Suzie nodded and walked out, too, her cell phone already in her hand.

Alone with Cindy at last, Patricia let the scales ruffle up her neck and down her arms. Leaning over her friend, she waited for her eyes to open. She didn't have to wait long. A few seconds later, Cindy's eyelids fluttered again, and she blinked a few slow times. Patricia knew the moment her vision came into focus, because Cindy flung herself back and squealed, sounding like the child she appeared to be. "Patricia! What the hell?"

"That's what I want to know," she responded. "What the hell are you doing? What have you done to us? What were you trying to do to Jessica?"

With a suddenness that took Patricia by surprise, Cindy's eyes filled with tears. Fat tears rolled down her face, and she made no effort to wipe them away. Cindy never cried. Even when her fiancé had died, she had cried very little, and only after consuming a great deal of alcohol. Patricia never knew what to do with tears. They made her suspect manipulation or feel embarrassed for the people who couldn't control themselves. In this case, she felt mostly confused. She wanted to hug her old friend and fling her across the room at the same time. She stood and stared at the woman-child on the couch, trying to decide what the best thing to do might be.

"Can I have some water?" Cindy blubbered out the request, wiping her face on the backs of her sleeves.

Patricia turned without saying a word, grabbed a bottle of water from the little cart that Suzie had thoughtfully brought and left in the main hall, and then stalked back to the room.

Cindy was standing at the window, swaying a little, unsteady on her feet. Patricia grunted to get her attention and threw the bottle of water to her. It landed at her feet, and Cindy bent to pick it up. Patricia stood with her arms crossed over her armored chest, waiting. Cindy downed the water quickly, in one long drink, and then stood there, crinkling the bottle in her hands. Patricia cleared her throat.

"They forced me to retire," Cindy said. Her voice was flat and quietly angry. Patricia wasn't sure what she expected, but this seemed a strange place for Cindy to start her confession. She raised an eyebrow and then realized Cindy probably couldn't see the gesture when her armor was up. It didn't matter; she went on. In a torrent of words, she told Patricia how the company she had been working for came to her and told her they had put a new mandatory retirement policy in place. They wanted to make sure they had jobs available for younger scientists, ones that would serve the company for many years. Ones that wouldn't put a strain on the company by using the medical insurance and their sick leave. They hadn't said that, of course, but Cindy knew that was part of what they were after.

"I was in my prime, doing the best work of my life, and, suddenly, they told me that I was too old!" The seeming-teenager vibrated with fury. "I decided they would never do this to another woman, that I would not be limited by a silly thing like expected lifespan. Not when I could extend it."

Patricia heard the fervor in her friend's voice and grew even more concerned. The last time she had sounded like this, she had ended up getting arrested for vandalism. Cindy had called it activism, but the police called it breaking and entering and destruction of property. The hospital had called it misplaced vengeance for the death of her lover. Patricia saw it as unchecked grief.

Cindy went on at some length about her experiments and the success she had found, first on animals and then finally on herself. She said the things that had happened to Patricia and the other women were not part of her plan, but lucky accidents. Patricia choked on the thought that Cindy believed they were lucky. Lucky to have had their lives uprooted and irrevocably altered without their consents? Anger began to win over her concern, and she stepped toward the window, intending to grab Cindy and shake some sense into her.

She had just rounded the couch where Cindy had slept off her drugs when she spotted the cell phone on the floor in front of it. Her own cell phone. It must have fallen from her pocket when she leaned over Cindy. She bent and picked it up, pulling in her claws on her right hand so she could operate the device. A message had been sent. "They have me at the college. Reed Hall."

Patricia ran from the room yelling for the others. Behind her, she heard Cindy laughing.

HELEN'S ALTER EGO

That afternoon, Helen had used a side entrance to the hotel and gotten to her room unseen, so far as she could tell. That was good, as she was sure she looked a mess. She was dirty and bruised and bloodied. Her hair felt like a rat's nest on her head. She was happy to note, though, the fire proof clothing had performed. There were no holes in her clothing! At least, not holes caused by fire.

Back in the hotel room, she pulled the curtain and locked the door, setting the security chain. It wouldn't stop that brute of a man, Leonel, if he came, but she didn't think there was much danger of that right now. They weren't trying to get to Helen. If anything, they were probably trying to hide from her, as well they should. When she got her hands on the three of them, she was going to burn them to ash.

In fact, she would have burned them to ash already, if she knew where to go. Crossing to the kitchenette, she turned on the television and flipped through the channels looking for local news. It took a few minutes to get to any interesting bits, during which Helen peeled off her tunic shirt and leggings and washed them out in the sink. Dr. Liu had warned against using harsh detergents or washing machines, saying that the chemical preparation would weaken, and the clothes would no longer stand up against her flames.

Her leg was throbbing, as was her head, so she took more of the painkillers she had taken from the Urgent Care office. She didn't have time for this crap. She needed to know where Dr. Liu was. She needed to get her back. Taking the painkillers reminded her to check on her other pills. She pulled the gym bag out from the closet. There were eight boxes of Surge Protector pills, the only boxes she could find in the entire city. They would hold her for a while. She took one, wondering briefly if it made any difference that she was also on painkillers, but shrugging off the concern.

The news came back on after the commercial, and she focused her attention on the television screen, wrapping herself in the comforter from one of the beds. There was a picture of Jessica's house, smoke billowing from the roof. The authorities were investigating the cause of the fire and reports from the neighbors of an altercation that took place in the yard. Pictures of that bitch Jessica and her mother were shown on screen, and information was asked about their where-abouts. Artist sketches of Leonel, Patricia, and Helen herself were shown next, and people were asked to call the number if they had any information. The reporter ended with a brief video clip with a boy of maybe ten or eleven years old who swore Mrs. Roark had flown above her house, and that fireballs had been flying. Her indulgent smile said that she didn't believe the story and didn't expect the viewer to, either. That was probably good.

There had been too much on the news here lately that could expose Helen and Dr. Liu. Patricia had apparently been involved in a fight at the mall, and she had also let people see her in her lizard form after breaking into Dr. Liu's house. That woman was incautious. Dangerous in more ways than one. Helen looked forward to taking her down. After this kidnapping, she knew that Cindy wouldn't stand in her way anymore.

Helen let the TV run while she took a shower. She had to shower mostly seated as the foot didn't want to take any weight. It was swollen and purple. Helen didn't touch it, knowing she would find it painful and tender to say the least. She had Jessica to thank for that. The impact that little flying squirrel had hit her with had been astounding. Helen's anger blazed through her, literally heating her entire body until the room became filled with steam, which billowed out into the hotel room when she opened the door and hobbled over to the closet, trying to ignore the pain that shot up her leg.

She had one more set of fireproofed clothes. The bright ones. Cindy had laughed at her, but Helen had wanted a costume set. If she had these powers, she might as well look, as well as live, the part. So, they had treated a pair of red leggings and a long yellow tunic. Helen had sewn a picture of a flame onto the shirt. There was a pair of red high top sneakers, too. Dr. Liu had said she didn't think she could do anything for the rubber soles, but she could treat the cloth material at least.

Helen would only be able to wear one of them because of the leg injury. The other foot she slipped back into the plastic boot and tightened the straps to support the injury. That left the mask and cape, both red. Helen checked herself out in the long mirror on the back of the bathroom door and grinned. She looked amazing. She held one hand out in front and allowed a ball of flame to gather there. "They call me the Flamethrower!" she told the mirror, wishing she could get a picture.

Squashing the flame between her hands, Helen went back to the kitchen. Her phone was on the floor. It must have vibrated off the counter. She picked it up, happy to see the screen had not cracked. There was a new text message. She didn't know the number, but it had to be from Dr. Liu: "They have me at the college. Reed Hall."

The campus wasn't even ten minutes away. Cindy would be free in a matter of minutes.

JESSICA RISES TO THE OCCASION

Jessica's conversation with Nathan hadn't gone well. In fact, she had hung up on him and turned off her phone at the end of it. She hadn't expected support, exactly, but she had thought he would, at least, be relieved to hear she was okay. She had barely gotten a sentence out when he began yelling at her, demanding to know what had happened to their house, but not giving her a chance to answer.

At least she knew the boys were safe at their other grandmother's house. Nathan's mother would let them stay up too late and ignore all their dietary rules, but they would be safe in her care. She'd deal with Nathan when this was all over. She knew now that it was unquestionably over. There would be a lot of turmoil yet, many battles over things like money and the boys, but knowing the marriage was over filled her with a feeling of relief. She could stop pretending, stop trying to make it all right.

The call ended, and Jessica turned to her mother. Eva sat very upright in the chair across the room. Everything about her posture spoke to her anger and stress. Jessica hated that she had gotten dragged into this. She hated Dr. Liu for messing up all their lives. She could hear the heated conversation, muted and indistinct through the thin walls, and hoped Patricia ripped off one of the woman's arms.

"How's your arm?" Jessica asked, taking the chair next to her mother and pulling back the sleeve to look at the reddened skin.

Eva pulled her sleeve back down over it and pushed her daughter's hands away. "It'll be fine. Suzie gave me some salve for it before she left to get the food. I've gotten worse burns trying to make cookies."

Jessica smiled at her mother's joke. She had inherited her lack of aptitude for all things kitchen from her mother. But she raged inside that Dr. Liu's flunky had hurt her mother. She wanted nothing more than to get her hands back around that woman's neck. But she had no idea where she even was now. They'd just left her in the yard in their haste to get away. Jessica felt so impotent, so unable to do anything that would help. She didn't even know how to comfort her own mother.

The two women sat in silence. Jessica closed her eyes and leaned back her head. She was exhausted, mentally and physically. She wanted to curl up in the chair, rest her head in her mother's lap, and cry for a while. It was just so much to deal with. She was just an ordinary mom and a wife, not a hero. How had she gotten mixed-up in all this? How would she get back out of it?

It was hard to imagine this ending well. Her brain ran scenarios that frightened her. She saw Leonel on fire, her mother crumpled on the ground. She imagined Patricia bleeding from beneath her scales. She envisioned Nathan pulling away from her in horror, Dr. Liu's intensely focused eyes. Her body shook. She wasn't sure if she was angry or scared or some impossible combination of both those emotions at once.

Still, when it had mattered, when she had really needed to, Jessica had managed to use her limitations as strengths, hadn't she? She could hardly believe she'd done it now. She'd thrown off her weights, thrown her body at the woman with fire for a hand, and had taken her down. And she hadn't drifted off into outer space. In fact, she had flown. She pulled the necklace from beneath her shirt and looked again at the emeralds. She felt certain they were the difference. Something about those rocks had made her able to control her flight for the first time.

"I'm so proud of you," Eva said.

Jessica jumped. "What?"

"You heard me. I'm proud of you. You were amazing. I owe you my life."

"Don't be silly. I owe you mine, Mom. At least three times." She patted her mother's hand, her other hand fondling the crystals in the bag around her neck.

Suddenly, Eva gripped her fingers hard. Jessica looked to see what was wrong. Eva was staring open-mouthed across the room, toward the windows. "Are those flames?"

Jessica jumped from the chair, flying across the room in a single long jump and landing by the window. Her mother gasped, but she hardly noticed. Pulling the blinds to one side, she peeked out at the quad. At first, she didn't see anything, but then she saw them, balls of fire, flying through the air and landing in the grass and trees. They fell in high beautiful arcs, streaking like comets across the evening sky.

That was when she heard Patricia yelling and realized it was her own name being called.

PATRICIA FINDS NO ME IN TEAM

Patricia ran into the hall at the same time as Leonel, Jessica, and Eva, still yelling for the others to come. "It's Helen!"

All of them started talking at once, their voices bouncing off the ceiling in the large empty foyer. Suddenly, a piercing whistle filled the air, making them all stop and cover their ears.

Patricia turned in surprise to see that it was Eva Roark, Jessica's mother, who had deafened them. "Where is Cindy?" she asked, each word spoken slowly and heavily.

Patricia pointed at the room she had just left and watched, stunned, as Eva turned and ran into the room. She and the others followed and found Eva on the floor, grasping one of Cindy's ankles with both of her hands as the woman-girl dangled halfway out the window and kicked fiercely at her. "A little help?" Eva called.

Leonel crossed the room in three long strides and grabbed Cindy by the waist, pulling her back into the room. The doctor grabbed the windowsill and resisted, but Leonel pulled her through with little effort and tossed her into one of the chairs. Then Eva surprised Patricia again by attacking Cindy, punching her in the face and screaming at her. "How dare you! How dare you! How dare you!"

She might have gone on forever, if Jessica had not wrapped her arms around her mother and gently tugged her away to another corner of the room. Patricia stewed, haranguing herself for her stupidity. It was her phone Cindy had used to contact Helen. She was the one who had run from the room, leaving Cindy to escape.

This was not going according to plan. Not that she'd had much of a plan. She was just going to get back in the car and drive away, find a place to take Cindy Liu and then figure out what to do from there. She wasn't good at making stuff up on the fly like this. She wanted time to research and think. She wanted to study charts with Suzie and make a recommendation to the board.

Instead, she had trapped herself, trapped all of them in a building on a college campus with a crazy woman in the body of a teenager while another crazy woman hurled fireballs at them from the quad. They should have dealt with Helen when they'd had the chance back at the house. Leonel and Cindy were both looking at her accusingly for different reasons. Leonel was probably thinking she was not fit to lead their little group, and he was probably right.

For the second time in the space of a few hours, Patricia hit her oldest friend to knock her unconscious. "Tie her up," she said to Leonel, who was still staring at her with big, brown cow eyes. "Here," she said, pulling off the tank top she wore over her sports bra and tossing it to him as she transformed into her lizard self. "You can use this."

Then she ran across the room and jumped through the window Cindy had just been trying to escape through, breaking the glass and landing in a crouch in the garden bed outside. Roaring in rage, she ran into the middle of the quad. Only when she was already there did she realize she didn't know where Helen was. She had to be nearby, but Patricia didn't actually see her. "Where are you? Come out and fight me, bitch," she yelled.

The only answer was a fireball that landed at her feet and set the grass on fire. Patricia fell backward and landed on her ass. She heard laughter that seemed to echo against the buildings, and more distantly, the sound of cars driving down the main drag on the other end of the quad. Patricia realized with a jolt how many people there were in the vicinity, how many innocents Helen would burn to get what she wanted. They had to stop her!

Suddenly, Leonel was beside her, grabbing her arm and pulling her down behind a piece of statuary, just as another fireball landed where she had been standing.

"She's on the other side of this fountain in the little ring of trees by the street light," he said, pointing.

Patricia peered into the night where Leonel had pointed and saw it when the next fireball formed and flew toward them.

Patricia pulled up onto her feet and turned to dash toward the trees. Just as she lunged to move, Leonel stuck out a foot and tripped her, forcing her to catch herself on the edge of the statue or face plant. "Don't be an idiot, Patricia. If you take her straight on, you're going to get hit."

"Don't you remember?" Patricia grinned, flexing to push out her spikes and armored scales. "I'm bulletproof!" Then she was off, running toward the ring of trees where Leonel had said Helen was hiding. Bulletproof, it turned out, was not the same thing as fireproof. Most of the fireballs missed making contact, whizzing past her with a crackle and pop or landing short, but eventually, one did make contact, square in the center of her chest.

It hurt. Patricia felt as though she had been stung all at once by an entire nest of wasps. Enraged, she spun, looking for Helen and not finding her. She looked back at the statue where she had taken shelter with Leonel. He was gone. More fire rained down around her, and Patricia dodged randomly, unable to pin down what direction the fire was coming from. She was feeling dizzy and getting tired. She heard voices, a lot of them, and the sound left her even more disoriented.

Then she heard a high-pitched whistle. It was Leonel, gesturing wildly on the far side of the quad, near the busy street. He had taken shelter behind a boulder with some kind of memorial plaque on it. Zigzagging as she ran to avoid taking another hit, Patricia threw herself behind the rock. She sat down hard, resting her back against the boulder. She was wheezing from the effort. Her body was nearly indestructible when fully armored, but it was also ridiculously heavy.

She was going to have to build up her endurance. If she made it through this, she'd start a new regimen at the gym.

Leonel clamped a hand on her shoulder and knelt to look her in the face. "If you run off like that again, I'm going to let her burn your skinny white ass, Patricia."

Patricia nodded. She was out of ideas. Maybe Leonel had a better one. Backs against the cool stone, the two of them sat shoulder to shoulder and thought. A crowd of college students had gathered at a short distance. They were going to have to get those kids out of there before someone got hurt.

Leonel clapped his hands and rubbed the palms together. "We need to work together here," he said. "We have three problems: Helen, Cindy, and these kids who are standing around gawking." Patricia nodded. Leonel pulled his phone out of his pocket and typed a message. The device lit up as a message came back. Leonel shook his head approvingly and put the phone back in his pocket. "Okay. Jessica will take care of these kids for us. You and I will see to Helen."

"And Cindy?"

"Eva will stand guard over her."

Patricia almost protested, but realized they had little choice. Cindy was tied to a chair, after all, and wasn't particularly strong or physically dangerous. She'd have to trust Eva could handle it.

Leonel went on with his plan. "Helen's in front of the building now, about three hundred yards on the other side of this boulder. She's been throwing fire wildly for more than fifteen minutes. I figure she's got to be getting tired. There's no way she can take both of us at once. I'll duck behind these trees and run at her from the left. You'll go around from the right. Whoever makes it there first should punch her out." Patricia pulled herself up into a crouch and peered around the right side of the boulder, poised to run. "Wait!" Leonel said, grabbing her arm yet again. "Wait for Jessica to get here."

She dropped from the sky just then, landing in a squat right in front of them. It was a move straight out of a Hollywood movie, and the crowd reacted with sounds of amazement. She turned and grinned at Leonel and Patricia, and Patricia could have sworn she saw a green glow through the thin, white cloth of Jessica's blouse. The emeralds.

Leaping into the air again, Jessica flew in a circle around the group, and the young people spun around, trying to keep her in view. She hovered for a moment in the lamplight, spreading her arms wide and throwing her head back. Then she zoomed away. The crowd of college students followed her, shouting and holding their phones and cameras. She led them out of the quad and out of danger. Patricia covered her mouth with her hands, eyes wide with amazement.

"Let's go," said Leonel. With one last look back at the dispersing crowd, the two women nodded at each other and ran in their assigned directions. The fireballs started flying again, but it was going well. Helen was whirling between the two of them, throwing fireballs and fire spears, but without focus and targeting. Nothing had come close to hitting either of them.

Patricia was starting to think it must have been a lucky shot that brought the fireball down on her chest. She was also starting to think this was going to work. She maneuvered her way nearer and nearer to Helen, dodging between statues, trees, and any other kind of cover she could find.

Then, abruptly, the fire stopped coming. Patricia stopped, too, and peered out from around the giant urn she had been using as shelter. She could see Helen, standing in the open in front of the Reed building, just as Leonel had said. The building's lights spotlighted her. Helen was dressed all in brightly colored spandex, her shirt clinging to her rolls of fat and featuring a picture of a candle flame. One of her feet was booted and the other was clad in a red converse sneaker. Was she wearing a cape?

Helen's attention was not on Patricia. Nor did it seem to be on Leonel, assuming he had stuck to his planned route. She was looking toward the main drag, a few hundred yards in front of her. She seemed transfixed. She had lowered her hands to her side, the flames in her palms touching the sides of her bright red pants, but, apparently, having no effect. Patricia craned her neck to see what had Helen's attention but couldn't see without stepping out into the open.

"Cindy," the woman yelled suddenly. "Stop! Wait! Where are you going?"

A figure on the path turned, waved, and then continued running toward the road. Patricia froze. Cindy had escaped? How? Patricia hesitated, trying to decide if she should chase her down or stick to the plan and take out Helen. She'd made enough bad decisions already today.

Luckily, the decision was taken out of her hands before she had to make it. "Oh no, you don't!" she heard from behind her and turned to see Eva Roark, running down the path with surprising speed. It was even more surprising when she tackled the seemingly young woman, rolling her into the grass. Patricia wondered if Eva had been a gymnast, too, and if that's where Jessica's skill had come from. For a moment, all three of them, Patricia, Helen, and Leonel, stood transfixed, watching the fight on the lawn of the college.

Helen was the first to move. But it wasn't the movement that attracted Patricia's attention; it was Leonel's scream. "No! Suzie! Get back!"

Patricia whirled around just in time to see the gleam in Helen's eye as she pulled her arm back and released a ball of fire that rolled across the ground like some kind of giant, flaming bowling ball.

Patricia knew she couldn't get there in time to help. She was just too slow in her armored state. "No," she screamed, staggering from her hiding place into the open plaza.

There was a whooshing sound, and Jessica streaked into view, flying back from where she had gone, her blonde hair blowing behind her like a flag. She flew into Suzie, knocking her backward and out of harm's way, the food boxes the intern had been sent to fetch flying into the air.

At almost the same time, she and Leonel ran from their hiding places, both rushing toward Helen. Helen's head whipped from side to side, her eyes wild, and her hair blowing out around her head in a blonde corona. She hunkered down like some kind of elemental wrestler, each hand curved around a swirling ball of fire.

Leonel reached out for Patricia's hand. "Trust me," he yelled. Not giving herself time to think, Patricia thrust her hand into his.

He yanked her arm, sling-shotting her ahead of him. She closed the remaining ground between herself and Helen in what felt like a single bound, flinging out a hand and slapping the woman so hard her head snapped back. Helen crumpled to the ground.

In the next moment, Leonel was there, grabbing Helen and holding her above his head. His face was contorted with rage and tears. He spun and flung the woman at the building's side wall. Helen flew. Even flying through the air, the surprise was evident on her face. She seemed to have forgotten fireproof wasn't the same thing as unbreakable. She was still vulnerable to brute force. When she collided with the brick wall, the crack of bones was sickening. Her body sank to the ground, her limbs bent at ugly angles that shouldn't have been possible.

Behind her, Patricia heard a strangled gasp. She turned. Jessica lay crumpled on the ground, her blackened arm pulled in to her chest. Patricia could smell the charred flesh from across the quad. Leonel ran to her side and scooped her into her arms, yelling for someone to get an ambulance. Patricia walked to them, calming her heart and willing her body back to its normal size. By the time she knelt beside them, she was herself again, a tall woman with short red hair, wearing stretched out yoga pants and a strangely torn up sports bra.

"Is she...?" She didn't finish the thought.

Jessica drew in a ragged breath and moaned horribly. Still alive then, for what it was worth. Patricia didn't hold out much hope for that arm. Stupid, brave girl. She should have stayed where she was safe. She brushed hair back from Jessica's face and noticed the necklace she had been wearing was gone. The emeralds.

Suddenly, Patricia stood. "Where's Liu?"

Leonel looked startled and twisted his neck to look down the lawn, where Eva and Cindy had been fighting. Eva lay in the grass, unmoving. Unmoving and alone.

Patricia cursed, scanning the area, but saw no sign of her erstwhile friend, just the still smoking bushes and trees and three women lying on the ground. It was all her fault. She was so angry and frustrated, she shrieked aloud, the sound echoing against the buildings like some kind of animal cry.

Then she heard the sirens of an ambulance or fire truck approaching. The least she could do was make sure the paramedics got to Jessica, Eva, and Suzie quickly. She got to the street in a matter of a few seconds.

As she ran to wave the emergency crew over, she spotted a girl at the bus stop right in front of the campus. She was a skinny kid, all knees and elbows, Asian, maybe thirteen years old. Just for a moment, she held Patricia's gaze. Then she smiled and waved, stepping onto the bus.

Patricia staggered a step or two toward the bus, but it was already pulling away. As the bus left, Patricia's mind finished processing what she had seen: the too big T-shirt and shoes, the familiarity of that smile. "Cindy?"

At the back window of the bus, she could have sworn she saw her again, waving goodbye, the emeralds in her hand.

She narrowed her eyes. "This isn't over," she promised herself. "Not by a long shot."

ACKNOWLEDGMENTS

ABOUT THE AUTHOR

Samantha Bryant is a middle school Spanish teacher by day and a mom and novelist by night. That makes her a superhero all the time. Her secret superpower is finding lost things. She writes because it's cheaper than therapy and a lot more fun.

When she's not writing or teaching, Samantha enjoys time with her family, watching old movies, baking, reading, gaming, walking in the woods with her rescue dog, and going places. Her favorite gift is tickets (to just about anything). You can find her on Twitter @mirymom1 or at her blog/website: http://samanthabryant.com

ALSO BY SAMANTHA BRYANT

Menopausal SuperHeroes

Going Through the Change

Change of Life

Face the Change